Praise for *The Witch of Willow Hall*

"*The Witch of Willow Hall* offers a fascinating location, a great plot with history and twists, and characters that live and breathe. I love the novel, and will be looking forward to all new works by this talented author!"

—Heather Graham, *New York Times* bestselling author

"Beautifully written, skillfully plotted, and filled with quiet terror… Perfect for fans of Simone St. James and Kate Morton."

—Anna Lee Huber, bestselling author of the Lady Darby Mysteries

"*The Witch of Willow Hall* will cast a spell over every reader."

—Lisa Hall, author of *Between You and Me*

"Steeped in gothic eeriness, it's spine-tingling and very atmospheric."

—Nicola Cornick, *USA TODAY* bestselling author of *House of Shadows*

"A creepy estate, juicy scandal, family secrets, ghosts and a handsome yet mysterious suitor make this a satisfying and quietly foreboding tale."

—*BookPage*

"Fox spins a satisfying debut yarn that includes witchcraft, tragedy, and love…. The inclusion of gothic elements adds a visceral feel that fans of historical fiction with a dash of the supernatural will enjoy."

—*Publishers Weekly*

Praise for *The Widow of Pale Harbor*

"A Gothic romance with the flavor of Edgar Allan Poe, this is also a suspenseful mystery novel…highly recommended."

—*Historical Novel Society*

"Sophy is a strong gothic heroine."

—*Publishers Weekly*

"*The Widow of Pale Harbor* is a delightful, fast-paced read. The perfect selection for fans of historical fiction who also enjoy a hint of romance."

—*Nerd Daily*

Also by Hester Fox

The Witch of Willow Hall
The Widow of Pale Harbor

The
ORPHAN
of
CEMETERY
HILL

HESTER FOX

GRAYDON
HOUSE

**GRAYDON
HOUSE**®

Recycling programs
for this product may
not exist in your area.

ISBN-13: 978-1-525-80457-1

The Orphan of Cemetery Hill

This edition published by arrangement with Harlequin Books S.A.

Graydon House
22 Adelaide St. West, 40th Floor
Toronto, Ontario M5H 4E3, Canada
www.GraydonHouseBooks.com
www.BookClubbish.com

Printed in U.S.A.

To my grandparents Pieta and Ben.

The

ORPHAN

of

CEMETERY

HILL

Remember me as you pass by,
As you are now, so once was I,
As I am now, so you must be,
So prepare for death and follow me.
—18TH CENTURY EPITAPH

1

IN WHICH WE MEET OUR YOUNG HEROINE.

Boston, 1844

TABBY'S LEGS ACHED and the wind had long since snatched her flimsy bonnet away, but she kept running through the night, her thin leather shoes pounding the cobbled Boston streets. She didn't know where she was going, only that she had to get somewhere safe, somewhere away from the bustling theaters and crowds of the city. Every time someone shouted at her to watch where she was going, or ask if she was lost, she was sure that they were one of her aunt and uncle's friends. Would they drag her kicking and screaming back to Amherst? Tabby shuddered. She wouldn't go back. She couldn't.

Her weary feet carried her up a hill lined with narrow houses, and gradually she left behind the streets choked with theatergoers and artificially brightened with gas lamps. After cresting the hill, she paused just long enough to catch her breath and survey her unfamiliar surroundings.

It was quieter here, the only sounds the groaning of ships in the harbor and the distant call of a fruit hawker trying to sell off the last of the day's soft apples. Going back down into the heart of the city wasn't an option, yet a wrought-iron gate blocked her way any farther, forbidding pikes piercing the night sky. Pale headstones glowed faintly in the moonlight beyond the gate. A cemetery.

Tabby stood teetering, her heart still pounding. Dry weeds rustled in the thin night breeze, whispering what might have been a welcome, or a warning. Behind her was the land of the living with house windows glowing smugly yellow, the promise of families tucked safe inside. In front of her lay the land of the dead. One of those worlds was as familiar to her as the back of her hand, the other was only a distant fairy tale. Taking a deep breath, she shimmied through the gap in the gate.

She waded through the overgrown grass and weeds, thorny branches snagging at her thin dimity dress and scratching her. Panic gripped her as she heard the hem tear clean away; what would Aunt Bellefonte say if she found that Tabby had ruined her only frock? Would she smack her across her cheek? Would Uncle lock her in the little cupboard in the eaves? *Aunt Bellefonte isn't here. You're safe*, she reminded herself. As she pulled away to free herself, her foot caught in a tangle of roots in a sunken grave bed and she went sprawling into the dirt. Her lip wobbled and tears threatened to overflow. She was almost twelve years old, yet she felt as small and adrift as the day she'd learned that her parents had perished in a carriage accident and would never step through the front door again.

This wasn't how her first day of freedom was supposed to be. Her sister, Alice, had planned their escape from Amherst last week, promising Tabby that they would get a little room in a boarding house in the city. Alice would get a job at a laundry and Tabby would take in mending to contribute to their room and board. They would be their own little family, and they would put behind them the trauma that their aunt and uncle had wrought, making a new life for themselves. That had been the plan, anyway.

When she and Alice had arrived in the city earlier that day, her older sister had sat her down on the steps of a church and told her to wait while she went and inquired about lodgings. Tabby had dutifully waited for what had felt like hours, but Alice never returned. The September evening had turned dark and cold, and Tabby had resolved to simply wrap her shawl tighter and wait. But then a man with red-rimmed eyes and a foul-smelling old coat had stumbled up the steps, heading right toward her. Tabby had taken one look at him and bolted, sure that he had dark designs on her. She had soon become lost and, in a city jumbled with old churches, hadn't been able to find the right one again.

Another thorn snagged her, pricking her finger and drawing blood. She should have taken shelter in the church; at least then she would have a roof over her head. At least then Alice would know where to find her when she came back. If she came back.

Tabby stopped short. Toward the back of the cemetery, amongst the crooked graves of Revolutionary heroes,

stood a row of crypts built into the earth. Most of them
were sealed up with iron doors and bolts, but one had a
gate that stood just enough ajar for a small, malnourished
girl to wriggle through.

Holding her breath against the damp musk, Tabby
plunged inside. Without any sort of light, she had to
painstakingly feel her way down the crude stone steps.
Lower into the earth she descended until she reached the
burial chamber.

Don't invite them in. As she groped around in the dark
for a resting place, Tabby tried to remember what her
mother had always told her. Memories of her mother were
few and far between, but her words concerning Tabby's
ability remained as sharp in her mind as words etched
with a diamond upon glass. *The dead won't bother you if
you don't give them permission, if you don't make yourself a
willing receptacle for their messages.* At least, that was how it
was supposed to work.

The only other thing she had learned regarding her gift
was that she should never, ever tell anyone of it, and the
lesson had been a hard one. She couldn't have been more
than six, because her parents had still been alive and had
sent her out to the orchard to collect the fallen apples for
cider. Their neighbor, little Beth Bunn, had been there,
picking wild asters, but she hadn't been alone; there was
a little boy Tabby had never seen before, watching the
girls with serious eyes from a branch in an apple tree.
Tabby had asked Beth who he was, but Beth insisted she
didn't know what Tabby was talking about. Certain that
Beth was playing some sort of trick on her, Tabby grew
upset and nearly started crying as she described the little

boy with blond hair and big green eyes. "Oh," Beth said, looking at her askance. "Do you mean to say you see Ollie Pickett? He used to live here, but he's been dead for three years." That was how Tabby learned that not everyone saw the people she saw around her. A week later she had been playing in the churchyard and noticed that all the other children were clustered at the far end, whispering and pointing at her. "Curious Tabby," they had called her. And *that* was how Tabby learned that she could never tell a soul about her strange and frightening ability.

But even in a place so filled with death, the dead did not bother Tabby that night. With a dirt floor for her bed and the skittering of insects for her lullaby, Tabby pulled her knees up to her chest and allowed the tears she'd held in all day to finally pour out. She was lost, scared, and without her sister, utterly alone in the world.

After the first night, it was too dreadful to sleep in the tomb once the sun had gone down. Bugs crawled over her and rats gnawed on the rotten wood of coffins, and on the bones inside them. The shadow of a spirit, thin and almost entirely transparent, had drifted by her in a cloud of incoherent moans and laments. But Tabby had held her breath, watching it pass by, and it had taken no heed of her. Now she slept during the day, coming out at night to look for the church, and to forage amongst the shuttered stalls of the market for dropped vegetables and crumbs.

She had lost count of the days since Alice had left her, and the gnawing thought that she had forsaken Tabby on the church steps on purpose was never far from the surface of her mind. Had that been Alice's plan all along, to abandon Tabby? In her twelve years Tabby had learned that you couldn't trust people, even family. But Alice was different. Alice had taken care of her, looked out for her after their parents died and their aunt and uncle took them in. Alice had suffered alongside Tabby from the interest their relatives showed in the sisters' rare abilities. No, Alice would not leave Tabby, not unless something terrible had happened.

One night, as dusk fell thick and dreary, Tabby watched as the caretaker shuffled about the grounds, picking up the rotted bouquets left on the graves. A tall, lean, dark-skinned man with graying hair and a pronounced limp, he made an appearance every few days to pluck at some of the more aggressive weeds and ensure that the gates were padlocked at night. It didn't seem to be a very active cemetery, with only the newer section at the other end being used for the occasional burial. Even with the harbor on one side of the hill and narrow brick houses on the other, the cemetery felt remote, safe.

She wondered what the caretaker did when he was not collecting old flowers and pulling weeds. He looked like a nice enough man, and more than once Tabby was tempted to show herself, to ask if he could help her find her sister, but she knew that while adults might look kind, they could be cruel and ruthless if you had something they wanted.

When she was satisfied that he had gone for the night, and the cemetery was empty of the living, Tabby stole out of the crypt. It was a brisk, damp night, probably one of the last before the frosts came. She tried not to think about how cold she would be down in the damp stone crypt soon without a blanket or a warm cloak. But those things cost money, and she didn't have a penny to her name. If only there was some way for her to earn money.

There was a way, but it was her aunt and uncle's way. It was sitting in a dark room full of the bereaved, the curious, the skeptical. It was opening her mind to terrible specters. It was a waking nightmare.

Tabby shuddered; she would rather beg or steal.

Just as she was preparing to slip out into the city night to scavenge for food, a rustling in the weeds stopped her. Ducking behind a grave, she held her breath and squeezed her eyes shut. *Please, don't be a spirit or the caretaker come back.*

It took her several long, drawn-out moments to understand what she was seeing, and when she did, she wished it had been a spirit.

The man was impossibly large and might have been Death himself, with his caped overcoat and black hood. But instead of a scythe, he carried a shovel and a bundle of cloth under one arm.

He might not have been the grim reaper, but his presence struck Tabby with no less dread. She watched in horror as the man plunged his shovel into the soft dirt of a grave. He gave a low whistle and a moment later another man appeared, this one carrying some sort of iron bar. After what seemed an eternity, there was a dull thud, and then the splintering of wood. Between the two of them, they hefted the shrouded corpse out of the grave and carried it to a waiting cart just outside the gates.

She had heard of such men before, whispered about

by adults when she was little. Robbers whose quarry was the dead, men who had no scruples when it came to the sanctity of eternal rest.

She waited until the uneven sound of wheels on cobbles had faded into the night, hardly daring to breathe. Tabby sat crouched, motionless, until the first traces of dawn were just visible in the sky.

She thought of the caretaker and wondered what he would do come morning. Though he didn't know she existed, she had come to see the older man as an ally, a living friend amongst the dead. Maybe she could pat the earth back down, and at least tidy things up so it didn't look as bad. She was just about to uncurl her cramped legs when the rustle of movement stopped her. Her breath caught in her throat; had the men come back?

But it was not the men, nor yet a spirit, but a boy of flesh and blood.

No, not a boy. A young man. For a home of the dead, the cemetery was well trafficked by the living that night. What was he doing here? Over the last week, the cemetery had become a sort of home, her home, and he was trespassing.

Though he wasn't much taller than Alice, he must have been at least sixteen, and was lean with fair hair that fell over his temples. If Tabby hadn't been so stricken with fright, she might have thought him terribly dashing.

Had he crossed paths with the grave robbers? A tear ran down the length of his breeches, and an angry bruise was blossoming across his cheekbone. He was leaning against a large column dedicated to the memory of those lost at sea, eyes squeezed shut as he gripped his right leg. He must have been fighting hard not to let out any noise, though she could see his throat working convulsively.

She should have gone back to the crypt and left him alone. He was part of the world of the living, and she was all but a spirit herself now, a being that lived in shadows and forgotten memories. But he had such a kind face, and she was so starved for kindness, for human contact. Besides, he wasn't an adult, not like her aunt and uncle and the others.

"Are y-you hurt?" It had been so long since she had used her voice that the words came out thin and cracked.

The boy's eyes flew open, but he did not so much as move a muscle as he studied her. Then a slow, brilliant grin crept across his face.

It did something to her, that grin, warming her all the way from her empty stomach to her frozen toes. It made her feel as if someone had seen her for the first time after being invisible for her entire life.

"Be a love and help me, would you?" He gestured at his torn breeches, revealing an angry red gash that ran the length of his thigh. "It's not much more than a scratch but damned if I can stand on it. Must have grazed the spikes scaling over the fence."

She blinked at the exposed skin and swallowed. She'd never touched someone like him before. Once upon a time her mother must have bounced her on her knee, and her father must have playfully tugged on her braids. But since those forgotten days, the only touch Tabby knew was Alice pressed tight against her at night to keep warm, and the clammy hands of clients she was forced to hold in her aunt and uncle's parlor.

When she realized that he was staring at her expectantly, she finally sprang into action, commandeering his neckcloth and tearing it into strips of bandaging. There was something in his smile, the easy openness of his demeanor that made Tabby absurdly eager to please him. He could have asked her to cut off her thick red hair, and she would have asked him how much he would have. Her head told her that she couldn't trust him, not completely, but her heart wanted more than anything to earn another smile from him.

As she dabbed at the wound, the question of how he'd come by his black eye burned on the tip her tongue. As if reading her mind, he said, "Found myself a bit down on my luck after a night of cards, and without the snuff to pay my debt." Then he cleared his throat and carefully shifted his gaze away. "There, uh, might also have been the matter of a kiss stolen from Big Jack Corden's sister."

Card debts! Stolen kisses! This boy—no, this *young man*—brought a sense of worldly danger and excitement into the cemetery with him. Tabby pressed her lips together, knowing that anything she might say would only give her away as a country bumpkin in his eyes.

Yet there was something in the way he kept clearing his throat, the downward shift of his gaze, that made her wonder if there wasn't another explanation, something not nearly so dashing, that he wasn't telling her. Tabby was well versed in the language of violence, and how adults visited it on the small bodies of children. She did not for one moment believe that his injuries were the result of an overprotective brother.

Tabby was silent as she wrapped the bandage around

the cleaned cut, the shadowy images of the grave robbers receding in her mind as the sky continued to lighten. "Didn't think I would meet an angel in the graveyard when I stumbled in here," he said, giving her another grin.

Heat rushed to Tabby's cheeks and she ducked her head, concentrating on tying off the knot. She should have been frightened of him, frightened that he might somehow know her aunt and uncle and toss her over his shoulder and deliver her back up to them, or tell the caretaker that there was a filthy girl living in the graveyard. But there was a warmth in his soft brown eyes and she felt a camaraderie with him.

"Well," he said, inspecting her rather sloppy handiwork, "that will have to do." He tested his weight on the leg, grunting a little as he righted himself. He cast a reluctant look at the brightening horizon and sighed. "I suppose I should be going."

But he made no move to leave. He was gazing hard into the distance, as if he was determined to stop the sun from rising by sheer force of will. When he spoke again his voice was so soft, so different from his previous bluster. "Do you... do you ever feel as if you don't matter? That your life is already mapped out for you, and your wishes are inconsequential? And that even if you accept your lot, bow down and take it gladly, it's still not enough. Just by virtue of being *you* you're a disappointment, with no hope of redemption."

It was a rather grown-up speech, and though Tabby didn't know the source from which it sprang, she did know what it felt like to not matter. She might have told him as much, but he was already smoothing back his curls and clearing his throat. "Well, I should be going back," he repeated with resigned conviction. "I won't ask what a little thing like you is doing all alone at night in a grave-yard, if you forget that you ever saw me." Then he gave her a heart-melting wink, and was gone.

Tabby stood in the cool night air, her blood pound-ing fast and hot. It stung that he referred to her as "a lit-tle thing," but one thing was for certain: Tabby would never, ever forget the dashing young man with kind eyes.

Every night for the next week, Tabby crept out into the cemetery, waiting with her heart in her throat to see if the young man would return. She knew it was foolish, knew that it was dangerous, but she couldn't help herself. Even just to catch a glimpse of him would help staunch the flow of loneliness that threatened to drain her com-pletely. As far as she knew, Alice had never returned for her, and whatever little flame of hope had flickered in her heart was well and truly extinguished now.

So on the eighth night when Tabby heard the rustle of weeds, she hardly thought twice before stealing behind the column and waiting for the young man to appear, her lips already curving into a smile in anticipation. But her smile faded as a sinister figure dressed all in black ma-terialized out of the gloom. A sinister figure whom she had seen before.

The next day, Tabby watched as the caretaker stood by the empty grave and rubbed a weary hand over his face. After the robbery the previous week, he had walked the perimeter of the cemetery, repairing the fencing and check-ing the locks on the gate, but had not summoned the po-lice. But it seemed that fences and locks could not stop the grave robbers. She had developed a sort of affinity from afar for the gentle man with the long, careworn face, and it made her bruised heart hurt to see him brought so low.

She had known that there was evil in the world, had seen the darkness and greed that had driven her aunt and uncle, had felt the devastating injustice of being robbed of her parents. But she had never known the depth of depravity that could lead men to steal the bodies of the dead. The trials of this world were bearable because of the promise of divine rest, of reuniting with loved ones on the other side; how could anyone endure life otherwise?

As she watched the caretaker heave a sigh and get to his knees to clean the gravesite, Tabby vowed that someday she would see the men that did such vile deeds brought to justice.

2

IN WHICH THERE IS A REUNION.

Boston, June 1856

THE CARRIAGE JUTTED and lurched over the steep cobblestoned hill, threatening to bring Caleb's lunch up all over his neatly pressed suit. Perhaps if it did then he would have an excuse to bolt. Caleb hated funerals. Well, he supposed that no one really *enjoyed* funerals, but it was more than that. They were just so…so *messy*. All that sobbing and wailing, and never mind the ridiculous costumes. (Caleb drew the line at those absurd weeping veils that men insisted on putting on their beaver hats— better to leave all that frippery to the ladies.) They were public displays of what should be private. When he died— which, God willing, wouldn't be for decades yet—he hoped that his friends would just quietly put him in a grave, raise a glass to his memory, and be done with it.

Across from him, his mother was exemplifying just the kind of fuss that Caleb was sure his father wouldn't have tolerated. She was burying her face in his last clean handkerchief, bawling and carrying on with seemingly endless stamina. He gave her an awkward pat on her knee. "There now, Mum. All shall be well."

But his words had no effect; if anything, she cried only the harder.

Caleb withdrew his hand. It wasn't that he didn't feel badly for his mother, it was just that this torrent of emotion had seemed to come out of nowhere. His old man had been hard on both son and wife, and Caleb was having difficulty grasping how his mother could be so grief stricken for the man who had never hesitated to raise his fist to her.

He shot a pleading look at the lovely young woman beside him, who had thus far been quiet during the journey from the church to the cemetery. "Can't you say anything that will bring her around?" he whispered to his fiancée.

"She's grieving, Caleb!" Rose hissed back.

"No, she's hysterical." He raked his hand through his carefully pomaded hair before he could stop himself. "She's gone and worked herself up into such a state that she can barely breathe." That very morning Caleb had come down to breakfast to find his mother had engaged the services of some quack medium. The woman had told his mother that her departed husband was in God's celestial kingdom, smiling down on her and waiting patiently for their heavenly reunion. What bosh. If his father was anywhere, it wasn't up above, and he most certainly would not have been smiling. When Caleb had informed the medium of as much, she'd had the nerve to screech at him that he had destroyed the fragile link between worlds and that it would cost them another ten dollars to reestablish it. He'd all but hauled the woman by her ridiculous black lace collar and thrown her out of the house.

Squaring her slender shoulders, Rose leaned over and placed an elegant gloved hand on Caleb's mother's arm. "There now, Mrs. Bishop. Look, the sun is out and you couldn't ask for a lovelier day. Surely that must be a sign that Mr. Bishop is giving you his blessing to leave off your tears and smile."

"Thomas hated the sun!" She let out a fresh wail and Rose gave Caleb an exasperated look. He shrugged helplessly.

Rose tried again. "At the very least, give your poor eyes a rest. You don't want to give the other ladies from the Benevolent Society the satisfaction of seeing you with puffy red eyes, do you?"

His mother snuffled back her tears and gave a jerky nod. "Yes, perhaps…perhaps you're right. Mrs. Craggs has been insufferable ever since she came back from that spa treatment in the Swiss Alps."

The crisis handled, Caleb settled back against the squabs and sent up a silent prayer of thanks for having such a clever woman for a fiancée. Not just for these little moments of feminine comfort she provided, but for all the practical knowledge she brought to their union, as well. His father had been dead only these three days, but already the transfer of his shipping business to Caleb had manifested in meetings with anxious investors, lawyers thrusting papers in his face that needed signing, and a hundred other irksome details. Having Rose there with her sharp eyes and easy grace had made all the difference. She was gently bred and knew just how to handle these matters. If she did not set his heart aflame with passion, well, that was hardly her fault, not when they'd both agreed that this would be a marriage of alliance and nothing more.

Ahead of them, the hearse was struggling to make its way up the steep hill, and Caleb wondered how often coffins simply fell out the back and went coasting down the hill like toboggans. But the groaning vehicle crested the hill without incident, and then they were following it through the iron cemetery gates.

The cemetery stopped just short of being derelict, and it certainly was not one of the fashionable garden cemeteries that sprawled around the outskirts of the city. The only reason that his father would be buried in this dreary location was that it contained the family crypt, the final resting place for Bishops going back all the way to the Mayflower. Their bloodline was a point of pride for his father, one upon which he had expounded enthusiastically and frequently.

The burial service was mercifully brief. It seemed that Caleb's father had not been a man to inspire fiery eulogies or long-winded remembrances. The reverend said a few words, Caleb threw a symbolic clump of warm spring dirt onto the coffin with a satisfying thud, and his mother made a pretty show of restrained sniffles. Then the black-clad pallbearers lifted the coffin and deposited it in the family crypt. All in all, it was a rather tidy affair.

Afterward, Father's acquaintances came up, offering

their condolences and promising Caleb that they were eager to continue doing business with the family. It seemed terribly gauche to conduct business at a funeral, but no doubt his father would have been appalled if the gears of industry were to grind to a halt on account of a minor detail like death. There probably wasn't a single person among the mourners who would have considered Mr. Bishop a friend. Despite his resentment of his father, Caleb felt a pang of pity for the old man. What a miserable legacy to leave behind.

Caleb stared into the gaping entrance to the crypt that now housed his father's mortal remains. There was a ridiculous bell contraption rigged up that his father had insisted upon. Supposedly, in the case of being buried alive, it would give him a lifeline to signal for help. Caleb doubted that if the bumpy ride up the hill hadn't roused his father from his deathly slumber, that he was going to wake up at any point in the future.

He jumped at a light touch on his arm and spun around, half expecting his old man's ghost to be standing there, wagging his finger in disapproval.

But it was only his lovely fiancée, her dark blue eyes filled with concern. "I didn't mean to startle you," Rose said, "but I think your mother is ready to go home."

He glanced over to where his mother was dabbing at her cheeks and his heart clenched at how lost the old dear looked. The tall form of his father's business partner, Richard Whitby, stood beside her. "Will you be a love and ask Whitby to take you both home? I'd like a little more time here."

Rose gave him a questioning look—she knew well that

there was no love lost between him and his father—but angel that she was, she only nodded. "Of course. I'll see you Wednesday for luncheon with my parents?"

"Just try and stop me." He gave her a chaste kiss on the cheek.

He watched as Whitby offered his arm to Rose, Caleb's mother trailing behind them. When the somber clip of the funeral horses had faded, Caleb was left alone with his thoughts and the soft chorus of birds. It wasn't that he really needed any more time to pay his respects or see the old man off, he just wanted a few moments of peace and quiet after a week of chaos. Good God, what was he going to do? His father had tried to drill the fundamentals of the shipping business into him, from how to balance the ledger to inspecting cargo, but Caleb had preferred to spend his days playing cards at the Beacon Club, and his evenings at the theater. Everything about shipping was dull and dry, and that was not to mention that a good portion of its success hinged on the trade of human souls in the Caribbean. Why could his father not have just left the business in the capable hands of Whitby? Caleb certainly didn't want it.

Before his old man's heart had stopped beating, Caleb had been secretly studying books on architecture at the Athenaeum, and putting together a portfolio of sketches in the hopes of securing an apprenticeship at an architectural firm. He had always been fascinated by the grand buildings around Boston, and had dreamed of one day leaving his own mark on the city. To tell a story in stone, to immortalize his vision for a more beautiful world, was the most noble pursuit he could imagine. But now he had a mother and a fiancée who relied on him to keep a roof over their heads and his plans of designing beautiful buildings would have to be relegated to the fancies of youth.

Sighing, Caleb stared into the gaping tomb that had swallowed up the last of his dreams, and felt only despair.

Tabby watched the funeral procession trudge up the hill from her window, a sluggish black stream of mourners. Burials were rare in the old cemetery nowadays, and anything other than a simple affair with a handful of mourners even rarer.

The spectacle of the glass hearse and the team of gleaming black horses drawing it was too captivating to watch from afar. She let the ratty lace curtain fall from her fingers, then threw on a light shawl and her straw bonnet and went outside to take a closer look.

The scent of hothouse funeral roses mingled with damp earth, and cheery sparrows, heedless of the somber occasion, dipped and chased each other among the stones. With the mild spring air on her neck, Tabby let her fingers trail along the worn tops of the headstones as she made her way toward the funeral party.

The minister had just finished his prayer and the crowd was beginning to disperse when Tabby caught sight of a young man standing by the crypt with his back toward her. His hair had lightened from chestnut brown to a warm honey blond, and he was taller now—though still on the slight, lean side—but she would have recognized him anywhere.

Creeping closer, it was as if she'd been thrown back to

that fateful night, when he'd appeared as if by magic and sowed the seed of longing in her. More than once she had wondered what had become of the handsome young man. But he had belonged to the world of the living, and since then she had learned the hard way that the people you cared about never stayed.

She was only a few yards away from him, so close that she could see the strong line of his jaw and his kind, expressive eyes that stared sightlessly into the crypt. As she was shifting her weight to get a clearer view, she accidentally stepped on a branch, snapping it and shattering the silence. The young man turned around, his gaze landing squarely on her.

"If you've come for the interment, I'm afraid you've missed it. He's quite at rest now, and not likely to get up again."

Swallowing, she stepped out fully from behind the tree and shook her head. "No, I just…" Just what? Was spying on him? Drinking in every detail of his face that had grown only more beautiful in the years since she'd seen him last? "My father is the caretaker, and he sent me to see if everything went well—if you needed anything."

This wasn't strictly true, but it wasn't untrue, either. Eli hadn't exactly asked Tabby to check on the young man, so much as he'd asked her to make sure that all the mourners were gone so that he could replace the stone over the mouth of the crypt. And he wasn't her father by blood, either. But over the years, Tabby *had* come to see the old caretaker as a father. It had been only a few days after she'd come upon the young man that long-ago night, when she was so hungry and cold that she'd had no choice but to go to his doorstep and throw herself on his mercy. He had taken Tabby under his wing, and treated the foundling from the crypt like the child he had never had.

"The caretaker is your father? But isn't he…" The young man trailed off, color rising in his cheeks.

Tabby was used to this reaction, though it didn't make it any less hurtful. She jutted her chin out, challenging him to finish his sentence. "Eli might not be my father by blood, but he's my family."

"Of course, of course." He cleared his throat, the flush of red on his cheeks gradually diminishing. "Everything went smoothly. Please give my thanks to your father."

Tabby nodded mutely. *She* certainly hadn't grown any more beautiful in the almost twelve years since she'd first met him. Her hair was still shockingly red, her eyes still cloudy on account of her cursed ability. In her worn, too-small brown calico dress, she could only imagine what she looked like in his eyes.

"You'll forgive the impertinence, but have we met? You look familiar."

She had thought about this moment often, half fantasizing about the romantic possibilities, half wondering if he would even remember her. But now, faced with his question and finally seeing him in the flesh after all these years, the words got stuck in her throat. It was foolishness, she knew that now. How could she think that a chance meeting over a decade ago as children would be as memorable to him as it was to her? Besides, her childish fancies were just that—fancies. She could enjoy the romance of the fantasy in her head, but it could never be played out in real life, not when she was an aberration, a curiosity.

He spared her the need to respond by giving a long, low whistle and snapping his fingers. "You're the girl! The girl from this very cemetery! You helped me that night I found myself here."

Crossing his arms, he leaned against an obliging stone and shook his head. "I always wondered about you."

She gave him a skeptical look. "You did?"

"Of course! How could I not? I stumble into a cemetery and a little sprite creeps out from amongst the stones. I half thought you were a ghost! The more time passed the more I was sure I had imagined the entire incident."

He hadn't just remembered her, he had *thought* about her over the years. She glowed at the thought. But the mystery of what had brought him there that night had stayed with her, as well. She studied him out of the corner of her eye. "Did you ever settle your debt?"

"Hmm?"

"Your card debt. You said you were hiding from some men to whom you owed money for cards. And there was something about a kiss as well, I believe?"

He frowned, as if searching his memory. "Oh, right. Yes. I'd forgotten. I did settle it, in fact. How clever of you to remember."

"But why the cemetery? Why did you come here of all places?"

"It's been so long now, I'll be damned if I can remember. I suppose I thought it would be the last place he—I mean, they—would look."

When it became clear that he wasn't going to elaborate, Tabby nodded toward the crypt. "I'm sorry for your loss," she said.

"Hmm?" He looked as if he had almost forgotten why he was standing in a cemetery talking to her in the first place. "Oh yes. The old man had a bad heart," was all he said. And then, "I'm being terribly rude, aren't I? I haven't even introduced myself." He swept off his hat and gave a neat bow. "Caleb Bishop to my friends, Mr. Pope if I owe you money from cards," he said with a devastating wink.

"Tabitha Cooke," she said. "Tabby to my friends, and I don't play cards."

She had been in earnest, but he threw back his head and let out a pleased peal of laughter. Her legs wobbled in spite of herself, and she felt happy to have made such a fine man smile. She might not have been in the same class as him, or even the same world, but it felt good to be normal, just for a little while.

"So, tell me, Miss Cooke, how is it that you come to be in a cemetery every time I see you?"

"I live here." She watched him carefully, gauging his reaction.

One golden brow shot up. "What, here in the cemetery?"

"Oh no, not anymore." She pointed to the narrow town house across the street where Eli rented the attic rooms.

But instead of looking uncomfortable or turning on his heel to leave, he only broke into a slow smile. "Oh, you're amusing. I like you."

Before she could explain that she hadn't been in jest, he was pulling out his watch and exclaiming at the time.

"Well, Tabby Cooke. I must be off. Business calls and all that. But I do hope it won't be over ten years until we meet again." He tipped his hat to her and, with a dazzling grin, was off, leaving her with a pounding heart and a flicker of happiness, the likes of which she hadn't felt since the last time they'd parted.

3

IN WHICH A CALLOUSED HEART STILL BEATS.

THE DEAD WON'T *bother you if you don't give them permission.*

That night, like so many others, Tabby's mother's words didn't seem to hold any truth. It was always in those liminal moments when the mind was not quite in the land of the wake, nor yet the oblivion of sleep. The dead would come, first soft and slow like a gentle snowfall, then mounting into a roaring and furious squall. They always wanted the same things: resolutions to problems unresolved in life, last words that had gone unsaid. The dead who had no such unfinished business never bothered her; they simply moved on to whatever it was that came after.

After escaping her aunt and uncle, Tabby had never told anyone of her strange and frightening ability, but if she had, this is what she would have described: A darkness like the deepest of sleeps, a soundless, stale void without confines. The outside world snuffed to nothing like a candle flame drowning in a pool of wax. With great force of will she could pull herself out of the void, but it took a tremendous effort, both physically and mentally.

She hated it. She hated the sickly sweet smell of rot, the sightless eyes. She hated that her mind was not her own, that she was nothing more than a vessel for outpourings of grief and anger.

Kicking off her quilt, she padded across the tiny room to the window. Below her, mist wreathed the cemetery, headstones just visible like buoys bobbing in the harbor. Passersby might think that the dead slumbered without regard to the outside world, that their trials were over. How comforting a thought that must be, what a solace when pondering one's own mortality. Tabby alone was privy to the burdensome truth that told her otherwise. When she finally crawled back into bed, her sleep was thin and fitful.

"Tabby, did you hear what I said?"

Tabby was sitting at the rickety table in the front room that served as their parlor, a rainbow of threads spread out before her as a weeping willow slowly took shape on her embroidery frame. When the scene was finished, it would depict a widower mourning at the grave of his beloved wife, the trailing leaves of the willow echoing his tears. Tabby was quick with a needle and thread, and though the memorial embroideries were not as fashionable as they once had been, they brought in some much-needed income. And, if she concentrated on the stitches hard enough, her mind was tight as a ship, with nary a crack in her defenses against the dead.

Frowning, she looked up Eli's words. "What was that?"

"I said that it looks like rain and I haven't been out to collect the old bouquets in weeks." Eli had been bent over his account book, but now he was peering at her. "Are you all right? You looked a thousand miles away."

Warmth flooded Tabby's cheeks and she ducked her head, concentrating twice as hard on pulling her green thread through the linen. Her mind hadn't been a thousand miles away, only a few yards, actually. She'd been thinking of young Caleb Bishop and the way he carried himself with such confidence, how he radiated charm. She was thinking of the way he made her feel as if she was the most important person in the world—no, the *only* person in the world—when he spoke with her. But at Eli's question she quickly pushed such foolish thoughts away.

"Just trying to get this stitch right," she said lamely.

Eli gave her a lingering look of doubt and then slowly unfolded himself from his chair. "Well, I'd better go collect them if we don't want the rats finding them first."

"Oh no, you won't," she said, jumping up. Eli's back had gotten bad over the past few years, and she didn't like the idea of him stooping over more than he already needed to. "I'll take a basket and do it. Besides," she added, giving him a sly look, "I saw Miss Suze yesterday, and she said she had a pie she wanted to bring over for you."

At the mention of the older woman's name, Eli obediently dropped back down in his chair. "Is that, ah... is that so?"

Eli was a quiet man who kept his own counsel, even from his daughter. Tabby didn't know everything of what went on in his mind, but she knew enough that she recognized the look Eli gave Miss Suze from the Baptist church as pure, unadulterated longing. Miss Suze was a widow with six grown children, at least a dozen grandchildren, and a propensity for making enough food to feed a small army. Occasionally she invited Eli and Tabby to dine with her, and Tabby always enjoyed the boisterous family meals.

"I don't know why you don't just ask her," Tabby said. "It's clear that she holds you in high esteem."

"It's not that simple," Eli said with a deflective grunt.

Tabby thought it was the simplest thing in the world. Miss Suze always made a point of sitting near Eli in church. Eli was a well-respected man in the community, never married, and clearly had feelings for her. Perhaps their living situation in the boarding house wasn't ideal for a married couple, but surely they could make it work?

As she was turning to fetch her shawl, Eli reached up and clasped her hand. "My Tabby cat," he said, his long face creasing with a smile. "You're a good girl. I don't know what I would do without you."

She looked down at her pink hand in his big brown one. The hands that had raised her were strong and capable, but she couldn't help but notice the knuckles were starting to swell with rheumatism. Eli had always been clever with a knife, and carved intricate figurines and talismans, including the death's head pendant that Tabby wore around her neck. He hadn't been a young man when he'd found her, and that had been twelve years ago. She often wondered how long he would be able to continue his work when it required so much labor. From what he had told her, he was the only one willing to take on the job as caretaker after this particular cemetery had fallen out of fashion with Boston's wealthy elite. The cemetery was filled with hundreds of unmarked graves of slaves and the African community, and Eli had left his job as a fishmonger and stepped up when no one else would. "Someone's got to care for them, remember them," he had told her. Because that was what Eli did; he cared for things that were broken and forgotten.

Brushing his cheek with a kiss, Tabby squeezed his hand. "And I don't know what I would do without you."

Thick banks of clouds were rolling in from the harbor, but the day was mild and perfumed with the fresh scent of pollen when Tabby stepped outside with her basket on her elbow. Spring in the cemetery meant lush grass beneath her feet, tulips and narcissus clustered about the old stones, and flowering crab apple trees that begged to be climbed—even if she was much too old for such things.

"Tabby!"

She spun around to see a young woman waving at her coming up the street. Tall and raven haired with ivory skin, Mary-Ruth turned heads as she walked by, but also cleared a path, like Moses parting the Red Sea. Tabby watched as one little boy, braver than his friends, darted right up to her to try to touch her skirt. Mary-Ruth stuck her tongue out at him, which sent him scuttling back to the safety of his playmates. Children always seemed to regard her with equal parts fascination and terror, as if she were some beautiful angel of death.

"What are you doing up this way?" Tabby asked her friend when she'd reached the cemetery. "I haven't heard of any recent passings."

Mary-Ruth linked her arm through Tabby's as they passed through the gate together. "Old Mr. Drew," she said, shaking her head. "The gin finally got the better of him. Just came from the house and thought I would see what you were doing."

Wherever there was death, there was Mary-Ruth. A layer, Mary-Ruth was summoned whenever someone had died and the family needed them dressed and laid out for burial. Almost all of the bodies that came through the cemetery gates first passed under Mary-Ruth's capable hands. Her blithesome, sunny demeanor may have seemed anathema to the somber nature of her vocation, but like Tabby, she was something of an outsider, and Tabby had gradually lowered her guard and let Mary-Ruth into her heart. Like Eli, Mary-Ruth was no stranger to the world of the dead, and so Tabby could trust her—to an extent. They talked about everything, from Mary-Ruth's patients to Tabby's embroidery projects, to the influx of Irish coming over on coffin ships just as Mary-Ruth had nine years ago. Everything, except the secret of Tabby's ability, which she guarded like a starving dog with a bone.

"Oh, nothing interesting." Tabby lifted her empty basket to show her. "Just out to pick up the old bouquets. I don't suppose you would want to join me?"

"Of course! It's a lovely spring day and I've been cooped up inside with naught but the dead to keep me company.

Did you know," she said, throwing Tabby a sidelong look, "that Gracie Peck has stopped watching? Her back is too bad now to sit up long nights anymore."

Gracie Peck was a watcher, or "watch woman," the counterpart to Mary-Ruth. She would sit up with the sick and dying until they exhaled their last breath, and then would watch them for hours to make certain that they were not like to draw a breath again. There was no greater fear for the dying than to wake up very much alive in a coffin. When their charge was well and truly dead, the watcher would send for Mary-Ruth.

Tabby shook her head, not liking the look in her friend's silver eyes. "I hadn't heard."

"Yes," said Mary-Ruth. She was quiet for a beat before adding, "I don't suppose you would consider taking up for her? There's good money in it, and I think you have just the sort of quiet, steady disposition that favors watching."

Tabby winced. She *would* be a good watcher, but not for the reasons Mary-Ruth gave. She would only have to open her mind the slightest bit and she would know if the person had passed. But Mary-Ruth didn't know about Tabby's ability. No one knew, not even Eli. To divulge the secret that she had carried all these years somehow felt like a betrayal to Alice, and Tabby had so little of her sister left. Besides, as soon as people learned of her abilities, she would become a curiosity, a novelty. Something to be exploited. She had only to think of Beth Bunn and the other children in the churchyard. Tabby could not jeopardize the fragile bonds she had worked so hard to forge and treasured so dearly with Mary-Ruth and Eli over the years.

Sidestepping the question, Tabby gave her friend a bright smile. "Come," she said. "Whoever picks up the most bouquets gets a licorice twist from Mr. Greene's."

Hitching up their skirts, they took off in opposite directions. Despite the lovely day and the good company, as Tabby darted between the graves looking for old bouquets, she felt a familiar sense of melancholy prick at her. If Alice had not abandoned her, could it have been Tabby and her sister running through the warm June air, laughing and enjoying themselves? Though she loved Mary-Ruth dearly, it was tiring to never be able to completely let down her guard. With Alice, she had been able to just be herself.

Tabby spotted a large bouquet of roses, once bright red, now browned and wilted, propped up against a headstone. No sooner had she set her eyes on it, than Mary-Ruth came from the other direction and saw it at the same time.

"Don't you dare, Tabby Cooke!" she squealed as she dashed to grab it.

Tabby had no intention of letting Mary-Ruth win, and lunged to scoop it up first.

"Aha!" Triumphant, Tabby waved the bouquet over her head, sending brown petals cascading down her shoulders.

But her achievement went unnoticed by Mary-Ruth, who had suddenly stopped in her tracks and was looking down toward the wall of crypts. "I say, Tabs, would you look at that?"

Tabby followed her gaze and sucked in her breath when it landed on Mr. Bishop.

"What's a coxcomb like him doing here?"

Protective, territorial feelings flared up in Tabby's chest.

He was standing by his family crypt, looking pensive and absurdly handsome in his beaver hat and a well-cut green frock coat. "The rich have to mourn, too. Come on," Tabby said, stuffing the bouquet into her basket and tugging at Mary-Ruth's sleeve. "We shouldn't intrude."

When Mary-Ruth didn't budge, Tabby looked back to find she was staring at her with a little smile. "You know him, don't you? You little minx!"

Tabby's cheeks burned. "Yes. I mean, no. His father was interred yesterday and he introduced himself. That's all."

She could feel Mary-Ruth's keen eyes on her. "All right, if you say so."

"I do," Tabby said firmly. She was just about to pull Mary-Ruth away, when Mr. Bishop must have heard their whispers and turned around.

He looked surprised for only a moment, but then he broke into an easy smile and waved. "Miss Cooke, was it? Out enjoying this fine day?"

Pushing aside the burst of happiness she felt that he had remembered her name, Tabby returned the wave. "Sorry to bother you, Mr. Bishop. We didn't mean to intrude."

"It's no bother," he said amicably, and indeed he didn't look bothered in the least. In fact, if Tabby wasn't mistaken, he looked almost relieved to see them as he drew closer.

Mary-Ruth elbowed her in the ribs, hard, and Tabby finally remembered her manners. "Er, Mr. Bishop, may I present Miss O'Reilly?"

"Mr. Bishop," Mary-Ruth said with an unnecessary curtsy.

This was torture. For all that Tabby would have been

content to just bask in Mr. Bishop's presence, she felt awkward and plain next to Mary-Ruth, and suddenly wanted to get far, far away. "Well, we'll leave you to enjoy your afternoon," she said, nudging Mary-Ruth to continue up the path.

As soon as the words left her mouth, Tabby wanted to kick herself. Enjoy his afternoon, indeed! He had come to mourn his father, and here she was acting as if he were out for a stroll in the park.

But to her surprise, Mr. Bishop only gave her a genuine smile. "No, please," he said, "don't leave on my account."

Mary-Ruth glanced between them, her eyes narrowing. "Do you know, I just remembered a previous engagement. You'll both excuse me?"

Before Tabby could ask her what on earth she was talking about, Mary-Ruth was saying her good-byes. And then just like that, Tabby was alone with Mr. Bishop.

"You have a…" He gestured to her bonnet. "And another one there." He pointed to her shoulder.

Reaching up, Tabby felt the dead rose petals from the bouquet, and hastily brushed them off.

They stood amidst the birdsong, the breeze teasing at his light hair under the rim of his hat. The clouds were growing heavier, and soon it would start to rain. Why had he wanted her to stay? She was not exactly the sort of sparkling company to which someone like him was no doubt accustomed.

"You must miss him terribly," she said finally, with a nod toward the crypt.

He let out a snort. "I can't say that I do."

Putting her basket gently down, Tabby moved closer. "Why did you come visit him if you don't miss him?"

Glancing around as if the dead might hear him, he leaned in conspiratorially. "I don't suppose you'd tell anyone?"

"Of course not!"

This earned her a wink and her heart skipped a beat. "There's a pet." He let out a frustrated sigh before continuing. "I've inherited my old man's shipping business and to be perfectly frank, I haven't the slightest clue what I'm about."

"Shipping business?" She wasn't sure what that entailed, but it brought to mind beautiful clippers with starched-white sails fluttering against cerulean skies. Cargo holds loaded with gems and exotic spices from far-off lands. Adventures.

"Bishop & Son Shipping," he said, incredulous. "Don't tell me you've never heard of it? Never seen the signboards down by the docks, or on the side of Boylston Hall?"

She shook her head. She rarely ventured into the thick of the city. Even if she had, she was forever looking over her shoulder to make certain no one was following her, and she didn't pay much attention to the riot of signboards and marquees that vied for attention.

"But surely your father must have prepared you?" she asked.

"That's just the thing. My old man didn't have a terrible lot of faith in me," he said with a valiant attempt at nonchalance that made Tabby's heart squeeze. "I suppose I wasn't the most attentive pupil if it came down to it, either. For the life of me I can't even remember where he kept the blasted ledgers."

Tabby absorbed this. She could just see the young Mr. Bishop going out on the town instead of squinting over papers all night like his father had wanted. What kind of things did a man like himself get up to? Well, card games and cavorting with girls, if she remembered his first foray into the cemetery correctly.

She studied the crinkled lines at the corners of his eyes that formed when he smiled, and wondered how many women before her had gazed upon them. How many women had felt themselves the center of the universe when he bestowed them with that lopsided smile? How many women knew things about him that Tabby would never know, like the feel of his palms against their breasts, the beat of his heart under their ear when they awoke beside him in the morning?

"But that's enough about me and my problems," he said, brightening. He glanced at her, looked like he wanted to say something, and then glanced back away.

"What is it?" she asked.

Biting his lip, he shook his head. "You'll think me terribly rude, but I must know."

She waited for him to continue, and he gestured to her cloudy eyes. "Your eyes, they're..." he trailed off, clearly realizing he'd gone down a path with no safe return. Tabby didn't say anything. It was oddly satisfying to render such a charming and urbane man speechless and stuttering. He cleared his throat. "Can you...that is, can you see out of them?"

She could see far more than he would ever know, see

things that would make grown men tremble in their boots. But she didn't tell him this. "Yes," she said, trying to keep a serious face. "I can see out of my eyes. For example, I can see you flushing up as pink as a tulip right now."

"Ah...erm, yes. Of course." He ducked his head, scrubbing at the back of his neck.

"Would you like to know if I can hear out of my ears? If I can taste with my tongue, perhaps?"

He sputtered and coughed. "No, no, that won't be necessary, I'm sure."

Tabby was enjoying herself immensely, but then she remembered that they were standing in front of his father's grave. His father who had only just died and been laid to rest. She composed herself, and steered the conversation back to him.

"What about your sister?" she asked. "Does she know anything of the business?"

"My sister? If I have a sister then my father has even more to answer for." He cocked his head and regarded her. "What on earth gave you that idea?"

"I—I thought I saw a young lady with you the other day." Now it was Tabby's turn to flush; she was all but admitting that she had watched him from afar.

He gave a little laugh. "What, Rose? I daresay she wouldn't be happy to hear she was mistaken for my sister. No, she's my fiancée."

The words made Tabby's chest twist in an unpleasant, unfamiliar manner. "Your fiancée," she echoed. The woman had been pretty, like a fashion plate come to life with her tiny waist, dainty slippers, and wide, guileless blue eyes.

"Just so. And," he said, pulling out his watch, "I promised to dine with her this evening. I hope I haven't kept you too long from your task."

Tabby had all but forgotten her half-empty basket of rotted flowers. She watched him leave, hailing down a hack when he reached the street. Of course Mr. Bishop had a fiancée; how could she have been so foolish? For all her years at Cemetery Hill, there had been little that Tabby missed of the outside world. There was Eli, her little room in the gables, Mary-Ruth, and her embroidering. She didn't need to fear her aunt and uncle anymore so long as she remained vigilant. She missed Alice terribly, of course, but the aching loss had grown familiar, had become as much a part of Tabby as the memories of her sister themselves.

No, she had no expectation or desire to marry. Her heart had grown calloused and hard, a necessary defense in her struggle to survive. Yet there was a vulnerability about him that inspired in her an absurd need to please him, to help him. She should thank her lucky stars that he wasn't available, that she had no reason to be tempted, yet all she felt was an empty longing that she knew would never be filled.

4

IN WHICH THE DEAD ARE DISTURBED.

CALEB WATCHED FROM the carriage as dusk settled over Boston, the gas lamps sputtering to life and passing by in a blur of yellow smudges. It had started raining shortly after he'd left the cemetery that afternoon and hadn't stopped since. His head had likewise been in a fog; his thoughts vacillating wildly between the mounting pressures of his father's business, his dashed dreams of becoming an architect, and a certain young lady who always seemed to be haunting the cemetery.

"Caleb? Darling?"

Caleb turned in his seat and belatedly realized that Rose had been speaking. "I'm sorry, what were you saying?"

"Are you all right? I swear, it seems your mind has been miles away lately."

"Has it? I suppose it's just—" he gestured vaguely at

the small carriage interior as if it contained everything that had happened over the past few days "—my father, the business. It's taking its toll."

"Of course," Rose said swiftly, taking his hand and squeezing. "I'm so sorry. You must take all the time you need."

Caleb gave her a weak smile, but he couldn't help but feel guilty when his thoughts turned right back to where they had been fixated: on the strangest girl he had ever met, the one with flaming red hair and eyes the color of mountains shrouded in mist. There was something about Miss Cooke that challenged him, yet made him feel instantly comfortable, as if he had always known her. Or perhaps it was the cemetery itself, the way time and all his worldly worries melted away amongst the graves and the gently bobbing flowers. It had felt so damned *good* just to spill out his troubles to a sympathetic ear. Rose would have listened to him—she always did—but he didn't want to burden her, didn't want her to have to offer solutions and feel as if she had to resolve everything for him. Sometimes a man just wanted to talk.

"Caleb? We're here."

The carriage had stopped and Rose was looking at him expectantly. Outside the theater, traffic streamed alongside of them, a throng of men in tall opera hats and ladies clutching at umbrellas. Caleb had been excited for the new French melodrama when he'd booked the box last week, but now he wasn't even sure he could sit still for three hours. He was also supposed to be in mourning, which meant no public engagements for at least a month, but Rose was still waiting for him, and she looked so fetching and hopeful that he had no choice but to shake free the fog from his head.

"Right," he said, hopping out and offering his hand to Rose. "Shall we?"

Tabby waited until Eli was sleeping that night before she swung her legs out of bed. She was already fully dressed, so she only had to grab her cloak and put on her shoes. Tiptoeing through their rooms, she took care not to wake the landlady when she reached the main stairs. Once she was outside, she let out her breath, hurrying through the cool spring mist that hung over the hill.

The streets were empty and quiet save for the yowling of a stray dog and the occasional clip of a passing hack. When she reached the church, she settled herself on the damp steps, and closed her eyes.

She had made this same trip down the hill and to the church once a month for the past twelve years. What she was about to do could have been done from anywhere—including the comfort and privacy of her own bed—but the church was where she had last seen Alice, and if there was anyplace where some little essence of her sister still lingered in the city, it was there.

Alice had once said that their mother had taught her never to try to contact anyone you had known in life. Alice had passed on the warning, cautioning Tabby against ever contacting their parents; it was too terrible to see someone you loved on the other side.

Pushing aside her sister's warning as she did every month, Tabby searched the cold, murky ether for the once-familiar face of her sister.

And just like every other month, no spirit came to her. There was hope that Alice was alive yet.

Rising from the steps, Tabby turned back to the hill. There was still one more spirit with whom she must make contact that night. Tabby had never willingly exercised her ability in this way except in her search for Alice, and she wouldn't have if it wasn't for the person she was trying to help.

After she had seen Caleb Bishop that morning and he had confided in her about his plight, she knew that she would do anything she could to help him. She didn't know why, but his story had touched her. He was a wealthy young man from a different world, and yet she had commiserated with his predicament. After all, she knew all too well what it was like to be funneled into a path that was anathema to one's character. And that meant that she must speak with his father, learn what he had to say about Caleb's business responsibilities.

At the cemetery gates, she lingered, loath to go inside even as she knew she must. They were open tonight, which was odd; Eli must have forgotten to lock them. Settling herself on a bench just inside the gates, she repeated the ritual she had just performed on the church steps not even half an hour earlier. This time it was Mr. Bishop who she invited to step through the veil. She did not know what he looked like, only his name; that would have to be enough.

She had learned that the dead did not like to speak of what became of their body after death. The disconnect was too great, the horror of seeing their mortal remains too much to bear.

Mr. Bishop. She spoke silently in her mind, her words echoing through the void. *You don't know me, but I am a friend of your son's. I know you want rest, but I believe that speaking with me could benefit us both.* If nothing else, surely the old man would not want to see his business flounder at the hands of his son.

It was a rare spirit that did not accept an invitation to speak with the living. There was always some message they wanted passed on, some last word added to the record. Tabby waited, bracing herself for the inevitable.

A stale wind whipped up through the void in her mind, and then the austere, wrinkled face of a man appeared. She sucked in her breath. No matter how much she anticipated the moment of contact, it always felt like an ambush, like the air was being stolen right from her lungs.

What do you want from me, girl? Don't you know who I am? I don't tolerate strangers meddling in my business.

So much for death being the great equalizer. Tabby forced herself to focus on the hard ground beneath her shoes, the faint scent of salt water from the harbor. She could not allow herself to get lost in the void. *I come on behalf of your son, Caleb. He—*

The spirit let out an impatient snort. *Caleb? That boy is not fit to handle his own allowance, never mind the business my father built up from nothing.*

Even though he was only in her mind, she could smell the rot on him, feel the cold air he brought wrap itself around her. More than anything, Tabby wanted to slam the door shut, build up her wall, and never have to see this awful man again. But she had come this far and Caleb needed her, so she pressed on.

You're wrong not to have faith in your son, but if you really care so little for him, then perhaps you will at least think of the success of Bishop & Son Shipping and answer me what I ask.

This seemed to capture his attention. His colorless eyes regarded her skeptically and it was all she could do to force herself to return his gaze in equal measure, willing him not to break contact. *Very well*, he finally said. *I will tell you what you need to know.*

When the interview was over and the smell of death had receded, Tabby leaned over with her head between her knees and heaved. At least she had what Caleb needed now. At least it hadn't been for nothing.

When her legs felt steady again and she could breathe, she stood up, ready to slip into the warm safety of her bed. But just as she was turning to leave the cemetery, the faint tinkling of a bell sounded in the still night air.

Quickly, she slipped back inside the gates and ducked behind a gravestone. There was just enough moonlight that she could make out a man dressed in dark clothes and carrying some kind of tool, a pickax, maybe. He was speaking to someone in a hoarse whisper, but a tree obscured her view. Tabby edged closer, using gravestones as shields until she had a clear line of sight to the crypts where the man stood.

There was the second man, his bobbing cap just visible in the recessed entrance of the crypt. The bell that had been installed on the door jangled in protest as they hefted the door aside. Few crypts were equipped with such a bell, and aside from particularly windy days, Tabby had never actually heard one of them ring. But now it rang in vain.

After the spate of robberies ten years ago, Eli had mended the fence and installed new locks on the gates, and, coupled with the diminishing amount of burials in the old cemetery, it had seemed as if the days of grave robberies were nothing more than a dark memory.

But now she watched in horror, paralyzed, as the wrenching sound of metal splintered through wood. The first man paced nearby, every now and then throwing a glance over his shoulder. This would break Eli. He took so much pride in keeping the cemetery safe, a sacred space.

The man in the crypt had disappeared from sight, but now he appeared again, hefting a pale bundle to the man above. Between the two of them, they carried the shrouded body to the far wall and clumsily hoisted it up and over to where a cart was presumably waiting on the other side.

Mouth dry as cotton, she crouched there for what seemed like hours, until her legs were numb. When the creaking of wheels had finally faded into the night, she clambered to her feet and crept over to the row of crypts.

The sourness in her stomach returned, and she felt as if she might faint, despite the anger pumping through her veins. It was a foggy night, and the moon had long since disappeared behind a heavy veil of clouds, but she didn't need to read the plaque to know what it said: it was the Bishop crypt.

5

IN WHICH A FORBIDDEN FRUIT IS TASTED.

AFTER THE RAIN of the previous night, Boston was enjoying a sunny, warm day. Couples picnicked on the Common, children ran down Tremont Street with hoops and sticks, and shop owners threw open their windows, the scents of roasting coffee and fresh-baked bread wafting out onto the streets. With his walking stick in one hand and the sun on his face, Caleb headed out into the city. He was just going to visit his father's grave one last time, and if he happened to bump into the intriguing Miss Cooke in the cemetery, well then, he could hardly be blamed for such a coincidence. That was what he told himself, anyway, as he briskly walked across town.

As he passed by the theater, a pretty brunette he recognized as the soprano from the other night threw him a wink. He tipped his hat, but kept walking. Since his engagement to Rose, he had been trying so hard not to slip into old habits, but he still enjoyed the attention of pretty girls. Pretty girls didn't expect lofty things from him, like running a business or carrying on the family legacy. All they expected was flattery and a bit of fun, both of which he was only too happy to provide. Seeing Miss Cooke would be a welcome distraction from the avalanche of responsibility that had come crashing down on his shoulders in the recent days.

He had hardly stepped foot through the cemetery gates when he spied the limping caretaker hurrying toward him. "Oh, Mr. Bishop. It's good you've come," Mr. Cooke said. "I was just about to send a messenger to fetch you."

Caleb blinked and grew wary, momentarily wondering if the man had somehow discerned Caleb's impure thoughts about his daughter. "You were?"

"I'm afraid there's, uh, been an incident."

So not about Tabby, then. Caleb frowned. "What kind of incident?" Scenarios ran through his mind, but none of them seemed particularly pressing. Had the silversmith botched the dates on the plaque? Had the payment from the bank not gone through? Mr. Cooke could have sent him an invoice or letter if any of that was the case.

Mr. Cooke pressed his lips tight together, looking exceedingly uncomfortable. "There was a robbery last night."

"A robbery?"

"Yes. That is…your father." Clearing his throat, the caretaker removed his hat and scrubbed at his graying crown of hair. "Rest assured, I've contacted the constable and he's aware of the situation."

Mr. Cooke was still speaking, but Caleb hardly heard him. "I'm sorry, but did you say my father was...robbed?"

The caretaker nodded.

Caleb considered this. "Are you trying to tell me that someone dug up my father's corpse just to *rob* the old fellow?"

Mr. Cooke looked taken aback at Caleb's language, but pressed on, exasperation creeping into his voice. "Sir, I'm telling you that someone dug up your father to rob him *of* his corpse."

Well. He certainly had not been expecting *that*. His father had been gouty and pockmarked; he hardly seemed like an appealing prospect as far as corpses went.

"Are you all right, sir? I know it's a shock, but—"

Caleb waved off his concern. "Yes, yes, quite all right. But," he said, "what on earth would anyone want with my father's body?"

"Er, I believe the freshly dead sell at a premium to surgeons and medical students. For dissection, that is."

"Well, I'll be." Caleb marveled at this. His father had been a miser and a hard man, but he certainly hadn't deserved such a fate. Caleb wouldn't be able to tell his mother about the desecration, of course; it would shatter the poor dear's nerves. Rose likewise should be kept in the dark, lest she become upset. "I thank you for bringing this to my attention," Caleb said, turning toward the back of the cemetery. "I'll bid you good day and take a walk to the grave site if it's all the same."

Mr. Cooke looked as if he would have thrown himself in Caleb's path to stop him if he could have. "I... You want to go to the grave? There's nothing to see there except a pried-open door and a splintered coffin," he said. "It might be most distressing for you."

But Caleb was already making his way to the back of the cemetery, scanning for a splash of bright red hair.

The crypt yawned at him balefully as he approached, debris and evidence of forced entry scattered about the ground. But it was the person he found there that caught his interest. "Hullo there."

Miss Cooke was crouched by the edge of the crypt with broom in one hand and pan in the other, sweeping up splintered bits of wood. She was wearing the same brown wool dress as usual, and without her bonnet her loose red hair shone brilliantly in the sunlight. At the sound of his voice she sprang up, sending wood and dust falling from her pan. "Caleb," she said. "I mean, Mr. Bishop. What are you doing here?"

Caleb was more than a little pleased at the way she breathed his name as if it were the most precious word to ever cross her lips, and the strange news of his father's body was momentarily forgotten. "What, is a man not allowed to pay his respects?"

She colored prettily at this, and he noticed that she had a light dusting of freckles across the bridge of her nose. "No, of course not, it's only—"

He stopped her with an airy wave of his hand. "Don't fret, I was only teasing." She was easy to tease, and though there was a guardedness about her, there was also a sensitivity, and he realized he would have to be careful with this rare cemetery bird, lest she take flight and leave him there. Because even though there was no accounting for it, he realized that he very much wanted her to stay.

They stood in silence, staring into the violated tomb, the only sound the clip of horses on the cobblestone street and a breeze lifting from the harbor and filtering through the trees.

When she spoke her voice was small, hesitant. "I—I am very sorry about what happened to your father's body. He..." She looked as if she wanted to say something else, but trailed off.

Caleb knew he ought to have been angrier about the robbery, but it was mostly just annoyance that it was one more unpleasant task on his endless list of obligations since his father died. The realization made him only loathe himself the more that he was such a vain creature, just as his father had always accused him of being. "I just hope the villains are brought to justice without too much fuss," he finally said.

"I doubt the police will be of much help. They could hardly be bothered when it happened before."

"You mean to say that this isn't the first time?"

She nodded. "The night we met, actually. I wonder that you didn't cross paths with them."

He gave a low whistle. "Is that so?" Then an unexpected surge of anger ran through him. "I say, they didn't bother you, did they?"

"No, they didn't know I was there."

A cemetery was no place for a little girl, even if her father was the caretaker. He wanted to ask her about how she had come to find herself there in the dead of night, but something told him he wouldn't get an answer.

"Do you think they targeted him in particular? He wasn't exactly well liked."

Miss Cooke shook her head. "I doubt they knew or cared who he was. They probably just wanted someone recently buried."

Caleb mused on this. "Do you know, my old man thought that a witch put a curse on him when he was a boy? Nothing was ever his fault. No matter that he was a bitter old drunk—if something went wrong, someone else always was to blame." The story of the witch always came out when he was deep in his cups, an angry, incohesive rant that explained everything from Mr. Bishop's lame leg to the bad luck that had plagued him throughout his sixty years. "It's all nonsense, of course," he continued. "Well, I hope wherever he is, he's in better spirits."

Miss Cooke hadn't said anything in a while. He looked over at her and found that she was worrying at her lip, staring at the crypt. "Miss Cooke? Are you all right?"

If she heard him, she gave no indication. "Mr. Bishop, there's something I need to tell you. I…"

He waited for her to finish, but she didn't seem inclined to go on. "Yes?"

"I… That is…" Pausing, she darted a furtive glance at him, then took a deep breath, and squared her shoulders. "I spoke with your father."

"You were acquainted with my father?" Caleb couldn't help his incredulous tone. This young woman was really quite extraordinary. She dressed as if she were the poorest church mouse, never seemed to leave the cemetery, and yet she had somehow crossed paths with his old man, who had always been notoriously proud when it came to mixing with the lower classes.

She bit her lip and twisted her hands together. "Well, not exactly... That is..."

Caleb groaned, leaning back against a tree. "Oh, don't tell me. You weren't one of his..." At her wide-eyed expression, Caleb cleared his throat and straightened. "Of course you weren't. I shouldn't have even suggested such a thing. I apologize."

Something in her seemed to shift, and her face shuttered. "It doesn't matter how or when I spoke to him," she said with a defensive bite in her voice. "He said that the ledgers are in a lockbox, behind a false panel in the bottom drawer of his desk. He knows that you aren't good at balancing the numbers, but hopes that with time will come diligence." With this, she crouched back down and resumed her cleaning.

This caught his attention. Drawing closer, he bent and took her by the arm. "How did you know about the lockbox?" he asked, raising her up. After he had gone home the other day, he had turned his father's study upside down, and sure enough, the ledgers had been in the bottom drawer of the desk. As for balancing them, he couldn't imagine a scenario in which his father had even a sliver of faith in him.

"Please," she said, twisting out of his grasp, "it doesn't matter how I know of them. I only wanted to help you, but now I see I shouldn't have bothered."

Her answer didn't satisfy him, but as he took her by the shoulders, studying the bitter disappointment, the earnestness on her face, he realized that he really didn't give a damn how she had found out. Someone had wanted to help him. For the first time since his father died, he didn't feel so utterly adrift. In fact, he felt rather calm and drowsy with the thin wool of her dress under his fingertips, and the sunlight cradling them in a hazy embrace.

"Mr. Bishop?"

Her tremulous voice tugged him out of his thoughts and when he looked down, he realized that he was still grasping her by the shoulders. He relaxed his grip, but just a little. She was looking up at him, her lips slightly parted, her eyes searching his. What did the world look like through those incredible eyes of hers? Did she see a foolish young man when she looked at him? Or something more? Did she feel the same inexplicable desire burning deep within her belly when they stood close?

Before he knew what he was doing, he murmured, "I think I will kiss you now."

She surely hadn't heard him right. Why on earth would he want to kiss her, here, now? His father's body had been stolen, the grave violated. And never mind that he had already told her he was an engaged man. But then he was leaning in toward her, the trajectory of his lips unmistakable.

She knew that it was wrong, for so many reasons, but she was helpless to stop herself as her mouth parted and she went boneless in his arms. She'd never been kissed before, and the temptation to experience this strange and wonderful phenomenon for herself was too strong to resist. Then he was deepening the kiss, pulling her against the length of him as she automatically twined her hands behind his neck.

It was glorious. Parts of her she didn't even know existed flared to life, her body flooding with warmth under his fingertips. There, amongst the carved death's heads and rasping crows, she felt more alive than she ever had before.

But then reality came rushing back. What was she doing? The girl with the calloused heart didn't fall into the arms of handsome young men. The girl with the curse of talking to the dead most certainly didn't partake in such intimate gestures. And he was *engaged*, the cad.

She pulled back and, before she could think twice, slapped him clean across his cheek, the force smarting her palm. She'd never struck someone before. Reeling back, he gave a yelp.

She shouldn't have hit him—it had been more to make herself stop than him—but he didn't look angry or even surprised, only slightly sheepish, breathing heavily as if awakening from a dream.

"I suppose I had that coming," he said with a crooked grin, and Tabby got the impression that this was not the first time he had found himself on the receiving end of a blow from a woman. But then his face darkened and his expression grew serious. "I'm sorry. I… I must be off. I shouldn't be here with you…doing this."

He was right, but the sudden sting of rejection hurt more than it had any right to. She watched him stride away, his gait still confident but unmistakably hurried, as if he couldn't get away from her fast enough.

Had that really just happened? She ran her tongue over her lips, reveling in the lingering taste of him. He had been so easy to talk to, and the fact that she had spoken to his father had just slipped out. How could she be so careless? All it had taken was one lopsided smile from him, one electric look from his probing eyes, and she had been ready to let all her secrets fly from her like birds from a dovecote. He was probably used to women spilling their secrets to him—he was clearly no stranger to kissing—but what would he have thought of her if she had told him the truth about how she had learned of the ledgers? At best, he would think her a charlatan after money from the grieving. At worst he would think her an aberration. It didn't matter either way, she reminded herself bitterly; he was not for her.

Hastily gathering up her broom and pan, she finished cleaning up the debris around the tomb. It had been her first kiss, and it certainly would be her last.

If Miss Suze had a surname or indeed any other name, Tabby didn't know it. Everyone from her own children to grandchildren simply called her Miss Suze. It was an endearment, a mark of deference. And though she was small of stature, Miss Suze commanded respect. A passionate abolitionist and active member of the church, no one of importance passed through Boston without sitting at Miss Suze's table and partaking in her legendary cooking and a lively debate. She could boast of having hosted everyone from Frederick Douglass to William Lloyd Garrison to Maria Chapman, earning her frequent mentions in the Boston emancipation newspaper the *Liberator*. So when Miss Suze's invitation arrived, Tabby had been quick to convince Eli to accept, knowing that it would go a long way to cheer him up from the robbery of the previous day.

Miss Suze lived in a modest, yet homey row house in the fashionable Back Bay enclave of Boston. With pink chintz wallpaper and cheery vases of flowers throughout the house, it seemed a thousand miles from the shabby rooms that Tabby and Eli rented. Every chair that was pulled up around the table was worn and comfortable. Children's footsteps pounded up and down the hall, adults halfheartedly admonishing them for being too rowdy. Tabby's elbows brushed against her neighbors on both sides as she hungrily spooned up Miss Suze's okra stew, the lively conversation flowing around her.

"Homer and Mary are coming by with the twins later," Miss Suze said as she set down a steaming plate of hoecakes. "You won't believe your eyes when you see how those boys have grown," she told Eli. "Gonna be tall like their daddy."

Polly, Miss Suze's eldest granddaughter, reached for a hoecake. "You know he puts cork in his shoes, don't you? He can barely see over the pew in front of him at church."

"Tch, you're just jealous 'cause you were born runty," rejoined a cousin or grandchild that Tabby didn't recognize.

"Was not! Pa, tell him I wasn't a runt," Polly implored her father.

"Oh no, I ain't getting involved." A neatly dressed man with lively eyes, Paul was a clerk in a law firm in the city. He diplomatically changed the subject. "Miss Suze, these hoecakes might be your best yet."

"You can thank Lemuel for those. He bought the corn-meal."

"You didn't go to Pratt's, did you? He always skims off the top."

Lemuel ducked his head.

"Lemmy is sweet on Isabelle Pratt," Polly piped up. "Ow! Why'd you kick me?"

Tabby was so fascinated by the back and forth of the siblings, that she almost didn't notice the little girl with braids that had crept up beside her chair.

"Tabby, will you play dollies with me?"

Tabby looked down to find little Ella with a collection of well-loved ragdolls. A shy girl of seven, Ella had always been Tabby's favorite of Miss Suze's grandchildren. She smiled. "I don't know how to play dollies, you'll have to show me."

Ella reached out to take her hand, but as Tabby pushed back her chair and stood, she felt her balance shift, as if the floor under her had tilted. Light-headed, she put her hand out to steady herself on the table.

Miss Suze shushed the conversation. "Tabby, are you all right?"

"I'm fine. I must have just stood up too quickly." But then she was assaulted by a familiar scent. The pungent, thick smell of death wormed its way inside of her and she doubled over, sure that she was going to be sick.

Ella shrank back, hugging her dolls to her chest. Tabby tried to reach her hand out, tried to open her mouth to reassure Ella that there was no need to be frightened. But she found herself powerless to say a word. *No, no. Not now. Not here!*

She concentrated every ounce of her being on closing her mind, trying to focus on the rapidly dimming table and family around her. But it was no use. Mr. Bishop came roaring into her mind's eye, a frightful apparition in the black expanse. *You lied, girl!*

She hardly had time to gather her bearings before his voice was ringing in her ears again.

You summoned me, requesting my help, yet I have no peace, no rest!

If you have no rest, it is not my doing. Desperate, Tabby tried to ground herself back in Miss Suze's dining room. Where was the pink chintz wallpaper? Where was the happy babble of children, the aroma of sweet yams and hoecakes? She tried to take deep, even breaths, but they came out shallow and fast.

Mr. Bishop was joined by another spirit, and then another. Soon Tabby's mind was filled with the grotesque faces of the dead, all clamoring for her attention.

I am lost! cried a woman with a gaping wound to her head.

I was laid to rest not three days ago and thieves came in the night, stealing my mortal remains away, lamented another. *Tell me, how am I to let go of this earthly plane when my coffin lies empty?*

You hear us, you see us, yet you do nothing. Have you no compassion for our plight?

You shall have no rest until we have rest!

Louder and louder they shrieked. Tabby's head filled with pressure, felt as if it were being cracked open from the inside. She was terrified, but a small, detached part of her could only think of the gathering that was happening around her in Miss Suze's dining room. What did she look like right now to them? How would she explain her episode when it finally ended?

Just when she thought that she would suffocate in the blackness swirling with death, light gradually pierced the void, the grotesque faces fading away like paint running in the rain.

The world came back into focus, the smell of hot food and summer flowers replacing the thick odor of decay. "Careful now," Eli said, helping her sit up.

Polly, who was crouched down on her other side, handed Tabby a cup. Tabby gulped down the water, the sharp coldness washing away the lingering bile in her throat. She was scared to know, but had to ask. "What happened?"

"You fainted clean away," said Polly. "One minute you were standing up, the next you were flopping on the ground like a fish on the dock."

Ella stared at her from the corner, wide-eyed, her dolls crushed to her chest. Tabby gave her a tremulous smile. "It's all right. I'm all right."

But when she tried to embrace her, Ella shrank back as if Tabby were a monster.

Eli and Tabby walked back home through the lingering summer evening, the setting sun gilding the Boston buildings in rosy light. As usual, by some mutually unspoken agreement, they took the back way, skirting the busy areas of the city. It would have been a lovely stroll if not for the pregnant silence that hung between her and Eli. Several times Tabby opened her mouth, trying to form the words to explain what had happened, but each time she lost her nerve. Never before had she experienced such an assault on her mind with so many spirits contacting her at the same time, and she had no idea how to explain it away. It ate at her soul, little by little, not to be able to confide in the man she trusted and loved above all else in the world.

6

IN WHICH IT ALL FALLS APART.

IT WAS NEARLY two o'clock before Caleb arrived outside of the Hammond townhouse. He hadn't had a chance to change his suit, and when he'd caught his reflection in a shop window, his rumpled clothes had all but loudly announced that he had just taken part in a clandestine encounter.

Tabby Cooke had tasted of licorice and sun-ripened strawberries, innocence and desire. He had never wanted the kiss to end. God knew he'd kissed his fair share of women before, but this had somehow been different. Even with Rose, the few times they'd shared a kiss there had been no real passion there. What on earth had he been thinking? It was a new low, even for him. His father's voice rang out in his head: *Good-for-nothing boy. Can't keep your filthy hands to yourself, can you? Someday you'll find yourself in real trouble and lord knows I won't be the one to get you out of it.*

It was just that he had been so *good* since getting engaged. Rose kept him honest and he wanted to please her, even if they weren't in love. Every time he let his eye wander, he hated himself a little more. So why did he continually do this to himself?

Taking the marble steps two at a time, Caleb rapped his stick on the door and stood back. A moment later, an older black man in tails came to the door and looked down at Caleb with one brow disdainfully raised.

"I say, Roberts, it's only me, no need to look so vexed. I've come to call on Miss Rose."

But the butler didn't budge. Perhaps the old man's hearing was finally starting to go. Pity. Caleb tried again. "I'M HERE TO SEE MISS ROSE," he said loudly, enunciating every syllable.

"Oh, for goodness' sake," said an irritated feminine voice. Rose swept out to the door. "Thank you, Roberts. I'll handle this."

The butler shot Caleb a scornful look, and then disappeared back into the house.

"Rose? What is this? Can I come in?"

"Caleb," she hissed, throwing a look over her shoulder into the hall. "You have some nerve. You were supposed to be here hours ago for luncheon."

He'd completely forgotten he had promised to come for luncheon today. He fidgeted with the brass head of his cane. He'd never had to beg permission to gain entrance to a woman's house before. "I can explain. Can I please come in?"

"Mama and Papa are out—they got tired of waiting. I know the past week has been hard on you," she said, softening a little, "but this is hardly like you. One moment you're whisking me out to the theater, attentive and full of good cheer, and the next you can barely look me in the eye or bother to honor your engagements."

He should have apologized and been on his way, but he had to get inside, had to explain to her how truly sorry he was for his behavior this past week. He couldn't live with himself if he was the heel who seduced virgins behind his intended's back. "Please? I won't be but a moment and Roberts won't let anything untoward happen." He nodded toward the butler, who was vigorously dusting a clean vase and pretending not to eavesdrop.

He could see the indecision wrestling on her face, but eventually Rose stepped back and opened the door the rest of the way for him. She was wearing a blue silk dress with full bell-shaped sleeves and tiers of lace on the skirt. On another woman it might have looked overly fussy, but Rose wore it with easy grace, the blue bringing out her intelligent eyes and setting off her delicate features. What was wrong with him? What had she ever done to deserve this sort of treatment? And for God's sake, why couldn't he cajole his stubborn heart into feeling something more for her?

In the foyer, Caleb deposited his hat and cane on the sideboard and then followed Rose into the parlor. She didn't offer him anything to drink, just perched herself on a settee and looked at him expectantly. "Well?"

"Look, I know I've been distant lately. You have to

understand that losing my father was a terrible blow, and everything with the business… Well, I'm a bit lost."

Massaging her temples with elegant fingers, Rose let out a long breath. "Caleb, I don't doubt that losing your father has been difficult, but this isn't like you. You could hardly stomach being in the same room as your father when he was alive." She paused, a vulnerable edge creeping into her voice that made him feel like the worst kind of scoundrel. "You promised me you would be here today to set a date for the wedding, and you made me look a fool waiting with my parents."

"I know, and I'm sorry. Truly, Rose. It's just…" he trailed off. He *was* a terrible scoundrel. It was one thing to indulge in such follies while in the bloom of adolescence, but for God's sake, he was nearly a twenty-eight-year-old man. In front of him sat the most beautiful, kind, and God knew, patient woman he had ever known, and all he could think about was someone he had met a handful of times, and in a cemetery no less. He gave a deep sigh, raking his hand through his hair. "The truth is, I was late because I was… I was with a young lady. It was a mistake," he hastened to explain. "It meant nothing." Though even as he said the words, they left a sour taste in his mouth.

Rose's silence was a censure, her stillness a weapon. What the hell had made him say that? She wasn't a priest, and she couldn't absolve him of his sins, and as the pain spread across her face, he realized he'd made a terrible mistake. The best course of action would have been to say nothing, to never do it again, and endeavor to be a better man. But it was too late now, and the damage was done. Who had said that honesty was the best policy? He'd wanted to be truthful, to make a clean breast of it, but as she sat there, radiating anger, he realized he had wounded her deeply. And was it any wonder?

Her face deepened three shades of red, and without so much as moving a muscle made Caleb melt into his boots with shame. "You were *what*?" she ground out.

"I'm so sorry, Rose. I—"

Standing up, she stopped him with a swift outstretched palm. "Don't, Caleb. I'm not so naive as to think that my husband would not have his dalliances before our marriage, but we have been engaged these six months without a wedding date in sight. To admit that you are still…" she trailed off, shaking her head, as if it were too terrible to even put words to his indiscretions. "Well, it is beyond the pale. And I *certainly* do not want to hear about them. What if someone saw you? What if they gave the story to the papers? Do you know who would pay the price of your indiscretion? It would be me! The competing papers would love nothing more than to paint the daughter of Boston's premier newspaper owner as a fallen woman. At the very least I deserve respect, and that means honoring our engagements and presenting a unified front."

"No one saw, I swear it." He could at least assure her of that much. There had been no one in the cemetery aside from him and Tabby. "And I do respect you."

"No. You. DON'T!" She slammed her fist down onto a side table, sending a vase of anemones crashing to the floor. "If you respected me you wouldn't go about cavorting with other women while you were supposedly visiting the grave of your dead father! If you respected me you wouldn't then *tell* me about it." She lifted a trembling hand to her temples and closed her eyes. "My God, Caleb."

She was right. Everything she said was right. He pulled at his necktie, sweat beading down his back. The gold medallions on the wallpaper swam and bled together. Why was it so bloody hot in here? "Rose, please—"

"I think you should leave now. I won't call off the engagement because it would break my parents' hearts, but I need time. Just, go."

Caleb opened his mouth to argue but clamped it shut just as quickly. There was nothing he could say to make it better, not right now anyway. He'd already irrevocably damaged the trust between them. Besides, he needed some air. The whole room was close and stuffy and hot. Standing, he nodded. "Send for me when you're ready," he said, but Rose had moved to the far side of the room, staring out the large window into the dusk. He threw one last hopeful look at her before placing his hand on the doorknob.

It was the last time he would ever see her alive.

7

IN WHICH THE VEIL IS BREACHED.

THE LAMPS WERE low on oil, and the small room where Tabby and Eli took their meals hung in flickering shadows. For an extra two dollars in rent, they could have dined downstairs with the landlady and other boarders, but Mrs. Hodge watered down her soup and served only the fattiest cuts of meat, so it was salted cod and potatoes made in the warming pan for them. When they were finished, Tabby would take out her embroidery, and Eli his whittling, and they would work together, heads bent low, close to the dim lamp. Sometimes Eli might sing a song, his velvet baritone filling the room. It was a comforting routine, and Tabby looked forward to it every day.

"You look worn down," Tabby said as she spooned out the last of the potatoes onto Eli's plate. She had never seen him so weary and stooped, and was afraid that the events of the other night were weighing heavily on him.

Eli took his charge as caretaker seriously, and it couldn't be easy to lose someone to whom he was tasked with providing eternal rest.

For her part, Tabby was still rattled from their luncheon at Miss Suze's. *We will give you no peace until we have peace.* If she had been under any illusion about the possibility of a normal life, that afternoon's events had swept them clean away. The look of terror on Ella's face alone was enough to convince her she could never have a family of her own. She had always known she would not have a normal life, but now it seemed she would not have a peaceful one, either. How was she supposed to help those poor souls? How could she care for a child when she could not control her own strange powers?

Sighing, Eli drew his hand over his face, as if trying to sweep away his troubles. "The police have been to Harvard and the hospitals, but they say it's unlikely they'll be able to find the remains. I thought we were done with this after the last time." He pushed the plate of potatoes away, and shook his head. "Boston prides itself as being a city of progress, but sometimes it feels like we're going backward."

Even if their bodies were used for the greater good and led to scientific advancements, it was hard to think about the dissections that took place in the sterile medical theaters for audiences of students and anyone else who could pay the five cents admission. It was usually the bodies of the poor, the insane, the unloved, that found themselves on a cold marble slab, and while Mr. Bishop certainly did not deserve such indignity, there was a sort of irony that for all his wealth and status, he had met the same fate. Like death, it seemed that the grave robbers did not discriminate when it came to reaping their grim harvest.

A knock at the door interrupted her thoughts and her stomach tightened. They'd been a little late with the rent, but Mrs. Hodge had accepted their money without complaint; could she really be back for more already?

"Stay," she ordered Eli when she saw him moving to get up, and answered the door.

When the door opened it revealed a young policeman in a starched blue coat with shiny brass buttons that winked in the dim hall light. "Miss Cooke? My name is Officer Hodsdon. I've come 'round to ask a few questions."

Had they found the body? Tabby shot Eli a questioning look over her shoulder, and found him with a stricken expression on his face. But then it cleared and he nodded for her to let the man in. "Yes, of course," she murmured, letting the officer step inside.

"Sorry to interrupt," he said, glancing at the remnants of their meager dinner on the table.

Eli pushed back his chair and stood, and Tabby winced as he wobbled a moment before finding his balance. "No trouble at all," he said gruffly. "Were you able to apprehend the robbers?"

"Ah, no, that's not why I'm here, I'm afraid."

Uneasiness swept over Tabby. Eli was a free man in Boston, but that didn't mean they didn't have to worry about hysteria whipped up over fugitive slaves in the north. All it took was one witness claiming that a black man resembled a newspaper advertisement they had seen for a runaway, and an officer willing to hear them out.

Tabby had to agree with Eli; Boston was certainly not as progressive as it prided itself on being. But Eli was well-known, a respected member of the community; surely no one would think to accuse him of being a runaway?

If Eli was thinking the same thing, his face gave nothing away. "And what would this be concerning then?"

The officer removed his hat and tucked it under his arm. "May I sit down?"

Tabby absently pulled up a stool for him, trying not to let her apprehension show.

"Thank you kindly," he said, seating himself. He cleared his throat several times, looking almost as uncomfortable as Tabby felt, before he finally said, "I've come because there's been a murder."

Tabby's hand flew to her mouth as her mind spun out in a thousand directions. Mary-Ruth? Her aunt or uncle? Oh God, what if it was Alice? "W-who?" she asked.

"Miss Rose Hammond."

Relief surged through her. Tabby had never heard the name before. Eli likewise shook his head. "Don't know a Rose Hammond," he said.

"I believe she was the intended for Thomas Bishop's son."

The young woman whom Tabby had seen with Caleb just three days ago. She had been so young, so vibrant and beautiful. How could it be possible that she was dead, murdered? And why would an officer come to notify them? Tabby had never even met Miss Hammond, let alone spoken to her.

"You'll excuse me, officer," Tabby said, "but why are you telling us this?"

"I understand you buried Thomas Bishop earlier this week, and that the young Mr. Bishop has been back several times?"

Tabby opened her mouth to ask him how he knew that, but thought better of it and closed it again.

"He came back after learning of the theft of his father's corpse," Eli put in.

"Ah, yes. That," the officer said. "Well, apparently the Hammonds' butler overheard the younger Mr. Bishop arguing with Miss Hammond a few hours before her body was discovered in the family's parlor."

Tabby stifled a little cry. It couldn't be Caleb. When he had kissed her, there had been an unexpected vulnerability in his touch. But then, what did she really know about the charming young man? This was why she couldn't let her guard down; men were wolves in sheep's clothing, waiting only for the first sign of weakness before striking.

"What I want to know from you," the officer said, producing a little pad of paper from his pocket and licking at the lead of his pencil, "is what state of mind you found him to be in when he was in the cemetery. Was he distraught over the grave robbery? Did you speak with him about anything particularly of note?"

Shifting a little in her seat, Tabby tried to tamp down her prickling conscience as she remembered the kiss. She'd had passing clouds of shame about it all day, but mostly the event had taken on an otherworldly glow, her memory making the sun softer, the air warmer. Now she felt only a deep sense of guilt, compounded by the uneasy feeling that the kiss they had shared could have been the precursor to something dark and tragic.

"He didn't seem particularly distraught," Eli said, be-fore quickly adding, "but he did seem taken off guard by the news. We didn't speak much beyond that."

The officer didn't lift his eyes from his notepad as he scribbled this down. "I see. Anything else?"

Eli shook his head. "No, sir."

Sighing, Officer Hodsdon flipped his pad shut and eyed the half-eaten meal on the table in front of him. "I must apologize again for interrupting your supper. Sometimes I lose track of the hour when I'm working."

All Tabby wanted was to see the officer on the other side of the door and enjoy a warm drink by the fire, but she knew how important it was to appease him, to make him feel welcome, lest he decide Eli would make an easy target in the future. "It is no imposition," she said. "Would you take a cup of coffee before you leave?"

He gave her a surprisingly warm smile. "That's very kind of you, miss. I'd appreciate that."

Tabby could feel Eli bristling as she relit the fire and put on more water to boil.

Officer Hodsdon made awkward small talk, his fur-tive gaze following Tabby as she moved about the room. She hadn't realized how young he was until he'd leaned in closer to the lamp, revealing fair hair and boyish fea-tures. For some reason, this put her more at ease, and a little of the tension she had been carrying between her shoulders relaxed. He was just a young officer who had drawn the short straw at the station. He held no malice against them, did not wish to make trouble.

"That's heaven," he said after Tabby had placed the cup in front of him and he'd taken a long draught.

She knew he was just trying to be kind—it was mostly water and sludgy grounds, supplemented with chicory root. Still, she was beyond relieved when he finally pushed his stool back and made ready to take his leave.

"Thank you again for answering my questions, Mr. Cooke," he said. "I'm sure nothing will come of it, but when investigating the murder of a respected member of the community like Miss Hammond, we must be certain to leave no stone unturned."

"Of course," Eli said stiffly.

Once the officer's heavy boot steps had receded down the stairs, Tabby slumped down into her seat. She hadn't realized how tense and prickly the air had grown while the officer was there, how she had hardly breathed the entire time.

Tabby's voice came out small in the quiet room. "Do you really think Mr. Bishop could have something to do with Miss Hammond's death?"

Eli looked up from his own private thoughts. "I suppose he could have. We hardly know the young man. He's a charmer, that's for sure, and sometimes the charmers are the ones with the most to hide." She must have looked crestfallen, because his look softened and he reached for her hand. "I know you took a liking to him, but you need to be careful, Tabby cat. Not everyone is deserving of your trust."

Tabby had never offered Eli the details of her early childhood besides the fact that she was an orphan, and he had never asked. He didn't know that the guardians to whom her parents had entrusted the care of their children would be cold and manipulative. He didn't know that

Tabby had learned to always be on her guard. He didn't know the things Tabby had done to survive in those early days. But his reminder was timely; Tabby knew that her greatest fault was that, once won, her trust was too freely given. It was the loneliness in her, the hunger for the warm heartbeat of human connection.

Caleb might have acted the rogue and kissed her, but it seemed a far leap to murder. She just couldn't see him being capable of that. But if her instincts were wrong about him, what else might she be wrong about?

She stood suddenly, rocking the stool back. "I… I have to go out."

Eli's gaze flicked to the darkened windows. "Now?"

"I have to find Mary-Ruth and learn what happened," she said, gathering up her cloak and bonnet. "What really happened."

Tabby hesitantly lifted her hand, and then rapped softly on the back door. She knew that she would find Mary-Ruth wherever the body of Rose Hammond was, and finding Hammond House had not been difficult; she had only to ask the lamplighter as he went about his rounds, and he had pointed her down a broad street lined with brick and marble houses.

The soft pad of footsteps from the other side of the door sounded, and a moment later Mary-Ruth appeared holding a lamp up into the night.

This was not the same carefree young woman that Tabby had run and laughed with in the cemetery the other day; this woman wore her abundant hair tucked up under a white turban like a nurse, and there were heavy smudges under her eyes.

"Tabby? What on earth are you doing here?"

Tabby glanced about the street behind her. Her childhood fear of being followed and discovered had never abated, and she had spent the entire walk darting between buildings, straining her ear for the sound of approaching footsteps. She wouldn't feel safe until she was inside with the door bolted behind her. "May I come in?"

Mary-Ruth ushered her inside and led her down a steep staircase into the bowels of the large house.

"The family is asleep," Mary-Ruth said when they reached the kitchen. "I was just about to go home. Now, do you want to tell me what you're doing here?"

Tabby fumbled for the right words. How could she tell Mary-Ruth that she had kissed the man accused of the murder? How could she explain that she was a burning mess of guilt and fear, curiosity and yearning?

So all she said was: "Rose Hammond... She's Caleb Bishop's fiancée."

Mary-Ruth crossed her arms. "Don't you think I know that? They're saying he's the one who did it!"

"It's not true," Tabby hurried to reassure her, the words rushing out despite her own misgivings. "He didn't do it. He couldn't have done it."

"How do you know?" When Tabby didn't say anything else, Mary-Ruth groaned. "Oh, Tabby. Don't tell me you're sweet on him. You had that look in your eyes the other day, but I thought it was just a passing fancy." She shook her head. "If it's true what they're saying, then you ought to stay far away from him, from this whole mess."

"I'm not sweet on him." She bristled. Brushing aside her friend's concern, she forced herself to ask the terrible question. "How…how did it happen?"

Pressing her lips together, Mary-Ruth looked as if she wasn't going to answer. After a moment of strained silence, she finally said, "She was strangled and stabbed. Repeatedly."

Tabby winced at the brutality of the truth, but it did not change the fact that she couldn't rest until she'd seen Miss Hammond for herself. "I just need to see her."

"See her! Tabs, why on earth would you want to do that?"

"I just… I need to. Please?"

Mary-Ruth looked uncomfortable, but she also looked tired, and Tabby pushed aside her guilt as she realized her friend hadn't the heart to argue. "Very well, but she… that is, it was a violent death. I could only do so much."

Tabby knew what Mary-Ruth was trying to tell her, but the shells that the dead left behind held no dread for Tabby, not after she had seen such horrors in her mind's eye since she was a small child. "I understand."

With a reluctant nod, Mary-Ruth led her down the narrow hall.

The room where Rose Hammond's body lay was cold and still as a mausoleum. A lone table stood in the center, a gauzy shroud draped over the motionless form. With the moonlight spilling in from the small street-level windows, the whole scene looked as if it was carved from marble.

"I'll dress her tomorrow," Mary-Ruth said quietly. "The poor thing has had enough for tonight."

"May I have a moment with her?"

Mary-Ruth's dark brows drew together in question, but she nodded. "I suppose a cup of hot tea might be nice. I'll be back in a few minutes."

The door clicked shut behind Mary-Ruth, leaving Tabby alone with only the sound of her breathing and the pressing heaviness of the room. The eucalyptus and lavender that Mary-Ruth had placed around the table mingled with the scent of bleach and lime. Taking a deep breath, Tabby closed her mind, and slowly approached the shrouded figure.

Gently, as if it were as fragile as a spider's web, she took up the corners of the shroud between her fingertips. A horse cart rumbled past on the street outside, the vibrations causing the shroud to quiver slightly. Just as she was about to pull it aside, she stayed her hands. She shouldn't be here. She had wanted to do penance for kissing the young woman's fiancée, and had hoped that seeing Miss Hammond would somehow convince her of Mr. Bishop's innocence. But now that she was here, she felt only guiltier than ever; she was a voyeur, and nothing more.

Her heart beat loud in her ears, and she could hear herself swallowing. The air grew heavier, like the building quiet before a storm. Suddenly Tabby didn't want to be anywhere near Rose Hammond's corpse or the too-thin shroud covering it. This had been a mistake.

She was just turning to leave when the smallest of noises stopped her. It was like the soft rustling of a curtain caught in a breeze, the predawn beating of a swallow's wing. But there was no breeze in the room, no birds, only Tabby and the corpse.

Though the hairs on the back of her neck were standing on end and her stomach had turned to lead, Tabby forced herself to turn slowly back around.

She had built up her wall. She had taken care to keep her mind closed. Yet it had mattered not one drop. The words took shape on Miss Hammond's veiled lips before Tabby heard them, hoarse and so quiet that she could not tell if they came from the corpse, or from inside her own head.

Help me.

8

IN WHICH AN ARREST IS MADE.

IT RAINED THE day of Rose Hammond's funeral, and everyone in attendance agreed that it was only appropriate that the heavens should weep for the loss of such a lovely young woman struck down in her prime. Tabby, who had witnessed more than her fair share of burials, might have told them that it was only superstitious nonsense, except that it did seem somehow fitting, as if the universe recognized the sorrow, the guilt, and the apprehension in Tabby's heart.

She had not gone to the funeral service at the church, but now she trailed behind the somber procession snaking its way down Tremont Street and into the large cemetery in the center of the city.

The last time Tabby had seen her, Rose had been nothing more than a vague shape under a gossamer shroud, and before that, a sparkling young beauty in the cemetery, vivacious and lovely. Now she was simply the contents of a polished black casket.

Nearly as old as Tabby's cemetery, the Granary Burying Ground was the final resting place of giants of the Revolution such as John Hancock and Samuel Adams. And now Rose Hammond would take her place amongst them.

The Hammonds had spared no expense for the burial of their only daughter; magnificent ebony horses with matching black ostrich plumes drew the glass funeral coach, trailed by a steady current of mourners. It seemed that Rose Hammond hadn't just been beautiful, but kind and well loved. How was Caleb bearing it? Tabby simply could not believe that he was capable of visiting the kind of violence on Miss Hammond that Mary-Ruth had described. Had they fought the night of her death? Perhaps. Had it been because of Tabby? She hoped not, though she couldn't help but feel it might have been. Had he struck her? Even that didn't seem likely, let alone that he could have stabbed her over and over until her flesh was raw and tattered. The man was a rake and a philanderer, but that did not a murderer make. Rumors were swirling about Boston that his arrest was imminent, but as far as Tabby knew, he was still a free man.

Miss Hammond's mournful words echoed in her head as the church bells pealed their sad song: *Help me. Help me.* Tabby was no stranger to requests from the dead, but there was something chilling in Rose's message, something that plucked a foreboding note on Tabby's heartstrings. As a rule, Tabby did not involve herself with the affairs of the dead, not after what she'd seen in her aunt and uncle's parlor, but she couldn't help but feel that she owed a debt to Miss Hammond. But then what if she did help her, and discovered something about Caleb Bishop that she would rather not know? What if Miss Hammond learned that Tabby was responsible for Caleb's straying? Would she seek vengeance on Tabby from beyond the grave? Was such a thing even possible?

As if on cue, Tabby looked up, and there was Caleb, slowly climbing out of a carriage and then turning to assist his mother. Tabby's heart sped up; he was here, which meant that he had not been arrested. Perhaps no charges had been brought against him. Perhaps it was all just a dreadful misunderstanding. Perhaps she was not such a terrible judge of character after all.

He was sharp and handsome as ever in his black tails and tall hat, but gone was the spring in his step, the boyish sparkle in his eyes. Her traitorous body jolted with excitement as she remembered the feeling of his arms around her, his lips on hers.

Once the Bishops had taken their place amongst the mourners, the service began. Tabby's cheeks burned with shame under her veil as the minister ruminated on the nature of resurrection, and made the sign of the cross over the open grave. She hadn't been the one to initiate the kiss, but she had enjoyed it all the same, had wanted it to go on forever. And now his fiancée was dead. Lifting her veil, Tabby swiped away a hot tear before it could overflow.

After the service, the mourners continued milling about the gravesite, kissing wet cheeks and shaking hands, making plans for dinners, all the little gestures that reminded them that they were still alive.

Mr. Bishop had been speaking with someone, but when he turned, he caught her eye and made his way toward her.

"Miss Cooke," he said, giving her a short nod. "How kind of you to come."

"I—I heard what happened. I'm so sorry. If there's anything that I can do…" she trailed off, knowing very well that there was nothing she could do for him, that she barely even had any business asking after what had transpired between them.

Taking off his hat, he ran his hands through his curly hair, heedless of the rain. His face was pinched and wan, dark circles under his eyes. "That is kind of you, but there's nothing that can be done now."

Though she knew she shouldn't get involved, Tabby couldn't help herself. She dropped her voice. "An officer came to see us the other night… He said that you're under suspicion." She watched his face carefully as she said this. She wanted more than anything to believe that he was incapable of such hateful violence, and against a woman that he was supposed to love and protect, no less.

To her surprise, he quirked a shadow of his crooked smile at her. "I'm honored they have taken such an interest in me, but it's a waste of their time. Meanwhile, whoever did this to Rose walks free."

Of course he would never admit his guilt if he had indeed done it, but she couldn't help but be reassured by this. Growing bolder, she asked, "What happened?"

Before he could answer, there was a ripple of murmuring, and the crowd of mourners parted as if for passing royalty.

"Lord have mercy," Caleb murmured. "Rose's parents."

"You have some nerve coming here." The woman who addressed Caleb was tall and straight, laced into her black silk mourning with all the precision and tension of a wound clock. Beside her, her much shorter husband stood on his toes to hold an umbrella over her head.

"Mrs. Hammond, Mr. Hammond," Caleb said, bowing deeply. "My deepest sympathies. You have no idea how sorry—"

But Mrs. Hammond had no intention of letting him finish. Tabby watched as the mourners around them broke off in their conversations, aware that something of interest was happening. The soft patter of rain on umbrellas intensified, a charged silence falling over the cemetery.

"Sorry indeed!" Her voice was growing shrill, her eyes unnaturally bright.

"Shouting at Mr. Bishop will not bring her back," her husband murmured. "Come along, my dear."

Caleb swallowed, his gaze flitting nervously around at the onlookers. "You must believe me. I—"

"I am not inclined to believe anything you say," she hissed. "We let you into our home, our lives, and you were nothing more than a…a…butcher, a *murderer* this whole time. You will pay for what you have done." And with that, Mrs. Hammond drew her head up high and swept toward her carriage with her husband slowly trudging in her wake.

Caleb's face had gone green, and rain rolled off the rim of his hat, slicking his cheeks. He looked so stricken, so

utterly lost, and Tabby wanted nothing more than to take
him by the hand and lead him somewhere dry and safe.
But he was a grown man, and it was not her place to offer
him comfort, and before she could even say anything anyway, there was a fresh ripple of excitement in the crowd.

"Caleb Bishop?"

He hardly had time to respond before two police officers were taking him roughly by the arms while a stony-
faced constable supervised. Tabby immediately recognized
the younger officer of the two: Officer Hodsdon. A terrible thought ran through her mind: What if something
she had said the other night had led him to Mr. Bishop?

Mrs. Bishop, who had fought her way through the
crowd, was swatting at the officers with her reticule.
"Unhand him, you brutes!"

"Can't do that, ma'am," the constable said. "Your son
is under arrest for the murder of Rose Hammond, and
he needs to come with us."

In the midst of the ensuing clamor, Caleb was the only
one who looked calm and resigned, and now he closed
his eyes as if for patience. "Really, Mother. I'll be fine.
Go home and I'll be along shortly after this misunderstanding has been cleared up."

"I am not going home, not without you," she said,
glaring at the officers.

Caleb sighed. "Miss Cooke, would you please escort
my mother home?"

Mrs. Bishop did not look like she intended to go
meekly, but Tabby gently took the older woman's arm.
"Mrs. Bishop, will you let me take you home?"

"But…but, my boy! What will they do with him?"

Tabby bit her lip. She didn't know what they would do with him. She could only hope that Officer Hodsdon would be as kind to him as he had been to her and Eli the other night.

Just as the constable was ordering his officers to escort the accused from the cemetery, Caleb twisted around, looking frantically about. "Tabby," he hissed as his gaze found hers once again. He briefly wrenched his arm free from Officer Hodsdon, taking Tabby by the wrist and looking her directly in the eye. "Whatever is said, I am innocent. You must believe me."

Before she could even do so much as nod, he was being wrenched back and led away, the great black sea of mourners swallowing him up.

After Tabby had finished her embroidery and said goodnight to Eli that night, she went to her room and latched the door behind her. With the image of Rose's parents and her funeral still fresh in her mind, Tabby took a deep breath and prepared to summon her.

After what seemed like an eternity, the smallest of breezes kicked up in her mind, carrying with it the cloying scent of decomposing flowers.

She forced down the dry lump in her throat. "Rose?"

Rose Hammond peered at Tabby from sunken eyes behind a stringy veil of dark hair, her shoulders slumped. Despite her fear, Tabby's heart ached for her. How terrible to be bound to that in-between place, with no justice and no peace, unable to move on.

"What can I do, Rose? How can I help you?"

If the spirit understood her, she gave no indication.

She stared through Tabby with unseeing eyes and when she opened the black hole that was her mouth, it was not words that came out, but a thin, sickly string of minor notes.

Gradually the notes grew fainter, and with them, Rose's pale face. When all that remained was a curl of smoke like a snuffed-out candle, Tabby opened her eyes, slowly coming back to the world of the living. She had hoped for answers, for some clue as to how to help Rose and find her true killer. Instead, all she had gotten was a song.

9

IN WHICH ALL HOPE IS NOT LOST.

PRISON WAS EVERYTHING the novels and serialized dramas Caleb had read in his youth promised it would be. His cell mates included drunks, vagrants, and a fellow who proclaimed loudly and frequently that he was the Duke of Wellington and was going to be late for a naval engagement if he was not released immediately. Time was marked by a leak in the ceiling which dripped slow and steady, day and night. The bread that he was given was somehow both mealy and stale, and the whole place smelled like piss. Yes, prison did not disappoint when it came to hopeless ambiance. His father must have been joyfully rolling over in his grave—or wherever his body was—vindicated that he had been right when he predicted that Caleb would someday find himself in jail.

Caleb wasn't terribly concerned that he would languish in here for more than a few hours. Mother would send

Mr. Whitby—his father's business partner and solicitor—with some money and papers and he would clear the whole mess up. The question was, when? How would it look to Caleb's business investors to see the new owner of Bishop & Son Shipping behind bars? How many meetings would he miss, and at what cost? It was like being granted a stay of execution from all those unpleasant business matters he had been dreading, only to spend it in, well, prison.

No, what *did* concern him was Rose and her terrible fate. What on earth had happened after he left Hammond House? Poor, sweet Rose. Who could have been cold-hearted enough to think her deserving of death? Thinking back to their argument and what an unforgivable cad he had been, he let out a groan. He had not loved her in the way a husband should love a wife, but they were supposed to have had a lifetime to find their path together. He imagined her dark blue eyes staring at him accusingly from across the divide, a life abbreviated. She had deserved more, so much more.

"Caleb Bishop?"

The rough voice snapped him from his thoughts, and he looked up to see the warden standing with crossed arms in front of the iron bars. "I'm the gentleman in question."

The warden scowled. "You've got a visitor."

That would be Whitby. About bloody time. Caleb stood up, waiting for the warden to unlock the door and lead him to some more hospitable chamber where he and Mr. Whitby could discuss the matter at hand, but instead the warden disappeared. When he came back, he had a young woman in tow.

Caleb's jaw nearly fell to the ground. "Good God, Miss Cooke?" He rushed to the bars, sure that his eyes deceived him.

"Get back!" The warden jabbed at him with his club through the bars.

Caleb just stared at her, shocked but also more than a little peeved. How he wished he had never given in to his incendiary desire and kissed the girl. She was a living, breathing reminder of the price both he and Rose had paid for their fight. "What are you doing here?"

Her eyes had widened, staring past him. Turning, he followed her line of sight to where a drunkard was relieving himself very loudly with a satisfied grunt in the corner. Jesus Christ, what a place for a young woman. He gestured to her to come to the other end of the cell, peering at her through the bars and was just about to ask her again why she had come when she spoke.

"I need you to know something..." she trailed off, twining her hands. "I... I know that you are innocent."

Hadn't he told her as much at the burial? "Of course I'm innocent!" His words came out much too loud, causing the Duke of Wellington to pick up a chorus of "Innocent! Innocent!"

She shook her head impatiently, the tattered ribbon in her plain straw bonnet nearly coming undone. "Yes, but no one will believe you unless we have proof. And to get proof I need you to tell me about Rose."

He stared at her. If her thoughts were following some

logical trajectory, he certainly couldn't see it. "What about Rose?"

"How long did you know her? Did she have any enemies, anyone who might wish her harm? Other suitors, perhaps?" The questions tripped off her tongue faster than Caleb could keep track of them until she suddenly stopped. She caught her lower lip between her teeth, worrying at it, and for a moment Caleb was transported back to their kiss at the cemetery, his regret tempered with a sudden jab of longing. "I can help you," she said softly.

"The only person who can help me is my lawyer. Now if you would be so kind, I believe I have some pensive brooding to do just over there on that bench while I figure out what the hell he can do to get me out of here."

Color rose to her face. "*You* may not want my help, but I promised Rose that I would bring her killer to justice, and I always honor my promises."

What on earth was she talking about? "You promised Rose? You didn't even *know* Rose! Don't you think you've done enough? She wouldn't be dead and I wouldn't be here if it weren't for you."

She jerked backward as if he had struck her, and he instantly regretted his sharp words. He knew full well that he had been the one to instigate the kiss, that it was his impulsive and base behavior that had caused this mess. The fault was his and his alone. Perhaps that was why he said what he did, because his own guilt was unbearable. "Look, I don't know what you're going on about, and frankly, I don't want to know. I'm just as much responsible for that damned kiss as you, but I think it would be better for all parties involved if you were to stay out of my affairs."

She gave him an unreadable look, her cloudy eyes seeming to see right through him. When she spoke again her voice was low and more forceful than he had ever heard from her before. "You forfeited that right when you came into the cemetery and kissed me. For better or worse, I would say I am already rather entangled in your affairs." With that she turned on her heel and marched out.

"Tabby!" he called after her. God damn it, she meant to get involved. "Tabby, wait! Stay out of this!"

But it was too late. The strange young woman was already floating down the hall as if she were a spirit herself.

Blinking back the brightness as she emerged from the dank prison, Tabby walked briskly through the city, too preoccupied to worry about being followed for once.

She had so carefully fortified her defenses over the years, and then this young man came along and they all but came crumbling down when he so much as looked at her. She should have been angry with herself for her lack of restraint, but instead she found herself irritated beyond all reason with him. He was a temptation, a threat to the life she had worked so hard to salvage. *Harden your heart against that which you can never have.* The old refrain ran through her mind as she walked. She would harden her heart against Caleb, but she was determined to help Rose. The dead, after all, could not break your heart.

Her feet carried her as her thoughts churned. Though it was less than a mile from the cemetery, Tabby had been to this part of the city only twice before: once to visit Mary-Ruth at Hammond House, and the second time to escort Caleb's mother home at his request. It was the latter to which she went now, feeling the smooth paved sidewalk beneath her shoes, listening to the pleasant sound of birdsong.

The Bishop home stood shoulder to shoulder among an unbroken row of other stately brick homes, generously bedecked with ivy climbing up the sides, and flower baskets of pink geraniums hanging from the windows. The day of the funeral when Tabby had taken Mrs. Bishop home everything had been a blur, but now as she climbed the front steps, she realized what a welcoming, pretty house it was.

A maidservant admitted her, and Mrs. Bishop intercepted them in the front hall, kissing Tabby's cheeks like she was an old friend, and not acquainted with her son by the strangest of threads.

"It is good of you to come, dear," Mrs. Bishop said as she led Tabby to an airy parlor appointed with cream-colored drapes and high crown molding. She was dressed in full mourning, her wide black skirts rustling as she seated herself, a brooch quivering with black crepe flowers pinned at her breast. When she caught Tabby taking in these details, she gave her a weak smile. "First Thomas, and then poor Miss Hammond. It feels as if I've lost Caleb now, as well."

Not sure if it was her place but too moved not to, Tabby reached out and patted Mrs. Bishop's hand. She liked the older woman, her comfortable, motherly demeanor making her easy to talk to. Mrs. Bishop gripped her hand in return.

Tabby didn't think it wise to tell her that she had seen her son in prison, so she forced a smile. "I'm sure Caleb will be out in no time. He is innocent after all."

"Yes, I'm sure you're right. He's too clever and spirited to stay there long."

A tawny cat with nicked ears and a crooked tail strode in, planted itself at Tabby's feet, and began mewing piteously at her. "Mind your manners, Buttermilk," Mrs. Bishop told the cat. "He must be missing Caleb."

Tabby eyed the cat, whose coat couldn't be further in color from its namesake. "Buttermilk?"

"Caleb named him," Mrs. Bishop said affectionately. "Found him on the street when he was a boy and would not be consoled until I allowed him to keep the mangy creature."

Buttermilk looked every inch the cat that had gotten the cream, a street Tom who now found himself living in the lap of luxury. Tabby scratched him behind the ears until tea was brought in. She had to force herself not to grab all of the mouthwatering cakes and fancies on the tray by the fistful. As she slowly chewed a fruit tart and Mrs. Bishop poured out the tea, Tabby let her gaze wander around the stylishly papered walls of the parlor. A few somber portraits of men in high, stiff collars, and women with overly large, expressive eyes dotted the walls, interspersed with framed pencil etchings.

"Aren't those dear?" Mrs. Bishop said, following Tabby's gaze. "Caleb drew them."

"Truly?" Putting aside her tea, Tabby stood to look

more closely at the etchings. Most of them seemed to be libraries and municipal buildings, but there were a few landscapes, garden scenes bursting with flowers and a lovely sense of movement. They were deceptively simple, executed in economic, confident pencil strokes.

"He's always sketching away. He's shy about his artwork, tries to keep it from me. His father didn't approve," Mrs. Bishop said, her lips tight, "but now that he's gone, I thought it would be a shame to keep them hidden."

Tabby was about to ask where her son had learned to draw like that, when the butler came into the room and cleared his throat expectantly.

"Yes, Larson?"

"Mr. Whitby is here, ma'am."

It was as if the son of God himself had been announced. Instantly, Mrs. Bishop's face lost about ten years, all the tension lines smoothing out and her heavy gray eyes lighting up. "Oh, thank goodness," she said in a flood of relief. Then, as if remembering that Tabby was there, gave her a sheepish look. "Tabby, I hope you don't mind, but Mr. Whitby was my husband's partner and our family solicitor. I expect he's here to discuss Caleb's release."

Tabby reluctantly placed her plate down, and stood to leave. But Mrs. Bishop stopped her. "Oh, do stay. It's so nice to have a young person in the house and it shouldn't take long. Larson," she said, "show Mr. Whitby in."

Larson gave a stiff bow of his head, and disappeared. A moment later a man of middling years in an immaculate navy frockcoat and dark trousers was striding into the room. Buttermilk let out a hiss, and then bolted back out past him.

Unfazed, Mr. Whitby gave Mrs. Bishop a neat bow. Tall and svelte, he looked about the parlor as if he were a wolf assessing prey, but as soon as his sharp gaze landed on Mrs. Bishop, his expression softened and filled with concern.

"My dear Mrs. Bishop." He bent over and kissed the older woman's hand. "You must forgive the tardiness of my visit. I came as soon as I heard."

His words rolled off his tongue like liquid silver, but Mrs. Bishop didn't seem to notice. "It has been so difficult since Thomas passed," she said with a heavy sigh. "And now Caleb has been taken away from me, under the most ridiculous of pretenses... As if he could even hurt a fly!"

Mr. Whitby drew back, his expression dismayed, but his eyes flat and unreadable. "Horrible, horrible business. I have not yet had the time to call on the young Mr. Bishop, but rest assured, I shall go as soon as my schedule permits it."

"He's been waiting for you," Tabby said, unable to stop herself. Regardless of how infuriating she might have found him, Caleb was innocent and rotting away in prison, the only thing giving him hope the promise of this illustrious family friend to swoop in and make everything right. And here the man was preening and posturing, claiming that he had not been able to spare one single moment to visit Caleb and put his mind at ease.

At her outburst, Mr. Whitby straightened and slid a cool gaze in her direction. "Indeed? And who might you be? I don't believe we've met."

"This is Miss Tabby Cooke," Mrs. Bishop supplied. "An acquaintance of Caleb's."

"A pleasure," he said with another neat bow. Turning

his attention back to Mrs. Bishop, he took a seat with a smart flip of his tails. "You know that I will do everything possible to make sure your son is cleared of these most heinous charges."

Mrs. Bishop's shoulders slumped in obvious relief. Reaching forward, she took Mr. Whitby's hand in hers, the crepe flowers at her breast rising and falling with her breath. "Oh, Mr. Whitby, you are indeed good to us. I knew that I could depend on you."

"How generous of you," Tabby murmured.

"I could not live with myself if I did not do everything in my power to see the family of my dearest friend and respected business associate cared for in their hour of need."

Mrs. Bishop's face shone with hope and gratitude. "You are too good to us," she said again. "I hope that it will be soon? Every day that my boy is away from me is an eternity. I am so very lonely now that I find myself a widow in this twilight hour of my life."

"Oh yes, soon. Very soon," he said absently. Pulling out a silver watch, he looked at it with a frown and stood. "I'm afraid I must be off. I have pressing business, but rest assured I will be paying a visit to Caleb as soon as it is possible."

After the door had closed behind him, Mrs. Bishop poured out fresh cups of tea, chattering happily about what a good friend Mr. Whitby had always been to the family, a residual glow of excitement on her cheeks. But Tabby wasn't listening; she worried at her lip, suddenly finding she had lost her appetite. She sprang up. "Mrs. Bishop, you'll excuse me but I must be going, as well."

10

IN WHICH AN ENEMY IS MADE.

MR. WHITBY HAD barely reached the corner when Tabby slipped out the door and into the flow of pedestrians, trailing behind him as quiet and soft footed as a cat. As she wove between strolling couples and hackney carriages, she could occasionally catch snatches of the tune he whistled. He seemed to be in high spirits, considering how distraught he claimed to be over Caleb's incarceration.

She hadn't expected him to go directly to the jail, and he didn't, instead heading in the opposite direction into the city, taking the broader streets lined with chestnut trees and tulip beds. It must have been very pressing business indeed.

They were just coming to the statehouse square when Mr. Whitby stopped in his tracks, and then turned quickly around. Tabby held her breath and froze in place, wondering if she had time to duck into a doorway. But it was too late; he had seen her and was making his way back to where she stood. For all her experience making sure that she was never followed, it seemed that the same could not be said of her abilities to follow someone else.

"Miss Cooke," he said, giving her a thin smile that did not reach his pale blue eyes. "How extraordinary to find ourselves taking the same path. You should have mentioned at Hammond House that you were leaving too and I would have been only too glad to escort you."

Bothered at herself for being so obvious, Tabby lifted her chin, determined to appear undaunted. "Thank you, but I don't need an escort."

"Of course," he said. "You appear quite independent." His unimpressed tone made it clear he did not consider this a compliment. "How can I be of assistance, Miss Cooke?"

Well, at least she had his attention. "Mr. Bishop needs your help. He's innocent and sitting in jail, and thinks you're the one to help him."

A dark brow rose. "You'll pardon me, but I don't believe I've heard your name come up before in connection to the family. I can hardly discuss such matters with a stranger. Who, or what, exactly are you to the Bishops?"

Tabby ignored his question. "I think if you cared half so much about the Bishops as you claim to, you already would have visited him, if not secured his release."

"Aha," Mr. Whitby said, stroking the sharp line of his chin. He paused, cocking his head ever so slightly at her. "You strike me as a young woman of strong opinions, but not well versed in the ways of the world."

Tabby opened her mouth to deny it, but he must have

seen the effect his words had on her, because he said, "Just as I thought. Well, Miss Cooke, let me give you a little advice, free of charge. In the business world, everything moves at a snail's pace until it doesn't. Young Mr. Bishop may well be innocent, but me storming into the city jail proclaiming that isn't going to sway the warden, now is it? No, I must go back to my office, compile a list of references of his good standing and character, and speak with the police about their investigation. *Then* I can go to the judge and present my case and see what can be done about releasing him pending a trial."

When he phrased it in such a way, it all seemed rather logical, and Tabby couldn't help but be annoyed at herself for her lack of understanding in such things. But that didn't change her dislike of Mr. Whitby and his cool, slippery way of talking. "You might have at least visited him and put his mind at ease."

The pale blue eyes narrowed at her in clear disdain. "Indeed. If you'll excuse me, Miss Cooke, you'll remember I have pressing business. Good day."

She did not for one moment believe that Mr. Whitby had Caleb's best interests at heart. And that meant no justice for Rose.

As he disappeared into the bustle of traffic, he took up his humming again. A chill washed over Tabby, the hairs on the back of her neck standing on end. And with a crawling sense of dread, Tabby remembered where'd she heard that song before.

It had been three days and Caleb's former life beyond the damp walls was rapidly becoming dreamlike and unimaginable. What did warm, fresh bread taste like? What about wine that wasn't vinegary? Had he ever really slept on a feather bed and not a hard bench with straw ticking? God, he was not cut out for prison.

"Caleb Bishop, you got a visitor."

Caleb sprang up. If it was Tabby again he would throttle her, the impetuous, determined thing. Yet at the same time he couldn't help the anticipation of seeing her again, found that he was desperate to see the sharp tilt of her chin, the shape of her extraordinary eyes in person. Desperate to feel the peace that seemed to surround her wherever she went. He compulsively smoothed back his greasy hair and straightened his collar.

"Oh." Caleb's face fell as the tall form of Mr. Whitby materialized from the dark corridor. Then he shook off his disappointment as he remembered just how much he needed him.

"Caleb," Mr. Whitby said with a short nod. "Don't look so excited to see me. I've only come to see what can be done about this mess."

"Of course."

"Were you expecting someone else?"

Was that a knowing glimmer in Mr. Whitby's eyes? "Of course not," Caleb said. "I try not to take calls whilst imprisoned."

"I'll keep it quick, then." Mr. Whitby produced a packet of folded documents. "I've secured your release—"

Caleb grabbed him through the bars, his disappointment instantly evaporating. "You brilliant man! I knew you—"

With a tight smile, Whitby extracted himself. "If you

would be so kind as to allow me to finish. I've secured your release until your trial, contingent on me vouching for your recognizance."

Caleb's elation was short-lived. "But surely they don't mean to bring up charges against me... I'm innocent!"

Whitby raised a brow, tucking the papers back inside his coat. "Yes, yes, I know, but they must play out the whole thing so that they can say justice has been done."

Caleb chewed at his lip. "I suppose. Well, for God's sake, get me out for now. My mother will be worrying herself half to death over this." And that was to say nothing of whatever scheme Tabby had gotten into her head.

Tabby slowly made her way back home from her encounter with Mr. Whitby, this time aware that perhaps she was not as inconspicuous as she had always thought. Hugging close to the sides of buildings, she checked that she wasn't being followed before leaving behind the statehouse and the city's bustling business district.

She had promised that she would help Caleb, and despite his orders not to, she had every intention of making sure that his innocence was proven. There could be no true justice for Rose so long as the wrong man sat behind bars. But how was Tabby to prove that Caleb was not the killer? The song that Mr. Whitby had been humming was the same one that Rose had sung, she was sure of it. But was that proof? Tabby didn't trust Mr. Whitby, but that didn't mean he was a murderer. What did he have to gain from killing her? If only Rose would speak to her again, help Tabby learn who was truly responsible for her death.

As she mused these problems, she turned onto Tremont Street and immediately came upon a roiling mob of people outside the Granary Burying Ground where she had stood not even one week before for Rose Hammond's burial. Large crowds had always unnerved her, but there was a hushed energy to this one, as if gripped by some singular fascination. She was just about to slip by when she noticed a familiar figure with dark hair standing toward the back.

"What's all this?" Tabby asked, coming up beside Mary-Ruth and linking arms with her friend.

"There's been another snatching," she whispered.

Tabby's heart flew to her throat. "It's not…it's not Miss Hammond, is it?" After all the poor young woman and her family had gone through, what a tragic postscript that would be.

"No," Mary-Ruth said, shaking her head. "God help the poor thing, but her body was too badly mangled to be of much use to the snatchers probably. It was a Mr. Goodwin, a patient I laid out the other day. He was only just buried."

Craning her neck, Tabby could see a police officer at the front of the crowd, pressing people back and trying to keep order. The last time she had seen that officer he had been leading Caleb away.

A man in a tweed suit and bushy side-whiskers heard them and leaned over. "It's the Spunkers Club," he told them in confidential tones. "They're a secret society, from Harvard. Medical men and professors and the like. They use the bodies for dissection. My brother writes for the *Gazette* and says that they have been dormant for decades, but they've resurfaced again."

"The Spunkers?" she repeated. It sounded like a made-up word, childish, not like a club comprised of doctors and professors.

Another man, overhearing the conversation, shook his head vehemently. "This isn't the Spunkers. Say what you will about them, at least *they* had the decency to leave the grave looking as pristine as the day the minister stood over it. I should know, they got my great-granduncle back in '01," he said, almost with a note of pride. "'Twas almost six months before we even noticed he was gone."

A familiar sense of outrage welled in her breast. Life was cruel enough; who would deny the dead the peace of eternal rest? The dead, who could not defend themselves.

She turned toward the man with the bushy side-whiskers who was puffing on a cigar. "Did your brother say why they have started up again? Why now?"

The man tapped his cigar, looking rather pleased to be asked. "Oh, I'm sure he has his theories. You hear rumors, you know."

"What kind of rumors?"

"Well, a gentleman doesn't like to say." It was becoming clear that perhaps he didn't know as much as he let on.

Mary-Ruth snorted. "Gentleman indeed," she muttered.

But the second man was more than happy to speculate. "Don't you know? It's because of all these Spiritualists. Now that science is making advances with talking to the dead, they need bodies for their experiments. Have you heard about High Rock Tower in Lynn?"

Tabby shook her head, not sure she wanted to know.

The man rocked back on his heels. "Some science-minded men are trying to build a new messiah, they say. Building mechanical men and reanimating corpses." He looked at Tabby expectantly. "Well, where do you think they get the corpses?"

The abundant sunshine couldn't stop a chill from running down her spine. She had a thousand more questions for the men, but Mary-Ruth was taking her by the arm.

"What rubbish. Come on," she said, pulling Tabby to the front where they could get a better view. They wove through the crowd which was finally starting to disperse once they realized there was nothing to see and there would be no answers.

When they reached the grave, Tabby caught her breath. As with Mr. Bishop's robbery, the gravesite before them was a mangle of iron bars and crumbled plaster. The hole in the ground gaped back at them, violated and hopeless. Whoever had done this had not been overly concerned with being discreet. Whoever had done this had wanted a body, and badly.

11

IN WHICH THE PRISONER IS FREED.

THE FIRST MATTER Caleb had seen to upon his release was getting a good strong cup of coffee and a plate of oysters at the public house. Bolstered by this, he'd been able to go home and face the grateful hysterics of his mother. Then it was calling for hot water for a bath and scouring the stink of prison off himself. He was under no illusions as to the permanence of his situation, but as he luxuriated in the hot water, he was grateful for the reprieve. He would have to appear in court, put together some sort of defense, and it still wasn't clear at all if there were any other suspects for Rose's murder.

When he was scrubbed clean as a newborn and dressed in a freshly pressed suit, he slipped downstairs, ready to go out and see what he had missed at the club over the past week. He was hungry for some amusement, for the company of a pretty girl and a game of cards, anything to distract him from how he had failed Rose.

Passing through the dining room, he grabbed a slice of toast and tiptoed behind his mother, who was absorbed in her lady's journal as she ate her breakfast. But the woman had the preternatural hearing of a cat, and turned in her chair.

"Caleb! Goodness, you gave me a fright, sneaking around like that. Come, sit down and have a proper breakfast with me."

He could have insisted that he had business to attend to, but the hopefulness and vulnerability in his mother's eyes was so palpable that he simply nodded, taking a plate from the sideboard and filling it with eggs and sausages before sliding into his seat. He found he had missed the old dear, her comforting chatter and even the gossip about the other ladies in her circle. The club would still be there after breakfast. "Pass me the *Gazette*, would you?" He could at least see what had been happening in the world while he had been stagnating in prison.

She obliged, but not without a little *humph* as he spread it before him. He knew he was not being the doting son she had missed while he was gone, but he hadn't the energy to cosset her, not when he'd only just begun to feel human again. For now, breakfast would have to be enough.

Buttermilk twined around his legs, and he absently scratched his head beneath the table. His gaze roamed down the page, skimming headlines about slave rebellions, cotton prices, and oil deposits, and stopping when he came to the small headline tucked in the corner of the page. "Resurrection men strike again: Have we returned to the dark days of dissection?" Quickly folding the page, he slipped it into his pocket while his mother was distracted buttering her toast. Caleb had somehow managed to keep the fate of her husband's body from her so far, and he would be damned if she found out now. If only the police spent more time investigating the theft of his father's person, and less time throwing innocent men into jail.

Pushing back his chair, Caleb downed the rest of his coffee and stood up. "Breakfast has been lovely, but I really must be going."

"Where are you off to anyhow this morning? You've barely had a chance to rest after…your ordeal."

He didn't tell her that he was starving for the touch of another person, that he craved distraction, and if he happened to run into Miss Cooke on the way to the club and set her straight, well, so much the better. Over the last few days his annoyance with her strange behavior had faded, and all he felt was a deep sense of gratitude that she had cared enough to try to help him. "Whitby wants me at the office to sign some papers."

She gave a sigh. "Good, dear Mr. Whitby. What would we do without him?" Her eyes got a hazy faraway look in them that all but declared that her mourning period for his father was already drawing to a close. She was still a handsome woman despite her years, with a lively demeanor and spades of affection left to give; why shouldn't she turn her eye to the future and the possibility of happiness and stability? After decades with the monster who had been his father, could he really blame her?

But there was something off-putting about Whitby, and he couldn't help but feel her affection would be better placed somewhere else.

Caleb was over halfway to the club when guilt overtook him. Not just that he'd lied to his mother about where he was going, but that he could even think of playing cards or enjoying the company of a woman when Rose was barely cold in her grave. An uncomfortable but familiar sense of self-loathing bubbled up within him. Didn't vain men like him usually learn some sort of profound lesson after finding themselves on the wrong side of a set of iron bars? He might still be the same vain man he always was, but he could at least try to play the dutiful son. Giving a deep sigh, he doubled back and headed toward Whitby's office.

He had just crossed the square when he stopped short at the sight of a young woman with red hair peering at Whitby's office from behind a tree. Well, let no one claim that he hadn't tried to avoid her; she was the one who had crossed his path. He came up behind her and tapped her on the shoulder.

Spinning around, Tabby Cooke looked as if she'd seen a ghost. "Oh, it's you! You're out of prison!"

Unable to help himself, he grinned at her guileless enthusiasm. "It is me, in the flesh. Now that we've established that, perhaps I might ask what you're doing hiding behind a tree?"

Pink touched her cheeks, and he could tell she was trying very hard to look dignified despite the compromising position in which he'd found her. Not meeting his eye, she mumbled something he couldn't quite catch.

"You'll have to speak up."

She gave him a peeved look. "I—I'm here to see Mr. Whitby. I'm just a little early, is all."

He coughed until he nearly choked. Regaining himself, he was only able to murmur, "Is that so?"

She nodded, still not meeting his eye. Goodness, when had she become acquainted with Mr. Whitby? She'd claimed to have known his father as well as Rose, and now it seemed she was acquainted with his family's solicitor. She really was the most peculiar creature. His question must have shown on his face, because she said, "He called while I was with your mother."

Of course the little love had gone to visit his distraught mother. He could have swept her up in his arms and kissed her. He could have done a lot more than that too, but he remembered what had happened the last time he'd given in to his baser desires with her. Clearing his throat and trying not to look as intrigued as he felt, he asked, "And you're here to see him because?"

"Because I don't trust him," she said simply.

"Why don't you trust him?"

She gave a little shrug. "I couldn't say exactly. It's just a feeling I get."

Caleb tilted his head, considering her. He might have dismissed her intuition out of hand, but the truth was, he got the same feeling from the cool and faultlessly polite Whitby. The man had been a fixture in their household since Caleb was a boy, a sharp, calculating man who quietly but firmly steered the business from behind the senior

Mr. Bishop. Caleb had been just as surprised as Whitby
when his father left him, Caleb, the business instead of
to his trusted partner.

When it became obvious that she wasn't going to elaborate on what had brought her here, he gave a sigh. "Look,
I have business with Mr. Whitby and— No, don't say it,"
he stopped her as soon as she made a face. "Like him or
not, he's the best man to handle my situation. I may be a
while, but please wait for me. We need to talk."

"Well?"

Tabby hadn't liked watching him disappear into the
imposing brick building. She didn't trust Mr. Whitby not
to clamp the irons around Caleb's wrists himself and drag
him back to that filthy cell. But despite all her fears, he
had emerged back into the sunshine with his usual devil-
may-care swagger, winking at her as he caught her eye.
She felt heat rise to her cheeks and chastised herself for
so easily falling under his charming sway.

"Well what?"

She gave him an impatient look as he laced her arm
through the crook of his elbow and led her away from
the square. "What did he say?"

"Oh, nothing of great import."

His easy manner made strolling with him comfortable,
familiar, and despite her natural instinct to pull away, she
allowed her arm to stay snugly in his. He may have been
acting like his usual self, but she didn't for one moment
believe that whatever had transpired between the two
men could have been of no "great import," not when she
could feel him stiffen at her question.

"Here we are." Caleb held the door open, and Tabby stepped inside. She had never been in a coffeehouse before, and the smell of roasting coffee beans and sweets wrapped around her, warm and comforting. Tables spread with white cloths dotted the cozy interior, the low hum of conversations and delicate clinking of china cups filling the space. Tabby discreetly folded her frayed sleeve cuffs under themselves.

As they made their way to an empty table near the window, Tabby noticed that all the other patrons had one thing in common. Leaning toward Caleb, she asked in a whisper, "Is this a ladies-only establishment?"

Ignoring her question, Caleb removed his hat and gave a short bow to a table of well-dressed women. "Ladies."

An older woman in a silk bonnet put down her cup. "Why, Mr. Bishop, where have you been? We haven't seen you in months! Prudie said she saw you going into the Beacon Club—you haven't forsaken us, have you?"

"Never," he said, sweeping a low bow and planting a chivalrous kiss on the woman's gloved hand. "Cards is all I'm after in there. I could never abandon your charming company, or your cause. If you'll excuse me, though, I have promised my friend here a pot of coffee and some of your renowned delicacies."

"Of course." She craned her neck to get a look at Tabby and gave her a warm smile. "I do hope you both enjoy. You must try the buns—Mrs. Denny made them."

When the woman had returned to her conversation with her friends, Tabby tugged Caleb's sleeve. "What cause?" she asked him. "What is this place?"

"It's a ladies' suffrage club, and they practice temperance," he finally replied as he pulled a chair out for her. "They run the coffeehouse, and use the proceeds to fund their work."

"Oh," she said, unable to hide her surprise. "I didn't realize you were interested in women's suffrage. Or temperance."

He gave her a look. "I don't take spirits," he said without elaborating. "Here." He handed her a little card that listed all the café's offerings.

After Caleb had ordered them a pot of coffee and a heaping plate of Mrs. Denny's sweet buns dripping with honey, Tabby broached her concerns again. "What did you and Mr. Whitby talk about? Would you tell me if you were in trouble?" She watched as he took a long sip of coffee as if he wasn't going to answer. "You would, wouldn't you?"

Sighing, he put his cup down and leaned back in his seat. "You're a love for your concern, but I am a grown man capable of handling my own affairs. Just because you stumbled into this mess doesn't mean you should be involved. Really, we hardly know each other."

The bun she had been holding crumbled in her fingers. His words stung. Of course she didn't have any claim over him, any right to know the first thing about his affairs. She hadn't even known that he was a sober man, or that he frequented a women's suffrage club for goodness' sake. Yet she had thought he might at the very least see her as an ally, a friend.

His expression softened and he reached forward, patting her hand. "I know you mean well, and I appreciate it. But I have enough going on without worrying if you're getting into trouble."

She nodded, but a shiver of foreboding ran through her. He didn't understand people the way she did. He didn't know that sometimes the hand that reached out to help you was also the hand that could strike you the hardest.

Caleb saw Tabby safely home, and then turned back to his own house with leaden feet. Despite what he had told her, the meeting with Whitby had not gone particularly well. As he had worried, several investors had pulled their funding on finding out that the new owner was in prison awaiting trial on charges of murder. Even worse, Whitby had told him that the police did not have any other suspects for Rose's murder. It looked as if he would have to stand trial, and hope for the mercy of a reasonable judge and jury.

"Well, how did it go?" His mother greeted him at the door, wringing her hands.

"Swimmingly, Mother," he said with a quick peck on her cheek. "Couldn't have gone better."

She followed him into the drawing room as he shrugged off his coat and poured himself a glass of water. "Does that mean that the charges have been dropped? Is the business safe?"

Downing his drink, he closed his eyes and gathered himself. He didn't like lying to his mother, but after a lifetime of safeguarding the woman's nerves and protecting her from his father's malice, he was surprisingly good at it. "We did lose an investor or two, but Whitby says all told that it could have been a lot worse. He's optimistic that we'll come out of this stronger than ever."

The tightness in her face melted into relief. "Oh, thank goodness. Your father would turn over in his grave if the business was in trouble."

Caleb inwardly winced at his mother's choice of words.

"I just keep thinking about poor Rose," she continued. "I do hope the police take the hunt for her murder seriously and not just bandy about ridiculous accusations. And you, my poor boy, I can't help but worry for you."

"For God's sake, Mother, don't waste your fears on me. I assure you they are entirely unfounded."

Nevertheless, she gave a put-upon sigh. "To lose your father—your mentor!—and then your betrothed, and so close together... Well, I mourn for your broken heart."

A stab of guilt ran through Caleb. Rose's sudden death horrified him. Because he had only heard bits and pieces of how it happened, his imagination filled in the rest, and he had a very colorful imagination. Every time he closed his eyes, he saw her sprawled on the floor, her limbs splayed like a broken doll in a pool of blood. But the horrible fact of the matter was he didn't miss Rose as much as he should. Oh, he did miss her, but not in the way of a tortured lover. He missed her easy manner, and the proficient way she had of handling things. He missed the security and companionship that she would have provided, but his heart was stubbornly intact. And, well, he missed his father not at all.

"Caleb?"

He snapped from his thoughts, looking up to see his

mother gazing at him with concern. "Sorry, what were you saying?"

She frowned. "Never mind." Standing up, she gave a weary sigh. "I'm retiring for the night. Mind that you don't stay up too late."

On a sudden impulse, Caleb stood as well, drawing his mother into an embrace, inhaling the familiar scent of talcum and lemons that had comforted him since he was a little boy. "You're a dear, do you know that?"

His mother blushed, abashedly swatting him away. "Oh, come now."

"No, it's true. Don't worry yourself about me or the business. I'll take care of everything." But even as he said the words, he doubted in his own ability to carry them out.

12

"AND THE EYES THAT CANNOT WEEP
ARE THE SADDEST EYES OF ALL."

IT HADN'T EVEN been a week, but Tabby couldn't wait a full month to perform her ritual of trying to contact Alice. Tea with Caleb—*Mr. Bishop*, she corrected herself—had brought the standing of their relationship into sharp relief. Just because her heart sped up and the sun shone brighter when she was with him didn't mean that he felt even remotely the same about her. And honestly, she should be thanking her lucky stars that he felt that way, as she had no business pining after a man she could never give herself to. Perhaps she mistook the throbbing in her chest as love, when in fact it was only loneliness.

Loneliness, at least, was a familiar ache. Though it would mean her sister was dead, Tabby longed to make contact with her, even if it was just a glimpse of her face through the dark ether. Would Alice still have the same auburn hair done up in plaits as when they were children? Would she open her arms to Tabby and welcome her into her comforting embrace? She would do anything to see her sister one more time, anything to soothe the burning ache of loneliness.

Settling down on her usual church step, Tabby took a deep breath and allowed her mind to open.

All was still, the night sounds of the city far away and subdued. Tabby kept her breath steady, her body tensed and expectant. But the apparition that appeared before her was not her sister.

Rose's spirit was little more than the pale husk of a woman, her skin sallow, her mouth slack. Rose did not speak, but Tabby could see the pain, the confusion in her sunken eyes.

She would not squander her opportunity to speak to Rose. *You asked for my help, but I need yours first. You must think back to your last moments as a living being. Who killed you? You sang a song that I heard Mr. Whitby humming before—was it him?* If Rose told her that it had been Caleb, Tabby was not sure that she could bear it.

The spirit opened her blackened lips, and a terrible choking noise came out, raising the hairs on the back of Tabby's neck.

I know it's hard, I'm so sorry. I would not ask if it wasn't of the gravest importance.

But if Rose could speak, she did not. *Was it...was it Caleb?* Tabby asked in a whisper.

Slowly, so slowly, Rose shook her head. Tabby let out a breath. Caleb, at least, was not guilty. *Was it Whitby?*

This time, Rose nodded. It was a jerky motion, her neck bobbling unnaturally. Any relief Tabby had felt quickly evaporated. She'd had her suspicions, but now they were confirmed. Mr. Whitby was wealthy, connected. He would not be an easy man to accuse of murder, especially when Caleb was already under suspicion.

Rose was trembling, a leaf clinging to a branch in the wind. Tabby did not know what toll it took on the dead to appear to her, so she let her go. *Good-bye, Rose. Go in peace.*

When Tabby was back in bed with the quilt pulled up to her chin, she lay there for hours, thinking. The encounter had set her mind at ease, but the fact still remained: the words of a ghost were not proof enough to free Caleb, and if he was to be acquitted, then she was going to have to find clear, irrefutable proof. Perhaps he would see her in a different light if she was the one to exonerate him. Perhaps he would take her seriously, less like a little sister and more like a grown woman with love to give.

It was only as Tabby was standing across the street from the modest brick home two days later, that she realized what a daft idea this was. She had gone to Mr. Whitby's office once again the evening before and followed him home, this time with an overabundance of caution, and found that he lived on Beacon Hill, not far from Hammond House. Satisfied that he would be at work for the day, she knew she would be able to get inside and look around without him the wiser. The only problem was she couldn't very well walk up to the front door and knock...

could she? What if she played the lost waif, frightened and hungry and in need of succor? She had done it before, though it had not been an act then. No, there was no guarantee that the staff would take pity on her and invite her inside. And even if they did, they would most likely take her to the kitchen, below stairs and far from Mr. Whitby's personal rooms. It was too risky; she would have to slip in undetected.

Hurrying around the side of the house, she found a worker leaning casually against the wall while he smoked a pipe. She froze, and waited for him to yell at her, but all he did was cock his head toward the open side door and say, "Deliveries through there." She nodded before he could question why she didn't have anything with her, and bolted inside.

She did not have much experience in the houses of wealthy folks, but thinking back on the layout of Hammond house, she found her way to the staircase and quietly made her way upstairs. When she reached the main hall, she stood still, straining her ear and trying to hear past the pounding of her heart. From somewhere upstairs came the muffled chatter of maids as they worked. The house was not empty, but Tabby would be quick. She would find what she needed and then slip out before anyone even knew she was there.

The carpet under her feet was plush, but the floorboards beneath it groaned in protest as she made her way down the dark wood-paneled hall, and she had to stop frequently, waiting for them to settle.

The first room off the hall was a drawing room, followed by a dining room on the opposite side. That left the last door on the right. It was ajar and she was just able to slip in without creaking it open any farther.

Perspiration was starting to gather on her brow. What was she looking for, exactly? Surely if Mr. Whitby had committed the murder, he would have more sense than to leave a bloody knife lying on his desk. But if there were going to be answers anywhere, it would be here in his study. She was certain of it.

Heavy damask curtains were drawn in the study, casting the room in melancholy shadows despite the bright day, but she didn't dare open them as she slowly tiptoed inside. An entire wall of the room was given over to books lined neatly on shelves. Unable to help herself, Tabby gravitated toward them. Eli always said that there was nothing so important in life than to be able to read and write, and had taught her how to when she first came to him. Yet books were expensive, and were a rare luxury in their household, with the Bible and a handful of short story volumes comprising their entire library. Instead, Tabby had read and reread the inscriptions on the gravestones, imagining the lives that had inspired such tender and heartfelt words. When there was enough money, Tabby bought cheap penny papers that left her with inky fingers. She couldn't remember the last time she'd felt the satisfying weight of a book in her hands.

Mr. Whitby's collection proved to be disappointing, however. There was an unsurprising amount of law volumes, treatises on British corn tariffs, an anatomy book from the last century, and titles in languages she couldn't even identify. Tabby allowed her fingers to trail over the leather spines, reveling in the gilded titles and embellishments. One, titled *The Fugitive Slave Act*, caught her eye. Had Mr. Whitby helped draft that reprehensible law? Wicked man. She wouldn't be surprised. With a shudder, she moved on.

The great desk which dominated the room seemed like the obvious place to start, and as she grew closer, she felt as if an invisible string pulled her toward it. The first two drawers opened easily, but after rifling through them she didn't find anything more than documents and paper packets. The bottom drawer was locked. Mr. Bishop's spirit had told her that he had kept his important ledgers in the bottom drawer of his desk behind a false panel. Perhaps Mr. Whitby did the same.

Just as she was feeling along the woodgrain for a latch, a noise in the hall stopped her, something that might have been the creak of a footstep or nothing more than the house settling. She froze, waiting for it to come again. When her legs had grown hot and tingly from sitting on her heels and she didn't hear the noise again, she let out her breath and resumed searching.

The bottom drawer wouldn't open, and she couldn't risk spending any more time trying to force it. Switching her focus to the top of the desk, Tabby ran her hands over the sparse items on the well-polished surface: a stack of newspapers, a handsome set of pens and blotting sand, a small wooden box inlaid with ivory. Gingerly, Tabby put her thumb to the lid of the box and pushed it up. To her surprise, it opened easily.

In the dim light she could just make out the hodge-podge of contents. There were a few loose buttons, stamps, and coins...the normal assortment of homeless items that find their way into a such a box, only to be forgotten. But then something caught the little bit of light coming through a crack in the curtains, reflecting back at her. Fishing it out, Tabby held up the small bauble for a closer look.

It was a sapphire or topaz, some sort of deep blue stone, and it was set in filigree and hung from an earring hook. It was exquisite; by far the most precious thing that she had ever held in her hand. But that wasn't what gave her pause. There was no question that it was a woman's piece of jewelry. Perhaps Mr. Whitby kept it as the relic of some doomed love affair, or an acquaintance had lost it and he had yet to reunite it with her. Or perhaps there was a more sinister explanation. Slipping it into her pocket, Tabby gently closed the box and returned it to its place on the desk. To stay any longer would be to press her luck too far, and even if the jewel was nothing, it was the closest thing she had found to a clue.

"Looking for something?"

The voice stopped her heart in her chest, and she spun around. A dark shape in the doorway stepped forward, revealing every intimidating inch of Mr. Whitby. "Miss Cooke, what a charming surprise."

No matter what he had seen, there was nothing she could do to explain her presence in his study in the middle of the day. Her tongue was suddenly thick, her feet slow. She just stared at him.

Moving into the room with lethal grace, Mr. Whitby came right up to her until she thought he was going to grab her by the shoulders and shake her senseless. But he continued moving past her to a sideboard and picked up a glass.

"You seem to have an inordinate amount of interest in me," he said casually as he fixed himself a drink. Did she have enough time to make a dash for the door? Before she could find out, Mr. Whitby turned, drink in hand, and placed himself between her and the only exit. "First following me on the street and now appearing uninvited in my study. I won't flatter myself that you have any sort of romantic designs on me, but I must say I find it curious that you make such an effort to put yourself in my path."

She forced herself to return his cold, unyielding gaze. "You killed Rose."

As soon as the words left her mouth, she regretted them. What was she thinking? The last thing she ought to do was provoke him. As the air between them grew hot and prickly from the accusation, some animal instinct inside of her screamed for her to flee. But before she could obey, he was lunging toward her, hands reaching for her like the talons of a bird of prey.

He was going to kill her, she thought numbly as his glass shattered on the floor. She had always prided herself on her survival instincts, had always thought that she was made of stronger stuff, but as she watched him approaching her at lightning speed, all she could do was shrink down into herself and pray that she was wrong about his intentions.

Stumbling back, she would have hit the desk except that elegant hands grabbed her by the collar and jerked her back up.

Time stopped and she froze in place, his hands still at

her neck. "How dare you," he hissed. His cold blue eyes were mere inches from hers, his breath hot and unpleasant on her skin. "You come into my house, rifle through my belongings, and then accuse me of murder."

Tabby's heart beat furiously. He was guilty, she was sure of it. But all her intuition would not help her if he decided to kill her, which right now it was looking very much like he wanted to do.

Her anger was stronger than her fear, though. It bubbled up and overflowed. If she could have spit venom like a snake she would have, but she had only her words and her outrage. "You let them lock up Caleb! He...he thinks you're his friend." The sickening injustice of it made her blood run hot. She had to warn Caleb.

The vein under Mr. Whitby's eye throbbed, and she knew that whatever reprieve she had just been granted was now gone. She might not be so lucky a second time.

"Let go of me!" She twisted and flailed, but he pinned her wrists, neatly avoiding her attack. "Let me go this instant!" Surely the house servants would hear her protests. But then, she was the one who had broken in like a common thief. Who would come to her defense?

He took her by her shoulders, his fingers digging into her flesh. "You can't possibly imagine that I can let you run back to young Mr. Bishop with these unfounded accusations now, can you?"

Her throat tightened as the reality of her situation slowly spread over her, her legs going wobbly. He gave her a mocking look. "Oh, come now, Miss Cooke. Don't think me a monster. I have no desire kill you." His assurance brought her no comfort, not when his piercing eyes bore through her as if she were no more than a rabbit caught pillaging the vegetable patch and in need of poisoning.

He was taller, stronger than her. She darted her gaze around the room, frantically looking for her best chance of escape. How could she have been so foolish to come in here without having an escape route planned?

As if sensing her plans to flee, one hand went around her neck, tightening just under her chin. "I don't *want* to kill you, but you seem determined to smear my good name."

The voice inside of her was screaming now, and she didn't even have to think. Groping blindly behind her, she struggled to find something, anything, with which she might fend him off. Her hand found the inlaid box and closed around it just as he was tightening his grip around her neck. With monumental effort, she brought it up and landed a glancing blow on Mr. Whitby's temple. He reeled backward, a bead of blood welling up on his hairline. "Goddamn you!" he spat.

It wasn't enough to knock him unconscious, but it bought her just enough time to free herself and make a dash for it.

He took a sidestep at her, his fingers grazing her skirt as she flew past him. She bolted back out into the hallway, practically knocking into a servant with an armful of linens. Running out into the street, she blindly wove around pedestrians and horse carts. She ran until the harbor stopped her, her heart pounding and her throat hoarse from gulping in air.

She had escaped with her life, but for how long?

13

IN WHICH FREEDOM IS SHORT-LIVED.

CALEB HAD JUST emerged from the smoky interior of his club, five dollars the richer after trouncing Debbenham at cards, when a dark-haired young woman waved him down from across the street. His eyes were still adjusting to the daylight, but she didn't look familiar. She made a frustrated gesture when he didn't return her wave, and then began weaving her way toward him. It wasn't until she was darting across the busy street that he recognized her from the cemetery as Tabby's friend.

He frantically searched his memory for her name before landing on it just as she stopped in front of him. "Miss O'Reilly, what a pleasant surprise. I—"

The young woman stopped him with an impatient flutter of her hand. "Have you seen Tabby?" she asked, still breathless from her dash across the street.

He finally noticed the frantic look in her eyes, the

flush in her cheeks, and the disheveled curls coming loose from her straw bonnet. He was just about to tell her that of course he'd seen her, they'd had coffee and buns just the other day, but then he closed his mouth, a feeling of dread creeping over him. He'd told Tabby in no uncertain terms that day not to get involved. If something had happened to her, he would never forgive himself. "Not since Tuesday," he said, his mouth suddenly dry.

Miss O'Reilly closed her eyes and nodded, as if he had just confirmed her worst fears. "She was supposed to assist me with a laying out this morning, but she never came. Tabby may be a creature of strange habits, but she always keeps her word."

A carriage clipped past them, sending dust and gravel spraying, and Caleb took Miss O'Reilly by the elbow, leading her away from the curb. "Have you checked her home? Spoken with Mr. Cooke?"

Scowling, Miss O'Reilly removed her elbow from his hold. "Of course I did! That was the first place I looked. Eli said that she went out to make some calls and never returned. He's sick with worry for her."

Caleb leaned back against the brick wall of a building and closed his eyes, letting the sounds of rattling carts and pedestrian chatter wash over him. God, what had Tabby gone and done? He should have known after she had pledged not to get involved the first time when he was in prison that she would do what she wanted regardless of her assurances otherwise.

When he opened his eyes, he found that Miss O'Reilly was studying him with a suspicious glare. "Yes?"

"You wouldn't know anything about it, would you?"

"What, that she's missing? You think *I* had something to do with it?"

Miss O'Reilly didn't answer his question. "What, exactly, are your intentions with Tabby?"

"My intentions?" He let out a little laugh, sure that Miss O'Reilly was in jest. But one look at her stony expression told him she was anything but. He cleared his throat. "Tabby is a fine girl, but I don't know that I have any intentions toward her. What do you take me for, a shameless rake?"

Miss O'Reilly's expression did not soften at this, if anything, her green eyes grew only stormier. "I see," she said in clipped tones. "Well, Mr. Bishop, let me tell you something. Tabby is more than just a 'fine girl.' Tabby is my heart outside of my body, my sweetest, dearest friend. I've heard about your exploits from more than one broken-hearted girl." At this, she threw a pointed look at the club across the street and Caleb felt like a chastened little boy caught pilfering sweets from the kitchen. "I know you were released from prison, though you are still a suspect in Rose Hammond's murder. If I hear so much as a *whisper* of your name in association with Tabby, I promise you I will not hesitate to make sure you end up back in prison, where you belong."

With that, Miss O'Reilly turned neatly on her boot heel, and swept down the street, mindless of the children that scattered from her path and the dust that her skirts kicked up.

Caleb watched her disappear into the busy afternoon foot traffic. How could everyone think him capable of such dark, nefarious deeds? When had he ever shown a disposition for such things?

The thrill of winning at cards had quickly worn off, and now he was consumed only with thoughts of where Tabby might have gotten to. Miss O'Reilly might have suspected him, but *he* knew that he had nothing to do with it, and that meant that Tabby was somewhere out there. It was no use going to the cemetery or the boarding house—Miss O'Reilly would have already scoured both places. At least at home he could dash off a few inquiries and make a plan. But he had to admit that Miss O'Reilly was right: he really didn't have any claim over Tabby Cooke. Hadn't he told her as much when she had insisted on helping him? He had told Miss O'Reilly that he had no intentions toward Tabby, yet the thought of her with a man—any man—made his chest twist. It was a hot, unpleasant feeling, and he did not care for it. Of course, he hoped she was just with a man and not in any sort of trouble, but that didn't make the thought any more palatable.

He was so preoccupied with his thoughts that he was almost upon the group of men standing outside his front steps before he even noticed them. At the sound of his footsteps, one of the men turned and Caleb's heart sank as he recognized the constable. "Mr. Bishop, we were just talking about you."

Behind him, his mother was standing on the steps, wringing her hands, her cap askew as if she had thrown it on in a hurry. Several curious neighbors hovered by their front doors, craning their necks to see what was happening.

"Is that so?" Caleb jammed his hands in his pockets, feigning a casualness that he did not feel at the sight of so many uniformed men. "And how may I be of service? Have you made some progress in Miss Hammond's case?"

"Well, yes, we do have some new information regarding the matter."

Caleb let out a breath of relief. "What is it?"

"Does this look familiar, Mr. Bishop?"

The earring the constable held out did look familiar. Caleb had given Rose just such a set of earrings and a matching necklace when he had proposed to her. "That's Rose's earring," he said.

The constable and officers shared a look, and Caleb caught sight of a pair of irons in one of the policeman's hands. They couldn't possibly be here for him, could they? Whitby had assured him that he was a free man until his trial, that there probably wouldn't even *be* a trial if they continued to investigate other possible suspects. "We found this in your parlor, shoved beneath the cushion of a chair."

At this, his mother couldn't contain herself any longer. She hurried to the bottom of the steps, as fast as her voluminous black skirts would allow, shaking her fist. "These men just forced their way in! I tried to stop them, but they are unmannered beasts!"

"I…" Caleb trailed off, the blue jewel winking at him in the afternoon sun. "I don't know how that got there," he said weakly. "But she was my fiancée, for God's sake—you can hardly fault me for being in possession of a piece of her jewelry!"

He racked his brain, trying to think how the earring

had found its way into his parlor. He supposed Rose might have dropped it during one of her visits, but Larson or Betty the housemaid would have surely found it before now. Rose had never mentioned having lost it. Glancing down the street, he wondered if he ran fast enough if he'd be able to chase down a passing carriage and catch a ride to freedom.

As if reading his thoughts, the constable raised his palms in a placating gesture. "Now, Mr. Bishop, no use making it harder than it has to be. Come with us willingly and I'll even ask Smith here not to use the irons."

The man named Smith looked a little disappointed, but Caleb nodded. The last thing he wanted was to further agitate his mother by ending up under a pile of burly policemen. "Lead away, Constable."

As the officer's hand clamped around Caleb's arm, it was not the prospect of returning to prison that made his heart plummet in dread, but the thought that Tabby was somewhere out there, missing, and he was powerless to do anything about it.

14

IN WHICH IT MAY BE TOO LATE.

"MISS COOKE!" THE guard stationed at the front desk sprang up from his seat as soon as she set foot inside the old prison. "What a pleasure to see you again!"

Tabby stopped in her tracks. Officer Hodsdon. His boyish enthusiasm at seeing her was at odds with the dreary walls and musty smell of the old building. "I've come to see Mr. Bishop," she said, trying to ignore the heavy staleness in the air, the muffled shouts that came from somewhere deep within the bowels of the prison.

Was it her imagination, or did Officer Hodsdon look disappointed at this? But then he was clearing his throat, and giving her a genuine smile. "Of course. It's not visiting hours, but I can let you see him for five minutes. Our secret," he said, leaning in and tapping a finger to his nose in a conspiratorial gesture.

It wasn't nearly enough time, but she knew it wasn't

worth arguing. Nodding, Tabby allowed Officer Hodsdon to lead her through a set of double doors and down a long hallway lined with barred cells. A few men leered as she passed and Officer Hodsdon yelled at them to mind their manners.

When they finally stopped, it was not in front of the general holding room in which Caleb had been the first time, but a solitary cell with a slit for a window, and a floor covered in musty straw. He was a sorry sight to behold, sitting on a hard bench with his head in his hands, his fine golden curls mussed and wild. Gone was the rebellious spark in his eye, the flippant air that he'd had the last time she'd visited him in this dismal place.

When he looked up and saw she was his visitor, he leapt to his feet, smoothing out his rumpled shirt. "Tabby? What on earth… You shouldn't be here."

"Shh, there isn't much time." She was right at the bars, aware that Officer Hodsdon was standing a polite distance away, but still within earshot.

Caleb just stood there, gawping at her as if he were seeing a ghost. "Miss O'Reilly told me yesterday that you were missing… No one knew where you were. I thought…" he trailed off, his throat working convulsively.

"It's all right, he didn't hurt me." She tamped down the memory of Mr. Whitby's breath on her cheek, the look in his eye that told her he would not only kill her if he could, but would relish doing so.

Caleb's brows nearly shot off his face and he rushed toward the bars. "Hurt you? Who? What are you talking about?"

She shook her head, annoyed at herself that she had let that slip. "Nothing, it doesn't matter."

"Doesn't matter! Tabby, I—" He broke off, running his hand through his hair and muttering something to himself that she couldn't catch. "Look, don't worry about me. Go home to your father. Mr. Whitby will sort all this—"

Tabby shot an alarmed glance at Officer Hodsdon, sure that he was listening, and then leaned closer through the bars so that she could lower her voice further. Despite the unsavory surroundings, Caleb still smelled delicious, like soap and peppery spices. She took a deep breath, composing herself. "Mr. Whitby is the one who had you arrested. He's the reason you're in here in the first place."

Caleb blinked at her. "Don't be ridiculous. I admit I have no great love for the man, but he's been with our family for years. He would never cast suspicion on me. Besides, he's the one who got me out in the first place."

Oh, but it was worse than that. Should she tell him the truth? Would he even believe her if she did? She had to, it was the only way to get him to understand the severity of the situation, to make him act. "I am not being ridiculous. I went to his house to—don't look at me like that—I went to his house to find evidence. Here," she said, producing the earring and holding it close to her body so that Officer Hodsdon wouldn't see.

Caleb's face drained of all color as his gaze alighted on the sparkling blue jewel, and he reached a tentative finger through the bars to touch it. "That…that's from a set I gave to Rose on our engagement," he said in a whisper. "The police claimed they found the other one in my parlor, but on my honor, I don't know how it got there."

Tabby knew how it had. It would have been all too easy for Mr. Whitby to slip the earring into a cushion or drawer in Caleb's parlor, and then alert the police. Her suspicions about the earring confirmed, she continued. "He killed Rose, Caleb, and he would have killed me if I hadn't—" She cut herself short, not wanting to alarm him unduly and incur his anger for trespassing in Mr. Whitby's house. "I don't know why he killed her, but he's letting you take the blame while he walks free."

When he didn't say anything, she returned the earring to her pocket. "Caleb," she said softly. "You'll hang for this."

He was pale as a sheet. "The business," he said in a hoarse whisper.

"What do you mean?"

From behind her came Officer Hodsdon's voice. "One more minute, Miss Cooke."

Caleb spoke quickly. "He wants the business. He thought my father would leave everything to him, since Whitby was his business partner, but he left it to me instead. He must want me out of the way." Then color flooded his face and his eyes narrowed and she saw real fury there. "Why would he have killed you, and where did you find that earring? When would he—"

"Hush!" She darted a furtive glance at Officer Hodsdon who was pretending not to stare at them. "You have to get out of here. You have to escape."

"Escape? You can't be serious." He looked at her like she had just suggested that he build a ship to the moon. "There's still the trial."

Tabby had no faith in the justice system, not when

she had seen Mr. Whitby pervert it so easily for his own gain. Besides, any evidence the jury would hear would be biased against Caleb. They would hear how he was the last person to see Rose Hammond alive, how they had argued that night. They would be shown the earring that was found in his house. She shook her head. "Mr. Whitby would have no problem making sure the court ruled against you. Please," she said, "you must find a way out of here."

Caleb didn't say anything and the silence stretched between them, growing heavier and tenser. Finally, he gave the smallest nod of his head. "But Tabby—" he gave her a stern look as her face brightened "—I don't want you getting any more involved in this. If Whitby is half as dangerous as you say, then I want you as far away from him as possible."

Tabby opened her mouth, but he stopped her. "No arguments. I can be a crafty dodger when I put my mind to it, and I'll figure this out. Alone."

She wanted to tell him that it wasn't just for his sake that she was concerned, but for Rose's, as well. It might have been the urgency of the situation, or how vulnerable he looked in his rumpled suit and unkempt curly hair, but this roguish young man had somehow found the chink in the armor around her heart. If he escaped—which was his only real course of action—she would never see him again. Would it really be so very terrible if she unburdened her secret, just this once?

These thoughts flitted through her head like an erratic sparrow in flight, and before she could let all the old arguments against it sway her, she was blurting out: "I can speak to the dead. That's how I knew your father, and Rose. That's how I know you're innocent and that Mr. Whitby is responsible for her murder. I've never told another living soul, except for my parents and sister, and they're all gone now."

The air around them had gone very still as she spoke, the noise of the prison melting into the background. He stared at her.

She shouldn't have told him. It didn't matter that she would never see him again. What mattered was that he didn't believe her. She could see it on his face, the wariness, the incredulity. She had been right to build up a wall around her heart. She could never hope to walk amongst the living, to thrive like a normal young woman. Her sister was gone, and with her, the only person that would ever understand Tabby. She was destined to wander through this half-life lonely and misunderstood.

She braced herself for his words, but it didn't make it any easier when they broke over her like frigid waves.

"You aren't serious." He searched her face, the corner of his mouth tugging up into a smile. But the smile quickly faded when she didn't say anything. "You are serious."

She just stared at him, hoping against hope that he would see her earnestness. He returned her look in full measure. "Tabby, love, all that spiritualism and speaking with the dead…it's all nonsense and parlor tricks, you do know that, don't you?"

When she still didn't say anything, he took a step back. "Oh Christ, Tabby. Is it money that you're after? You know, I'm quite familiar with your kind. A woman claiming to be a medium fleeced my mother of twenty dollars after my father died. Has that been your aim all along? Is that why you're so determined to involve yourself in my affairs?"

Suddenly she was back in the churchyard, Beth Bunn and the other children's taunts ringing in her ears. He may have had her secret now, but he would not have her dignity. Before he could see the hot tears welling in her eyes, she turned and fled.

15

IN WHICH THERE IS A PAINFUL GOOD-BYE AND AN UNLIKELY PLAN FORMED.

AFTER SHE HAD emerged from the prison, Tabby had headed toward the docks, where she would blend in with the crowds of servants and housewives at the fish market. More than anything she wanted to run to Eli, but what if she led Mr. Whitby to him? She didn't know how badly she had injured Whitby, but it would only be a matter of time before he came looking for her, if he wasn't already. For all she knew, he might have someone chasing after her. She didn't doubt that a man like him could find anyone he wanted in this city.

She just had to see Eli one last time, and then she would disappear, leave the cemetery, and ensure that she never put his life in danger. Eli had once told her that there was a warren of tunnels that ran beneath the cemetery, once used by privateers in the old days, and now abandoned.

But Tabby didn't know where they originated, so instead she took a long, circuitous route to ensure that no one would follow her.

She found Eli stooped over in the back of the cemetery pulling weeds, perspiration beading his balding temples. When he heard her approaching, he looked up, the plants falling from his hands. "Tabby," he said, slowly rising. "Where've you been, girl?"

Had it really been only that morning that she had been in Mr. Whitby's house? Only an hour since she had stood opposite Caleb with nothing but iron bars separating them?

She let herself be folded into his embrace, his familiar scent of pipe tobacco and shaving tonic wash over her.

"I—I was helping Mary-Ruth with a laying out."

Pulling back, he studied her with a frown. His dark eyes swept over her torn collar and disheveled hair. "Mary-Ruth was here, looking for you."

"Oh, that must have been before we crossed paths," she said lamely.

Tabby didn't know if she was a good liar or not; she so rarely had to do it. But he only gave her an unreadable look and nodded. "Well, you're home now."

She didn't say anything else. How could she tell him that this wasn't permanent, that she had to leave? The flowering tree boughs swayed gently in the breeze, the sweet scent of pollen making her want nothing more than to stretch out on the warm grass and drift off to sleep.

She was just about to tell him that she couldn't stay, when the heavy-set figure of a woman came bustling along the path.

"Tabby Cooke! Are you coming for supper? I haven't seen you in church lately, but then, you never came regular. You sure your pa is feeding you right? You know that you always have a seat at our table."

Tabby gave Miss Suze a weak smile, trying not to dwell on the memories from the last time she had been there. "I'm afraid not today. I was just telling Eli that I have to go away for a while. You see, I've found a relative— a cousin—that lives in Rockport, and she's invited me to visit."

Eli gave her a long look. "A cousin?"

"Yes, it was a surprise to me, as well." Shifting in her boots, Tabby forced herself to push on. "It's just for a month or so, and then I'll be back in time to help in the winter." The lies tasted like acid on her tongue.

Squinting up at the cloudless sky, Eli scrubbed a weary hand over his stubbled chin. "I don't like this, Tabby, not one bit. You only just came home and you look like you've been through the mill. How come you never mentioned this cousin before?"

"I never knew her. I only just discovered that she lived in Boston."

"I thought you said she lived in Rockport," Miss Suze said.

"Her family summers in Rockport," Tabby quickly amended. "That's what I meant."

"I don't like this, Tabby," Eli repeated. "You're a grown woman and you can come and go as you please, but I worry about you. At least stay for supper."

She opened her mouth, but Miss Suze tutted. "Your

pa is right. At least come in and sit with us for some supper. You can't travel on an empty stomach."

Tabby wavered in her resolve. Her stomach *was* growling and it would be so nice just to sit down with Eli at their little table again, for one last time. She could leave at first light in the morning and make certain that no one saw her. "All right," she relented. "Just for supper."

After Tabby left, Caleb sat on the hard bench covered in straw ticking that served as his bed. Through the narrow window the sounds of a city at work drifted in, as familiar as his own heartbeat, yet foreign as a half-forgotten dream. Here he had thought that Miss Cooke was an innocent, but she was nothing more than a charlatan, taking advantage of the grieving just as the medium had done with his mother.

But what was more important was the message she had brought about Whitby. If Tabby was to be believed, then he was dangerous, malicious. *Could* she be believed about anything, though? His brief, unbelievable conversation with her played through his mind over and over. If what she said was true, then his situation was hopeless, dire, even. But why would Whitby work to get him out of prison the first time, only to make sure he was arrested again shortly thereafter?

Rubbing his stiff knees, Caleb finally stood and stretched, the rush of fresh blood that pumped through his body revitalizing him. The most sensible course of action would be to hire a good lawyer, see the trial through, and hope that the jury was reasonable. But that was in a perfect world where things were fair and actually worked the way they should, not in a world where greedy men killed innocent young women for their own gain. It was a gamble, and while he relished a good game of odds, he was not particularly keen to do so when the stakes were his life.

If Whitby was truly the murderer, as Tabby claimed, then Caleb would be sitting in this cell until his hair turned gray or he was executed, whichever came first. Whitby would never fall under suspicion, and even if he did, he would quickly be cleared thanks to his connections and name. As the sounds of carts and fishmongers transitioned into the laughter and chatter of dock workers making their way home for the day, the only possible solution became clear: Tabby was right. He had to escape.

As Caleb took stock of his miserable cell and what was available to him, he couldn't help but let out a grim laugh. If someone had told him a month ago that his father would die and leave him the business, and then his father's scheming business partner would murder Caleb's fiancée in order to exact a perverse revenge and gain control of the company, he would have slapped them on the shoulder, saying it was the best joke he'd heard in a long time. But here he was, plotting his escape from prison so that he would not risk standing trial and being found guilty by a bribed jury. God worked in mysterious ways, as his mother was so fond of saying, but he would have paid good money to ask God what He was thinking with this level of absurdity.

His thoughts were interrupted by an officer bringing Caleb's evening tray of stale bread and thin barley soup. Caleb recognized the blond man with the close-cropped hair as one of the officers that had been present at his first arrest, and then had supervised his visit with Tabby earlier that day. Officer Hodgeson or something to that effect.

It wasn't until the next morning when the same officer came to collect his tray that the spark of an idea took root in Caleb's head. An inventory of his cell the previous night had made it clear that Caleb was not going to carry off some daring escape involving a tunnel or scaling walls. He hadn't the patience for digging, let alone the musculature. No, there was only one way out of here, and it was to use his wits.

Caleb had noticed the way the officer had watched Tabby's every move, the quick duck of his head when she turned her gaze in his direction, the color touching his cheeks when she addressed him. Despite the officer's look of wide-eyed innocence and his boyish demeanor, he was well built and tall, bigger than Caleb.

Officer Hodsdon—as Caleb learned his name was eventually—did not come every day. Sometimes it was the warden or some other nameless officer. But when he was on duty, Caleb made a point to chat with him, find out everything he could about him. He learned that the young man had injured his hand in the line of duty, and that he had been relegated to work within the prison until he mended. He'd recently lost his mother, and her dying wish was that her son reach the rank of sergeant.

"Back on dinner duty?" Caleb asked in a pleasant tone.

Officer Hodsdon was juggling three trays in one hand, grappling with his ring of keys in the other. He grunted in answer.

"Seems like you could use some help."

Slipping Caleb's tray through the slot in the bars, Officer Hodsdon gave a little shrug. "We used to have a girl that handled all the meals and linen collection, but it became clear that her presence was a distraction to the prisoners and guards alike, and she was let go."

As far as steering the conversation went, it was rather clumsy, but Caleb had only a few seconds before Officer Hodsdon moved on to the next cell, so he took his chance. "Speaking of girls, do you know that young woman who visits me? The one with red hair and the clouded eyes?"

Pausing, Officer Hodsdon regarded him with something between wariness and suspicion. "Miss Cooke."

"That's right." Caleb gave him an encouraging smile. "She mentioned you the last time she was here. Said you looked too kind to work at a place like this."

If Officer Hodsdon was intrigued, his face didn't betray anything. A flush of shame ran through Caleb that he would dangle Tabby in front of this man, like some sort of pretty fairground prize. He decided to try a different angle. "She's a medium, you know." Caleb held his breath, trying to look nonchalant as he waited to see if the officer would take the bait.

Now this seemed to pique his interest. "She is?"

Caleb rubbed at the back of his neck. God, he was dirty and in need of a bath. "Oh yes. I'd wager she could contact someone for you. Your mother, say."

Unmistakable interest crossed the officer's face, and immediately there was a shift in his demeanor. "You know, we see each other every day. You might as well call me Billy," he said.

When Billy was done with the trays, he came back, a pack of cards in his hand. "I don't suppose you play? Half the men in here can barely count to ten and I'm fit to expire of boredom."

Caleb was only too happy to oblige. Dragging a little table right up to the cell, Billy began dealing and Caleb scraped his chair over to position it between the bars.

They played their cards in silence, Billy occasionally getting up to patrol the other cells in the hall, and Caleb making sure to play well, but not well enough to beat his guard.

"I could put in a good word for you with her," Caleb said carefully as he laid his cards out.

He didn't say who, and he didn't need to. The cards in Billy's hand stilled. "You would?"

"Of course!" Caleb exclaimed, like they were the oldest friends in the world.

There was silence as Billy considered his play before sliding Caleb a sly look. "You're sweet on her, aren't you? You're sure you're not just trying to see her again?"

Caleb feigned intense interest in his cards. He gave a one-shouldered shrug. "She doesn't mean anything to me. Just a friend of my mother's."

Billy rubbed at his chin, presumably to hide the pink flush from creeping up farther. The man really was smitten with Tabby, and could Caleb blame him? She might have been a fraud and a liar, but she was an uncommonly striking young woman.

"I don't know," Billy said at last, folding his cards on the table and leaning back, his fingers laced behind his head. "I can't just accept favors from prisoners. If I want to make sergeant, then I have to walk the straight and narrow."

"Well, let me know if you change your mind." Caleb flashed him his most charming smile. "I'm not going anywhere."

After four days and no sign that Billy would take Caleb up on his offer, Caleb's hope began to wane. Was it imperative that Billy did? No, but it would certainly make Caleb's plan easier. He needed Billy to let his guard down, so to speak, in more ways than one.

So it took Caleb by surprise when bringing him his tray one morning, Billy slid him a curious, almost sheepish look.

"Is she really a medium?" he asked. "She can speak with the dead?"

Caleb chose his words carefully. "That's right. She's not like some of the charlatans peddling false promises and nonsense around Boston. I've witnessed her gift for myself." How anyone could believe such tripe was beyond him, but Billy seemed intrigued.

Leaning against the wall, Billy folded his arms in consideration. "I'd like to see her again. If you're still willing to arrange something, that is."

Caleb's pulse beat faster but he kept his voice steady. "Of course. I'm afraid that we left on rather poor terms the last time I saw her, but fetch me paper and pen and I'll write to her."

"Well, I'd wager you will have more luck with her than I would. She would hardly look at me when she came last time, even though she was nothing but courteous when I called on her at home."

When had Billy met with Tabby outside the prison? But he couldn't very well ask without sounding suspicious, so he kept his questions to himself.

If the weak shaft of light coming from his sliver of a window was any indication, then it was still daytime. It wasn't ideal timing, but an opportunity was an opportunity. He would have to be fast and take extra care not to be seen.

When Billy returned, he was carrying a sheaf of paper and some lead. "I'm afraid I couldn't commandeer a pen, but hopefully this will do."

Caleb accepted them through the bars, and after making a show of trying to write with the paper braced on his thigh, he turned a sheepish look at Billy. "Say, you don't think I could write this at your desk, could I? I'm afraid the light in here is rather poor. You could watch as I write and make sure the letter is to your satisfaction."

"I can't let you out, Caleb. You know that."

"Of course, what was I thinking," he said, pausing for effect. "Would you come in here with a lamp, then? You can still look over the letter, and we'll have it off in no time."

He could see indecision warring on Billy's face, not wanting to be impolite, but clearly uncomfortable with the request. Caleb pushed away the guilt of lying to the man who had been nothing but kind to him during his time here.

Sweat trickled down Caleb's neck as he waited for what felt like an eternity. Eventually, Billy unclipped the heavy ring of keys he kept at his belt and then he was opening the door and breaching the boundary between freedom and confinement.

Caleb kept his breathing even as Billy set down a lamp and then settled next to him on the creaking bench.

"Better be quick about it," Billy said as he craned his head to peer out the door. "The captain or warden could walk by anytime and I can't be caught."

"Of course." Caleb began writing, flicking one quick glance at Billy before he fumbled with the lead, dropping it and sending it skittering across the floor. "Damn. Can you see where that went?"

Billy dropped to his knees, reaching for the lead, which had rolled across the cell and come to rest against a clump of straw.

Taking a deep breath, Caleb reached for the lamp beside him. "I'm so sorry," he murmured.

Billy didn't even look up. "Hmm? For what?"

"For this." And with that, Caleb brought the lamp down on the back of his head, hard.

The butter on the johnnycakes was starting to congeal.

Usually when Eli made the special breakfast, Tabby was already wolfing down second helpings before the butter had a chance to so much as soften. But today she sat poking at the cooling cakes, lost in a heavy fog. She had slept poorly the night before, waking every time a stray dog barked outside or a branch rustled in the wind. She'd stolen to the window more than once, peeking out from behind the curtain at the cemetery across the street, certain that she saw a shadowy figure watching her. Dawn had found her with dry red eyes, but there had been no knock at the door from Mr. Whitby, no one come to find her and drag her back to him.

Her last day at home had stretched into a week, then two, as the cooler winds of autumn swept away the sweet, grassy summer evenings. Every morning she awoke from her fitful sleep, determined that it would be the day she finally left and disappeared into some anonymous city. But where would she go? She'd had the lie about a cousin in Rockport at the ready, but hadn't actually thought about where she would go. Eli hadn't said anything as each day she sat inside, tense and withdrawn.

Tabby poked at her johnnycakes. For all the thoughts swirling in her head about Mr. Whitby, there was something about his motive for killing Rose that didn't sit right with her. How did he know that Rose and Caleb would have argued that night? And why would a rich man like him get his hands dirty? If Caleb were to be hanged, would the shipping business actually revert to Mr. Whitby? It was a convoluted and precarious plan, and Mr. Whitby struck her as anything but.

Eli set down his fork with a sigh and leaned his elbows on the table. "You're not eating. You need to eat."

Tabby gave a weak smile and skewered some of the cake on her fork and made an effort to lift it to her mouth. "Just tired," she said.

He gave her a long look. "There was a prison break last night," he said finally. "Mrs. Hodge told me when I paid the rent this morning."

Tabby stopped chewing, the johnnycake turning to ash in her mouth. "Oh?"

"Caleb Bishop." Eli's gaze was still trained on her, as if he could see every half-truth and secret she was keeping from him. "He created some kind of havoc and then slipped clean away. Gave a guard a good lumping on the head."

Slipped clean away. So, Caleb was gone. A light rain was starting to fall, pattering against the window and turning the world inside small and quiet. Would she ever see him again? Was he somewhere safe at least? Good, she reminded herself; it was better this way. A dangerous temptation had been removed. He was nothing but trouble, and the farther away he was, the better. But then why was there an entirely new and unwelcome ache in her chest? It seemed that the great ocean of time had claimed yet another person she cared about, and that she was destined to sail alone through life.

As if reading her thoughts, Eli broke the silence. "Do you ever think of marriage, Tabby?"

She nearly choked. "Marriage?" she asked weakly.

"You're almost twenty-four, a full-grown woman. Now, I'd keep you here with me forever if I could, but that's no life for you."

"I—I hadn't given it much thought."

That was only partly true. She hadn't given it any thought until she'd recognized the young man with chestnut hair standing beside an open crypt. Since then she'd had many vivid—very vivid—thoughts about what it would be like to marry one man in particular. But the golden fantasies quickly turned to dust when she tried to envision day-to-day life with a rakish young man. He would irritate her to no end with his careless behavior.

Besides, who said that he even would have wanted to marry her? Kisses and smoldering gazes were one thing, but young men like Caleb traded in those as easily as breathing. Never mind that he came from a different world, a world of plenty, a world of sparkling ladies and sumptuous entertainments. Never mind that he thought her a fraud and a liar. He was gone now, and she was still Curious Tabby. She would never know what it was like to take vows, never know the warm, satisfying weight of a baby in her arms, never know what it was to be loved unconditionally.

Eli gave a sigh, folding his napkin and pushing back his chair. "I know I'm not the family you wanted or needed, but I want to do right by you, see you happy. And settled. I won't be around for—"

"Don't say it," Tabby begged, a sob choking in her throat. "Please." His hair was turning grayer, his stoop more pronounced, but like the death's heads etched in stone in the cemetery, she wanted him to stay the same forever, to never leave her. In that moment she vowed that she would not let Mr. Whitby get anywhere near Eli and the little life they had built together, even if it meant she could never see her father again.

After she'd kissed Eli on the cheek and watched him shuffle across the street to the cemetery, she went to her room and locked the door behind her. It was dark and gray, the soft September rain still falling outside. Crouching before her bed, she pulled out her carpet bag, the one she hadn't used since she'd run away with Alice, and began piling her few belongings inside it. When it was full, she perched on the edge of her bed, paralyzed by the enormity of what she had to do next. Hours passed as she watched the weak shadows on the wall fade into nothing.

The sky was growing dark, and Eli would be back soon. It was now or never. There was no cousin in Rockport, nowhere to turn. The old feeling of desolation flooded over her. She was to be a runaway again, an orphan without a home.

Taking up her bag, Tabby closed the door to the little room in the eaves. She folded a note addressed to Eli and left it on his place at the table. She couldn't tell him everything, but she could tell him that she loved him, and that she would see him again someday. Then she walked down the creaking boarding house steps for the last time, and emerged out into the world, a lost child once again.

Caleb stood on the deck of the ship, salty wind whipping his hair and biting into his cheeks. The cold air felt good, refreshing, after weeks in the hold with his head in a bucket. It'd been nothing short of a miracle that he'd gotten passage on a ship at all, given that all he had to offer was his labor (which he'd been unable to perform given the whole head in the bucket situation) and a promise of payment on docking (which he was still not sure how he would provide).

He hadn't been able to return home to pack anything or to say good-bye to his mother. When it was safe to do so, he would write to her from his new home. Perhaps Tabby would visit her and reassure her, calm her. Poor old dear, he'd certainly made a hash of everything, and his mother would be suffering the consequences.

Home. The word should have brought his smart brick

house on Beacon Hill to mind. It should have brought images of the stuffy Bishop office where he'd spent so many long hours since he was a boy. But it was Tabby's cloudy eyes looking up into his, seeing more in him than anyone else ever had, the soft touch of her lips, that filled his thoughts.

He'd known he couldn't say good-bye to her, but he'd gone to the hill anyway and stood outside the dark cemetery, staring up at the top floor of the boarding house. He'd just wanted to get a glimpse of her, even if it was no more than a silhouette passing the window. But he hadn't seen her there. Instead he'd found her standing beneath a tree in the cemetery, gazing out toward the harbor and looking as lovely and ethereal as the day he had met her. It had nearly been his undoing, watching her from behind the gate, so close and yet not being able to go to her. But it would have been too dangerous, for both of them. For her because she would have been complicit in his escape. For him because he knew if he wrapped his arms around her, he would never be able to let go. After weeks at sea with nothing to do but think, he found that he didn't care that she had lied to him about her motive for trying to help him. Perhaps she even believed her own delusion, and was convinced that she could speak with the dead.

By the time Caleb roused himself out of his reverie, his skin was wet and cold, his hair plastered to his head, and the outline of the English coast had appeared through a bleak layer of fog.

16

IN WHICH THE DYING GAIN
A NEW COMPANION.

TABBY SLIPPED OUTSIDE into the mild, rainy dusk. She paused before the cemetery gates, the fresh scent of damp earth and honeysuckle filling the air. The cemetery, which had always felt like a sanctuary from the bustling world of the living, now was the most dangerous place she could be.

If she had had time, and if Eli had not been there, she would have gone inside, bid farewell to some of her favorite stones. She would have lingered at the Bishop crypt, where she had spent her first nights as a runaway, and where she had reunited with Caleb all those years later. But there was no time, and she could not risk seeing Eli again for fear that she would lose her nerve. She had already slipped out to walk through the cemetery the other night, and had felt as if someone had been watching her.

Turning, she began walking down the hill. She had decided to accept Mary-Ruth's offer to be a watcher for Boston's dying. While she didn't relish the idea of spending time with those near death, she would need the money to start a new life far away from Boston and Mr. Whitby. The orders for mourning embroideries were few and far between, and did not bring in much. Watching would be a small thing; she could provide comfort to the dying, and perhaps even send money to Eli to help with expenses at the same time.

Tabby found Mary-Ruth in a shabby tenement in the west end of the city, hovering over a partially covered corpse. In the corner, two little chubby-faced boys in torn and dingy smocks watched solemnly. When Mary-Ruth saw Tabby she sprang up, her ministrations forgotten. "You're back!" Throwing her arms around Tabby, she squeezed her so tight that Tabby thought her ribs might crack. "I was worried sick about you. Where have you been?"

"I was visiting with a cousin," she said weakly.

Mary-Ruth gave her a long look before turning to the little boys and bending down to offer them a penny. "Why don't you two take this to Greene's and pick out a sweet to share."

When the boys had shyly accepted the coin and scampered out of the grimy room that served as both kitchen and parlor, Mary-Ruth picked up her sponge again and began gently dabbing dirt and blood away from the body. The woman on the table might have been anywhere from twenty-five to fifty, so careworn was her face, so sunken her eyes. "Childbirth," Mary-Ruth said without looking up. "Poor woman lost too much blood as well as the babe, and now there's two little boys with only a drunk father to raise them."

They fell into respectful silence as Mary-Ruth worked. Finally, she put down the sponge and turned around. "You don't have a cousin, and you wouldn't have gone all the way to Rockport without telling me first." When Tabby didn't say anything else, she sighed. "Well, you don't have to tell me, but you might have at least given me the courtesy of letting me know before you disappeared off the face of the earth."

"I'm sorry," Tabby said, but she did not offer any more details about the past weeks or why she had been hiding at home.

Mary-Ruth moved around the body, rubbing it down with a silk cloth as carefully as if she were polishing marble, while Tabby stood in awkward silence.

"I've been thinking, and..." Tabby toed at the worn carpet with her shoe, trying to put her words in order. "I'd like to do some watching."

Mary-Ruth's eyes lit up, any lingering sourness about Tabby's lies evaporating. "Oh, that's such good news! You'll be wonderful at it, and I'll get to see more of you."

Tabby wasn't as enthusiastic, but she managed a smile. The hours would be long and fraught, giving her mind time to wander to all those places she tried to avoid: spirits, death, and now Caleb. But at least she would always have a place at night, so long as she had a patient to watch.

"You know," Mary-Ruth said without looking up, "I saw that Caleb Bishop the other week."

Tabby's chest went tight. "You saw him?"

"I have to say, Tabs, I don't know that I trust him." Mary-Ruth slid her a sideways look.

Tabby worried at her lip. "When did you see him exactly? What did he say?"

"During my search of the city for you, after you never came for the laying out. When I informed him that you were missing, he acted surprised."

So, before he had escaped. Tabby desperately wanted an account of every word Caleb had uttered, but something in Mary-Ruth's closed expression told her that she would only get half the story.

"Now he's the one missing," Tabby said gloomily.

Mary-Ruth shot her a look. "What do you mean?"

"He escaped from prison."

"Escaped from prison!" Mary-Ruth straightened from her washing and wrung out the sponge in the basin. "I knew it. They must be convinced of his guilt in the Hammond case. I can't say I'm sorry to hear that. I only hope that they catch him quickly."

"He didn't have anything to do with it!" Tabby's words came out more forcefully than she intended. She took a deep breath. "It was his father's business partner, a Mr. Whitby. That's where I was... I found evidence that implicated him in the murder, and he caught me. I only just managed to escape with my skin."

"Tabby, you didn't!" Mary-Ruth looked over her shoulder as if worried that the corpse might hear. "Is it safe for you to be out around the city? Do you think he'll come after you, looking for Mr. Bishop?"

Tabby closed her eyes. She was so weary of running

and hiding her entire life, of being afraid. "I don't know," she said. "But it's likely, so don't tell anyone."

She stood and threw one last glance at the corpse on the table. "Next time there's need for a watcher, send for me. And whatever you do, don't go near Eli. The last thing I want is for him to know anything about this."

17

IN WHICH AN OLD FOE IS FACED
AND A FRAUD EXPOSED.

TABBY SLUNK THROUGH the city, hating that she felt like a rat, clinging to the shadows and scurrying with her head down. She despised Mr. Whitby for everything he had done, and what he had reduced her to. It was risky to go to the Bishop house, when she knew Mr. Whitby to be a visitor there on occasion, but as with Eli, she just needed to see Mrs. Bishop once more before disappearing.

As she neared the house, a line of carriages with stomping horses at the curb greeted her. Mrs. Bishop often had other callers, but this looked as if she was hosting a party or one of those fashionable charitable events. So long as Mr. Whitby wasn't in attendance, she would go and give her regards to Mrs. Bishop and then be on her way.

Larson, the butler, greeted her at the door and took her cloak and bonnet.

"What's all this?" she asked. "Is Mrs. Bishop having a party?"

Larson shook his head and glanced over his shoulder into the house before he leaned down to whisper to her. "Not a party—a séance."

"A séance?" A heavy, sour pit formed in Tabby's stomach. "Why?"

The butler shrugged. "I believe it's a fashionable pastime for ladies these days."

Her heart began to beat a dreadful alarm of *Run. Run. Run.* But Tabby forced herself to ask, "Do…do you know the name of the medium?"

"It's a Mrs. Bellefonte."

All the air went out of Tabby's lungs, and vivid memories that she thought had disappeared long ago flashed through her mind: sharp backhanded slaps that sent her stumbling to the ground; dark, airtight cupboards where she was forced to spend hours until she would submit to opening her mind; meager meals of porridge and sour milk.

She should go, turn around and flee. But what could they do to her here? She had to see them, or she would never be able to breathe easy again. "Do you know," she said to Larson, "I think I will keep my bonnet after all. Is Mr. Whitby in attendance?"

"No, miss. Ladies only today."

Pulling her bonnet low over her face and wishing she'd worn a veil, Tabby allowed Larson to admit her to the large drawing room. The drapes had been drawn, and the opulent room was dim and stuffy. Mrs. Bishop was large and resplendent in the billowing black taffeta of her widow's weeds as she conferred in low tones with a group of other ladies.

Tabby easily blended into the small gathering of women in somber colors and veils, who no doubt hoped that the famed medium would have a message for them from their loved ones.

How had her aunt carried it off? She didn't have a stitch of clairvoyance, and Tabby doubted that she had developed any in the past ten years, yet somehow she had managed to become a notable medium.

A maidservant moved about the room with a silver tray, loaded with dainty cakes and finger sandwiches. Putting aside her tea and standing up, Mrs. Bishop cleared her throat. "Ladies, we will be beginning shortly. If you would all be so good as to take a seat." She gestured to three rows of chairs facing a circular table draped in a long cloth.

Excited murmurs rippled through the group as ladies in voluminous layers of petticoats swept over to the chairs and lowered themselves. How many of them were here not because they wanted to contact a loved one, but merely for the morbid entertainment of the spectacle?

Taking a seat in the back, Tabby breathed slowly and evenly as the lamps were lowered. The room took on a hazy glow, the building anticipation of the women making the air thick and expectant.

A door off to the side opened, and a petite woman in all black glided in. The lady next to Tabby leaned over to her and whispered, "She's so small! I had imagined she would be tall and slender. I have never seen her in person, but my brother saw her do a demonstration and said that it put to rest any doubts he had about the existence of an afterlife."

Tabby couldn't respond; she was too transfixed on the diminutive form of her aunt, seating herself at the table. Was this the same woman who had instilled such bone-deep terror in Tabby as a child? Had she always been so small? Her uncle was nowhere to be seen, but he would probably be off to the side somewhere, orchestrating whatever tricks they would have to use.

The woman beside her was perched on the edge of her seat as Mrs. Bellefonte began. "To make this a welcoming place for spirits, I must have absolute quiet." She made a show of arranging herself on her seat and holding her hands out, palms up.

A preternatural calm fell over the drawing room, and it was so still and quiet that Tabby could hear the rise and fall of a dozen taffeta bodices around her.

Then, all of a sudden, Mrs. Bellefonte let out an eldritch groan and swayed back in her seat. "There is a spirit near," she said in a hoarse whisper.

The women gave little cries and fanned themselves with their black lace fans. Even though Tabby knew that it was all a sham, she couldn't help the chill that ran down her spine.

"It's a male spirit...a grown man." Her aunt squinted into the air, as if he was standing right before her. "He has a mustache and a very distinguished air about him."

"My Henry!" A woman shot out of her chair. "Oh, but it must be my Henry."

Mrs. Bellefonte nodded solemnly. "Yes, he says his name is Henry, and that he is here to speak with his wife."

The woman's black veil quivered as she spoke. "Tell him that I am sorry, that my…transgression…meant nothing. He was the only one that I ever truly loved."

"He says that he forgives you, that he knows that his illness was difficult for you in the last months. He looks forward to having you at his side in the kingdom of heaven someday."

With a little gasp, the woman slumped back into her chair, her friends swarming around her like butterflies to a black-petaled flower, as they administered salts and fanned at her with lace handkerchiefs.

More husbands were contacted, as well as mothers, fathers, children. Mrs. Bellefonte had a neat little message for nearly everyone before she finally came to Mrs. Bishop.

Tabby held her breath, waiting for her aunt to claim that she had reached the late Mr. Bishop. But to her horror it was not him whom she claimed to find.

"I see a young man, quite handsome. Light hair and brown eyes."

Mrs. Bishop let out a strangled gasp. "My…my Caleb," she choked out in between labored sobs. "He's dead?"

Frantically, Tabby opened her mind. If there were truly spirits here as her aunt claimed, then she would find them. *Please no please no*, she chanted to herself as she let the ether envelope her like a cloud bank. But no spirits came, Caleb or otherwise.

Her aunt was a fraud, and thank God for that. There was a daguerreotype of Caleb on one of the tables in the parlor that her aunt had probably seen and used to describe him.

She might have been a fraud, but she was convincing. She knew when to wait for her client to offer more details before continuing, and when to gamble and offer a snippet of information. It was clear that she had done some research on Mrs. Bishop before accepting her invitation to hold a séance. When she claimed that Caleb had died running afoul of scofflaws, Mrs. Bishop gave another cry. It broke Tabby's heart to see Mrs. Bishop reduced to tears, believing that her only son was truly dead.

"He's gone," Mrs. Bellefonte said quietly, and a pregnant hush fell back over the room. "I believe all the spirits have left us today and—"

Tabby's cheeks had grown hot, and every little sound in the room was amplified. Before she knew what she was doing, she shot up and raised her hand. "My aunt," she said in a choked voice. "I lost my dear aunt when I was but a child. Please, you must find her for me."

There was a moment of hesitation from Mrs. Bellefonte, surprised as she was by the passionate outburst. But then she was nodding and gesturing for Tabby to come to the front of the room. "Come here, young lady. I will need to join hands with you to reestablish a connection and create a conduit by which the spirits may speak through me."

Swallowing, Tabby slowly walked to the table and sat across from her aunt. With her bonnet still pulled low on her face, she placed her hands in the older woman's. She hadn't known what she was going to do when she'd raised her hand, but now a plan formed rapidly in her mind. For all the years that the threat of her aunt had hung over Tabby like a specter, now that she was finally in front of her, Tabby felt only determination. In the last twelve years, Tabby had grown callous, yes, but also strong. She had survived the streets of Boston as a child. She had escaped Mr. Whitby. The small woman in front of her held no power over her anymore.

Her aunt began humming, a low, tremulous sound that would have been laughable if not for the gravity of the situation. Then her hands went stiff and she broke off in her humming. "A spirit has shown itself to me."

The audience whispered and shifted in their seats, craning their heads as if they too might see it. Tabby feigned surprise. "Oh, is it my aunt?"

"I believe so. The spirit is a woman."

Tabby's courage grew and so too did her confidence in her acting. "What is her name? What does she look like? Oh, it must be her! I can feel her near!"

From behind her veil, Mrs. Bellefonte's eyes flashed, and Tabby could tell that she was surprised her young customer was so fervent. But she played along, using Tabby's enthusiasm.

"Her name... Spirit, what is your name?" There was silence for a moment before Mrs. Bellefonte shook her head. "I can't make it out. Perhaps if you were to provide her initials..."

Tabby persisted. "What does she look like?"

There was a flash of irritation behind her aunt's gauzy veil. "The connection is not strong enough to see her. But I am sure that she is your aunt. She says that you were always a good girl, and that she loves you very much."

This was Tabby's moment. If she wanted to reveal her aunt for the fraud she was, then she was going to have to risk exposing herself, as well. It gave her no pleasure to dash the hopes of the women here, but at least she could put poor Mrs. Bishop's fears to rest. She had not come here with the intention of divulging her abilities, but she at least took some small satisfaction that she was turning the very ability that her aunt had so coveted back on her. When word got out that there was a true clairvoyant in Boston, it would be in every paper, but by then, Tabby would have made enough money to go somewhere far away.

"Does she really? How very odd. I never knew my aunt to speak in such kind terms. But you are right about one thing: she is very near indeed. I can feel her hands in my own, almost as if she were flesh and blood."

"It is not uncommon that you might feel such sensation—the dead are often desperate to be seen, heard, and even felt."

"I never said my aunt was dead, though."

Mrs. Bellefonte's hands went limp in hers. "What do you mean?"

"In fact, I see her right before me. Her name is Minerva Bellefonte, and she is wearing black satin gloves and an embroidered veil."

"Child, I don't know what kind of nonsense you think you're about, but—"

Before her aunt could finish, Tabby was pulling off her bonnet and, for the first time in twelve years, facing down the woman who had instilled such fear, anger, and hatred in her.

Her aunt's body went completely still, and the disbelief in her voice was delicious. "Tabitha?" she said in a breath.

"What is the meaning of this?" Mrs. Bishop was standing, her gaze snapping back and forth between Tabby and her aunt. "Miss Cooke, do you know this woman?"

"I know her very well. She is my aunt. And..." She hesitated, aware that she was about to dash many of the fragile consolations the ladies there had found that day. "She is a fraud. She cannot speak with the dead."

A collective murmur of outrage went up from the audience.

"And why should we believe you?" said the woman whose husband Mrs. Bellefonte had contacted earlier in the séance.

Tabby took a long, unsteady breath, drawing in all the shame, fear, and anxiety of a lifetime, and exhaling the truth. "Because I can."

18

IN WHICH A POINT IS PROVEN.

CHAIRS UPTURNED AS ladies sprang to their feet, and more than one delicate glass of sherry went shattering on the floor. A man in plaid trousers and matching waist-coat materialized from behind one of the heavy drapes, fretting at his mustache and watching the chaos unfold. Her uncle. He had never terrified her the way that her aunt had. He was short and slight, and while her aunt had been the architect of Tabby's misery, he had been the one to simply follow along. He looked around in a daze until he met Tabby's eye. "Tabby? Is that you?"

Her aunt's shrill voice cut through the rabble. "You un-grateful chit! We have been out of our minds with worry about you and your sister for the past twelve years!" She threw a look around the room, as if only just now won-dering if Alice might be among them.

"If you have been out of your mind with worry, it has

only been for the money you have surely lost when we left."

The room had grown unnaturally still, as the women watched this unexpected drama play out in front of them.

It was Mrs. Bishop who cut the silence. She turned to Tabby's aunt. "Is what she says true? Have you no true clairvoyant powers?"

Her aunt made a nervous gesture. "Of course not, madame. I do confess that the child is my niece, but there is no truth in what she says. She always was touched in the head, and that's why we have been so worried about her since she ran away. It is a cruel world for an unprotected young woman, never mind one that is so ignorant." An artificial smile stretched across her aunt's mouth. "Isn't that so, Harold?"

Her uncle, who had been fiddling with his watch chain, snapped back to attention. "Oh yes. Quite right, my dear. An unprotected simpleton, just as you say."

"They lie," Tabby ground out.

Mrs. Bishop looked between them. "I don't pretend to be well acquainted with Miss Cooke, but from the time we have spent together I can say that she is one of the most levelheaded young women I have met. She might be a little unpolished, but she is no simpleton."

"And how do we know you aren't just another charlatan?" the same woman asked again as she looked Tabby up and down. "Can you offer us any proof that Mrs. Bellefonte is a fraud? Or that you are not?"

She had known that this was coming, but it didn't make it any easier. "I can, on both counts." Turning to one of the women, she said: "Your husband, Henry, was a banker. He worked long hours and was often away from home. But he loved you dearly, and he says that you broke his heart when you carried on with his brother."

The woman gasped, but Tabby was already moving on. "Mrs. Orson, your son was killed after taking too much drink and trying to rob a bank with nothing more than a pocket knife."

Mrs. Orson sniffed. "Anyone could know that. It was in the papers. It doesn't prove anything."

Tabby bit back a retort. How easy it was for everyone to believe her aunt's smooth and palatable lies, but when faced with the truth, they balked. "He says that it was your idea to rob the bank, that you wanted the money to start a new life in California, and that he will never forgive you."

At this, Mrs. Orson went very pale, and slumped down into her seat. Tabby turned to a quiet older woman who was still seated, her hands demurely crossed on the head of her cane.

"Mrs. Sprague," she said softly, coming and kneeling at the woman's feet. "Jenny wants you to know that there was no pain at the end, that she knows you did everything you could for her. Though she was only a babe, she loved you so much, and was so glad that you were her mother."

A dry sob broke from Mrs. Sprague's throat. "It's been forty years since I lost my Jenny, and I think of her every day. I always wondered if there was something I could have done differently, something that would have saved her from that fever."

Tabby shook her head, trying to contain her own welling emotion. "Nothing," she said. "There was nothing you could have done differently. You loved her and she says that was enough."

There was taut silence as the other women watched Tabby and Mrs. Sprague, and then an explosion of clamoring voices.

"Me next!"

"No, me!"

Throughout all this, Tabby was only vaguely aware of her aunt and uncle taking their leave, slinking away like the snakes they were. She had no doubt that they would be back, now that they knew where she was, but for now, they couldn't show their faces here again.

When at last everyone who had clamored for a message had been satisfied, Tabby turned to Mrs. Bishop. Sustained contact with so many on the other side had left her exhausted and weak, but she was determined to put Mrs. Bishop's fears to rest. "Caleb is not dead."

Mrs. Bishop let out a gasp and would have collapsed if not for the lady next to her catching her by the arm. "Where is he? I would give anything to see him again, to hold him. I know in my heart that he is innocent."

Tabby looked at her feet and shook her head. "I wish I knew, I'm sorry. I only know that he is alive. He is a clever man, though, and I'm sure wherever he is, he's thriving." She did not have to lie or sweeten her words; they were the truth.

"I miss him so much," Mrs. Bishop said softly.

"I miss him, too." She hadn't even realized it until the words slipped out. For as much as the young man had confounded her, she found herself missing him with an intensity that rivaled the loss she felt for her sister. She hated that she missed him, especially after he had accused her of lying, but she did. She missed the appreciative glimmer in his eye when she said something clever. She missed his quick smile that was no less special for its frequency. She even missed his cocky banter.

But now was not the time to mine the depths of her heart. No sooner had she given her message to Mrs. Bishop than the parlor door was opening and Larson was clearing his throat expectantly.

"Madame, Mr. Whitby is here. Should I tell him you're busy?"

Tabby froze. She shot a pleading look to Mrs. Bishop, but of course the older woman had no clue what had transpired between Tabby and him, and so the urgency of the situation was lost on her.

Mrs. Bishop gave a heavy sigh. "No, that won't be necessary. The séance is concluded, I suppose, and he may be here with news about Caleb."

Panicked, Tabby darted her gaze around the room, looking for a way out. If she moved fast, she might be able to slip out the servant's entrance and into the back hall.

"I—I have to go," Tabby mumbled. But as she started for the door, she was waylaid by the gaggle of women.

"Miss Cooke, I'm hosting a party Tuesday next, and I simply *must* have you there to perform a séance."

"How much do you charge for a sitting?"

"Do you offer private sittings? I have a question for a spirit, but it is of a delicate nature."

Bombazine skirts pressed in around Tabby, feathered fans snapping open and shut as the women all pleaded for her attention.

When at last she had broken free, mumbling vague promises of appointments, Tabby threw a glance over her shoulder at the other door just as a well-pressed suit stepped inside. For one brief, terrible moment, her eyes locked on his, and then she was gone.

19

IN WHICH THERE IS A GRUESOME REVELATION.

THERE WAS A clock on the mantel and with every heavy movement of the minute hand, it let out an awful, grinding *tick, tick, tick*.

After being admitted by a distracted adult son and daughter-in-law, Tabby had been left in the stately bedroom with the dying man, her first patient as a watcher. Robert Graham had obviously lived a comfortable life as a dean of Harvard, his chamber well appointed and tastefully peppered with mementos of a career spent in academia. The doctors had come and gone, done what they could for Mr. Graham's chronic chest complaint, and told his family that all was left now was to make him comfortable in his final hours.

Tabby sat up in the armchair by Mr. Graham's bed,

stretching her aching legs and willing her scratchy eyes to stay open. She was not just being paid, after all, to keep him company; she was responsible for making sure that if and when he stopped breathing that he was well and truly dead.

All she wanted to do was sleep, and put the chaos of the séance that afternoon behind her, but she had promised Mary-Ruth, and she needed the money. Besides, she would be safe here, a roof over her head for so long as the sick man lingered. And when he took his last breath, she would find another dying patient, and so it would continue.

Mr. Graham's chamber was oppressively hot, but Tabby was mindless of the sweat that beaded down her back. The image of Mr. Whitby's cold eyes finding hers across the room had seared itself into her mind. They had held a threat, a promise. She knew that he had killed Rose, and he knew that she knew. He would find her.

A hoarse voice pulled Tabby from her thoughts. "Shh," she said, rising and placing her hand on Mr. Graham's clammy forehead. "You mustn't exert yourself. Here." She poured out a glass of water from the china decanter and held it to his lips.

He drank but a short time and then feebly turned his head away, water dribbling from the corner of his mouth. Then he was trying to speak again.

Tabby leaned down close, trying to catch the broken and raspy words. She had thought he was past the time for speech, but he seemed agitated, desperate to get words out.

"They must not… Do not let them take me…" His glazed eyes were wide with panic, his chest rising and falling much too quickly.

Tabby dabbed at his perspiring temples. It was not uncommon for the dying to express last fears or terror of the unknown. "Let me fetch your son and his wife."

Even as she made the offer, she knew that it would bring him little comfort; she had seen the way his family disdained him, had no desire to sit with him in his final hours and leaving him in the care of a stranger.

"No," he rasped. "I have done wicked, wicked things. But I beg of you, do not let them take me when my time is come. Do not let them do to my body what I allowed to happen to so many."

Something in his tone made Tabby pause and take notice. This was more than just the ordinary regrets of a dying man. "Who?" she asked. "Who would come for you?"

Mr. Graham went on, as if he hadn't heard her. "Such terrible, terrible things. For science, yes, but at the cost of morality and God's will. Oh, just let my aching body rest in peace, even if I prevented others from doing so. God must forgive me."

The clock ticked away, and Tabby wet her lips. "What terrible things?" she managed to whisper.

Suddenly he was sitting bolt upright in bed, letting out a hair-raising howl as the sheets fell away from him. "Let the dead lie! Let the dead lie! Let the dead lie!"

Tabby stood to try to cajole him back down, but then his eyes went lucid, and he grabbed her by the wrist. She sucked in her breath as he yanked her down close to him. His breath was hot and sour. "The things they do are unnatural, unholy. I am as guilty as the rest, but I repent! I repent now!"

She willed herself not to flinch at his touch. "What do you repent for? Can you tell me?"

He turned his gaze on hers, holding it with startling intensity. "The resurrection men. They have taken to heart the full meaning of their name. At first it was just paupers and criminals, and when it was for the advancement of medicine that would save lives, it seemed a small enough price to pay. But now they go too far, it has all become too terrible."

He closed his eyes before continuing. "To bring back the dead. Oh, but you have never seen such a ghastly sight as an electric current running through a corpse, making them jerk and dance like puppets. And does it work? Never! The poor souls are no more alive than they were before, and their mangled bodies are fed to the pigs." His eyes flew open, spittle gathering at the corners of his mouth, "Now do you see? You must swear to me that you will not let them take me. Swear it!"

He broke off in a fit of phlegmy coughing. Tabby pressed him further. "Who are the resurrection men?"

He gasped for breath. "Powerful men, men you wouldn't want to cross."

"How am I to stop them from taking you if I don't know who they are?"

It looked as if he was just about to say something when another coughing fit overtook him. When it had passed, Mr. Graham closed his eyes, his head slumping back against his pillows as he labored to breathe. "Harvard.

They hide behind the veneer of learning, but what they do has little to do with education and progress, and everything to do with hubris and the desire to play God."

Tabby's mind raced. She grasped his hands in hers and squeezed hard, as if that could wring more information from him. "Who at Harvard? Who else is involved? Did Rose Hammond's murder have something to do with it?"

But her questions fell on unhearing ears. Mr. Graham gave a rattling breath, and then was still.

The clock ticked on, and, left alone with her roiling thoughts, Tabby sat and watched. Watched and watched and watched until the body stiffened and grew cold, and there was no doubt that there was not an ounce of life left.

Frost tinted the windows and a bleary September sun was just starting to climb into the sky when the younger Mr. Graham dropped the coins into Tabby's hands and sent her on her way. They should have felt like hope, like satisfaction, but they only sat cold and heavy in her palm.

As she walked through the early-morning streets, Tabby pulled her cloak tighter around her, the coins clinking in her pocket. She should go tell Mary-Ruth that Mr. Graham was ready to be laid out and dressed, but she couldn't bring herself to come back to reality and the world of preparations.

Mr. Graham's last words burrowed into her gut like maggots, making her squirm. She had always thought that robbing a grave for the supposed sake of science was reprehensible, but this was worse, so much worse. She'd read serialized stories about mad scientists and desperate men who tried to bring the dead back to life, and while the stories had always been framed as ambitious and even romantic, she found them revolting. But they were just stories. This was real.

20

IN WHICH AN OPPORTUNITY IS WASTED.

FROM THE FOGGY coffee shop window, Caleb watched the higgledy-piggledy buildings of London weep dark streaks in the rain, and pedestrians with black umbrellas hurry down the street. His vantage made him feel small, safe, and very, very lonely.

London was an old city, so much older than Boston, yet it felt new and full of possibilities. If ever there was a place made for the ambitious imagination of an architect, it was London. The new and the old stood shoulder to shoulder, the classical juxtaposed with the new, just like the citizens of its vast empire.

It was not Caleb's first time on British soil; as a boy, his father had sent him to Eton for an education, thinking that it would give him a polished edge in the world of American business. In the end, his father had been disappointed in his investment, saying that Caleb had come back only dandified. During his schooling, Caleb had not been beyond the suffocating brick walls of the college, and so the ancient city was ripe for discovery now.

He had been in London for nearly a week and was slowly but surely amassing a small fortune from the card tables he visited every night with what little money he had left from his journey. His abstinence from drink meant that he was sharp, while his opponents made risky bets and played long after they should have stopped.

But that was in the evenings, and the days were long and lonely. Caleb downed the rest of his coffee, shrugged into his overcoat, and plunged into the jostling traffic of the narrow, muddy street. It was time to find his mark for the night.

He would find his man in a pub. It had to be just the right sort of pub, a place that was dark and dull enough that the men who frequented it would be willing to part with a couple of coins, but not so rough that he would risk incurring the wrath of an angry loser.

He was sopping wet and chilled to the bone by the time he laid eyes on the Crown & Cabbage, a narrow door tucked into an alley with a peeling sign depicting the pub's two namesakes.

Inside was dim and soggy, the wet scent of wool and corduroy mingling with stale beer and body odor. It was warmer than the street, but only just. When he had enough money, he could go to the gentlemen's clubs where the stakes were higher, the men a better caliber. But until then, places like the Crown & Cabbage would have to do.

As he surveyed the pub for a likely mark, he caught

the eye of a woman lounging with one elbow propped up on the bar, her red hair loose and uncoiled. She raised her cup and winked at him in an unmistakable invitation.

His heart beat a little faster, his skin tingled with awareness. Here was his chance to be a new Caleb, a better Caleb. Or perhaps a new person all together. Caleb Pope? No, he needed something completely new, something he had never used before. Daniel... Daniel Cooke had a nice ring to it. He'd always liked Tabby's surname, and figured she wouldn't mind if he borrowed it now. Daniel Cooke had a strong work ethic. Daniel Cooke certainly would not take up with the first pretty girl who looked his way in a dark pub. Daniel Cooke was strictly here to play a fair game of cards and be on his merry way.

But of course, the pretty girl in question didn't know if he was Caleb Bishop or Daniel Cooke or the prince of Liechtenstein, and before Caleb could figure out just what Daniel Cooke *would* do, she was making her way over to him. Old habits died hard, and Caleb found himself sliding over on the bench to make room for her to sit.

The woman glanced at his cup of coffee. "I didn't even know they served coffee here. Bit of a strange choice, isn't it? Come into a pub for a cup of old coffee?"

He raised a brow. "Bit of a presumption, isn't it, to question a man's choice of beverage in which to drown his sorrows?"

She clapped her hands together, squealing in delight, and sat down beside him. "You're an American! Well, I 'spose your strange habits can be forgiven then. Ruby," she said, sticking out her hand for Caleb to kiss.

He obliged. "Daniel Cooke."

"Well, Mr. Cooke, I've not seen you in the Crown before. What brings you to our dark and dreary corner of London?"

"Business," he said. "Architecture, to be exact." It felt good to lie, to be someone else, even if the someone in question was shaping up to be just as much of a scoundrel as Caleb Bishop. "I was looking for a bit of hospitality when I saw the sign from the road."

"Architecture!" Her green eyes lit up. "That sounds lucrative."

He bestowed one of his winning smiles on her. "Oh yes, very lucrative," he lied. "But I daresay a woman such as yourself isn't interested in the humdrum workings of my business. Tell me, what is a rare flower like yourself doing here?"

He fell easily into the routine of flirting, letting the flattering words fall off his tongue at the right times and giving the right smiles. Ruby knew her part well, playing the coquette, laughing prettily, acting as if he was the most interesting man in the world.

As they talked, she leaned in closer, her skirt brushing his leg. Her perfume was artificially floral, too strong. He should have felt the old thrill of the dance, but all he felt was emptiness.

He drained the last of his cold coffee and dug in his pockets for some coins. If he didn't leave soon, he would almost certainly do something with Ruby he would regret. He had to find a mark for a game of cards or he wouldn't have enough money for his boardinghouse rent. "Miss Ruby, your company has been delightful, a warm draught on this cold night. But I'm afraid I must be going."

Ruby pouted, her namesake-colored lips looking altogether too inviting. "Have a drink, love, a real one. 'Twill warm you up before you leave." Ruby pushed a mug of something brown and frothy toward him.

Outside, the London wind howled and banged the pub sign into the wall. Heavy cold rain pelted against the bottle glass windows. Caleb did not relish the walk back to his boarding house. London in the day was expansive and exciting with its many parks and storied architecture, a bustling metropolis of people from every corner of the empire. London at night was a warren of oppressively narrow streets filled with cutpurses and all sorts of depraved characters.

He wavered, one arm in his still-wet coat. "I don't drink," he said, eyeing the cup and wishing that it didn't look quite so inviting.

"Don't drink!" she exclaimed loudly, drawing a few guffaws from the old men at the bar. "You really are American, so puritan and sober. Come, join the rest of us down in the gutter, love."

He was about to shrug the rest of the way into his coat and be on his way, but something stopped him. Why not have a drink? He couldn't sink any lower than he already was. If the possibility of starting a new, fresh life stretched before him, then so too did the emptiness of it. He missed his mother and their house on Beacon Hill, though he would have died before admitting as much to her. He missed Buttermilk's watery purr. He missed the broad streets of Boston and the blooming gardens. He missed Rose and her kind smile, the gentle touch of her hand on his arm. God help him, he missed Tabby. He'd spent so long chasing that elusive feeling of belonging, of being good enough. It would feel so good to let go.

Ruby wrapped herself around his arm and laughed in approval as he grabbed the cup and downed it in two gulps. The liquor blazed a warm trail throughout his body, pleasantly fuzzing the edges of reality. He'd spent so long trying not to be like his father, and look where that had gotten him. The card tables could wait. His new life could wait. Right now, he just wanted to slip into comfortable oblivion. He wanted to feel the warmth of a woman beside him and forget everything else.

"Do you have somewhere we can go? Somewhere private?"

Ruby grinned. "I thought you'd never ask. 'Ave another drink first, won't you?"

The muddy street dipped and weaved under his feet, and Caleb had to brace himself against the slick shop walls as he made his way back from Ruby's room. Hacks driven by mud-drenched horses trudged past, spraying him with fetid water. Misery was a pair of boots saturated with London mud. How had his father managed to drink himself into this state so regularly? It had been only one night of indulgence and between the pounding of his head and the acid in his stomach, Caleb was certain that he would never see the light of day again.

He staggered past shuttered shop windows and beggars under blankets tucked into doorways, trying to remember what streets he had taken, but London was a dark labyrinth of alleys and dead ends. An occasional gas lamp glowed in the thick darkness, but other than that, the heavy fog blocked any moonlight. Bracing himself against a lamppost, he doubled over and retched. Just as he was wiping his mouth on the back of his sleeve, two figures stepped out of the shadows, blocking his path.

"Well, well, well. What do we 'ave here?" said a thick cockney voice. "Looks like someone's been a little too deep in 'is cups."

"That's him. The fancy American toff I was tellin' you about," a familiar voice said. Caleb struggled to bring his gaze into focus, and he caught a glimpse of red hair and a low-cut bodice. "A rich architect, and sauced off his ass."

The man grunted as he advanced on Caleb, backing him up against a wall. "You done good, Ruby girl."

From somewhere beyond the panic and the haze of alcohol, Caleb almost laughed. They thought him a rich architect. They thought him Daniel Cooke, and not Caleb Bishop, the most wretched man to ever walk the earth. Well, they were in for a sore disappointment. Caleb Bishop had only had a few coins to his name.

"I don'know whatyouthink—" Caleb slurred.

A meaty fist slammed into his jaw, drowning the rest of his words in blood. Hot pain exploded in his face. Stumbling back, Caleb lost his footing in the mud and went sprawling.

He was about to get robbed, beaten, and possibly killed, and all Caleb felt was a numbing sense of disappointment; he'd had every chance in the world laid before him to start fresh, and he'd thrown it all away because he'd felt sorry for himself. He'd wasted his chance at happiness with Rose, and it occurred to him from somewhere deep down in a sober corner of his heart, that he perhaps *had* loved Rose, but had been too stupid to recognize his feelings of affection and respect as love. He could have made an honest living here in London, and instead he'd played cards and cheated weak men out of their money. His father had been right about him all along: he was a failure and a disappointment.

"Don't need to be so rough," Ruby said from somewhere beyond his vision. "Can't you see he's only a slip of a thing? Stiff breeze could knock 'im over."

The blow to his pride hurt almost as much as the blow to his jaw. Almost. Hauling him up by the collar, the man pinned Caleb's neck with his elbow, while his other hand rooted inside his coat pocket.

Pulling back, the man spat in disgust. "Where's the rest of it, then?"

"That's it. That's all my money," Caleb said through the blood. He kept one shilling squirreled away in his boot as an insurance policy, but he somehow doubted even that would appease the man.

"I thought you said 'e was rich."

"He said he was. Guess the little fellow was lying."

"I'm not little," Caleb protested weakly. "I'm fine boned."

But the man wasn't listening. "Maybe I should kill 'im. At least get some money for 'is body then."

That sobered him up right quick. The man was busy counting out the sorry collection of coins in his palm. Gathering his strength and what little balance he had,

Caleb was able to put his head down and ram all his weight right into the man's stomach.

Ruby screamed as her partner fell backward. "Charlie!" She crouched over him as he swore and wheezed. She wrenched back around and faced Caleb. "You bloody rotter! You bloody liar! To think, I spent all night plying you with beer and kisses. Not even a bloody guinea to your name!"

Caleb doubted that he'd done more than knock the wind out of Charlie, but he wasn't eager to find out. Stumbling and nearly slipping again in the putrid mud, Caleb staggered out of the alley and back into foggy oblivion.

21

IN WHICH THERE IS A FAMILIAR FACE.

TABBY HURRIED THROUGH the city. Wet leaves slicked against the cobblestones and a cold breeze carrying the scent of wood smoke clung to her cloak. The brilliant, early days of autumn had come and gone, leaving the trees bare and a bitter promise of snow in the air.

In the past two months, she had survived by watching and embroidering, taking in mending. It was a lonely existence, and aside from occasionally crossing paths with Mary-Ruth, she had become a creature of silence and solitude. She missed Eli and their little routines, their shabby yet homey rooms in the boarding house. Only occasionally did she allow her thoughts to turn to Caleb, and wondered where he was.

But tonight there was no dying person to watch, and so she would have to sleep at the flea-ridden room she shared with six other girls in a rickety tenement. They slept two to a bed, the straw mattresses damp and moldy. The last time she had slept there, someone had stolen her stockings as they'd hung on the grate to dry. As if reminding her that she had no other option, the wind kicked up, frigid air biting her through her thin cloak.

People hurried home from work, doing their last errands before the snow began. Tabby had always loved the bustle before the storm, the sense of camaraderie that it inspired. In that brief window of anticipation, all differences were forgotten as people made predictions about how much snow would fall, laughing and greeting fellow last-minute shoppers. For those few moments, even Tabby belonged.

She stopped at a crossroads, taking care to keep her face covered. If she turned right, the street would take her to the north end of the city and to her cemetery. To Eli. More than once she had teetered on this corner, fighting the urge to run home and see him. But she had a chance to make things right, not just for Rose, but for all the nameless dead who had been robbed of their dignity and eternal rest. There were answers out there, and they only needed to be found. If what Mr. Graham had said was true, then the men in power were the ones responsible and would never do anything. But she could.

Turning in the opposite direction, she made her way across the city to find answers.

Caleb's head was pounding, his jaw ached, and his mouth tasted like blood. The sound of shops opening and heels clicking on cobblestones ricocheted through his pounding head. Cracking one eye open, he was met with a horizontal view of a London gutter. The smell hit him shortly after that.

Good God, what had happened last night? He vaguely remembered drinking piss-poor coffee in a pub, the shrill laugh of a woman.

He groaned as the memories became clearer. Red hair, too many cups of ale, and a fist connecting with his jaw in an alley. In a panic, he sat himself up and frantically went through his pockets. His money was gone, all of it. That money had been his seed, his chance to rebuild his life. And now he would have to start all over. A passerby looked askance at him as he hurriedly removed his boot and pounded on the heel until a coin fell out. His last shilling. Well, that was something at least.

Grunting, he hauled himself up and divested himself of a rotting piece of cabbage that had somehow found its way onto his coat. If he had been disoriented last night, he was downright lost now. The street was broader, the shops more respectable. He was the lone degenerate. A lady in a tall, feather-bedecked hat held her handkerchief to her face in disgust as she hurried past him.

"That hardly seems necessary," he muttered as he brushed off as much mud as he could from his coat.

Still dizzy, he'd barely gone three steps when he doubled over and was sick. Once he was upright and there was nothing left in him, he felt the first stabbing pains of hunger. He passed a bakery, the warm scent of bread enticingly wafting out into the street. Instinctually, he turned to go in, before remembering that his shilling would carry him only so far, and he would have to ration it carefully. Being poor was one thing, but being poor *and* hungry was a bridge too far. Oh, for the days of comfort and plenty, when Larson would bring in a tray brimming with all his favorite cakes and sandwiches.

With the rumble of his stomach goading him on, he went inside and bought all the buns and coffee that his shilling would get him, and promptly devoured them. Now he was officially penniless.

Cursing the day he had ever thought it would be a good idea to partake in drink, he trudged down the street, continuing to offend the delicate sensibilities of several ladies along the way.

What he should have done as soon as he'd made enough money from cards was invest it in drafting supplies and built a portfolio, taken it to some of the firms in the city, and tried to find a position as an apprentice or clerk. But he'd gotten swept up in the thrill of the game, and now it was gone. He would have to start all over again, perhaps pawn the fob from the watch that he had already used to pay for his journey across the Atlantic. One thing was certain: no more cards, no more women, and absolutely no more drinking.

This was much too nice a section of the city, so he cut across down to the Thames where mud larkers kept the rag and pawn shops in business. As he looked about for a promising pawnbroker, he passed a portrait studio, photographs of somber faces exemplifying the photographer's skill pasted in the window. The sign advertised that they were portrait artist to HRH the Prince of Wales. But that wasn't what caused him to stop short.

A picture stood in the center of the window, propped up on a small easel. The face that stared back at him was familiar, yet different, a young woman, her eyes so pale and clear as to appear colorless, with long, loose curls spilling over her shoulders. Without a second thought, he was pushing the door open and ringing the bell on the counter.

A tall, stooped man came out from a curtained room in the back, his face buried in a stack of papers he was leafing through. "May I help you?" he asked without looking up.

Caleb hardly knew where to begin. "There's a portrait in the window...a young woman. I was wondering—"

"Of course, of course. I can replicate any pose you see there." Finally putting the papers aside, he looked up and ran a critical eye over Caleb's muddy and soiled suit, and the bruised and bloody spectacle that was his face. "I don't supply the costumes, though, the sitter is responsible for their own costume. A portrait costs one pound two shillings," he added, as if convinced the price would be a deterrent.

Caleb shook his head impatiently. "It's not the picture, it's the girl in it. I think I know her...that is, I was wondering if you could tell me who she was, and when the likeness was made."

The man looked skeptical. "I pride myself on professionalism, and I cannot simply give out information about my clients, either past or present. I am, after all, portrait artist to His Royal Highness the Prince of Wales," he said with a condescending sniff.

"Yes, yes, I saw the sign." If only Caleb hadn't spent his last coin on those buns. He needed something, anything to convince the man to tell him what he needed to know.

Caleb pulled out his watch fob and placed it on the counter. The fob had belonged to his father, and his father's father before that. It was solid gold, inset with polished jet, and it was a minor miracle that the crook hadn't found it last night. The fob would have easily paid for his entrance into a high stakes card game at a reputable club and then some, but this was more important.

Eying the fob, the man nodded. "Which picture is it you're wanting to know about then?"

Caleb went to the shop window and plucked the daguerreotype from its place. "This one. When did she come in? What's her name?" Looking at the picture was like being transported back across the ocean. It couldn't be Tabby, yet there could be no doubt that the sitter was somehow related to her.

The man's face shone with pride. "Ah, yes. *Her*," he said with a wistful sigh. "I saw her walking past my shop one day and knew that I had to have her sit for me. In my ten years behind the lens, I have never seen eyes like that. She was hesitant, said that she didn't want her likeness immortalized. But I wore her down," he said proudly. "Offered her a handsome sum, and even told her she could have a copy of the portrait free of charge. But she never came back to collect it, so I keep it in the window for business."

"What was her name?" Caleb asked, breathless.

The man shook his head. "If she told me, I've long forgotten. It had to have been going on three years now."

Caleb studied the picture again. "Does she live nearby?"

"I couldn't say. She used to pass by frequently, but I haven't seen her since her sitting."

The shop door opened, and two well-dressed women came in. The shopkeeper excused himself and left Caleb with his thoughts.

Any hope that Caleb might have felt on seeing the picture was quickly deflating. London was a vast city, and finding a girl with no name would be nearly impossible, and that wasn't even taking into consideration the fact that she might not be in the city at all anymore.

Why did it matter so much anyway? It was probably a coincidence, and nothing more. But as he stared into the face that was so like Tabby's, he knew he had to find her.

Outside, he looked about him in a daze. Without his watch fob, he had nothing left to pawn except the clothes on his back, and those were in a rather sorry state after the events of the previous night. He stopped in front of a cart where an old woman was selling wilted bunches of watercress, and took stock of what he had.

He had the clothes on his back, which he had already established were both undesirable to anyone else, and necessary to his (relative) decency. He had a quick wit and was clever at cards, but had no money for a buy-in. He had a gnawing hunger that had quickly returned after his breakfast. He had an overwhelming need to find the girl in the picture and find out who she was, but no resources to do it. All in all, he was in a rather hopeless situation.

So deep in his thoughts was he, he didn't hear the old woman at the cart speaking to him. "I'm sorry?"

"I said, ye're scaring away me costumers, standin' there a-gawping and gaping."

Caleb looked around but, aside from a few pigeons pecking about in the mud, didn't see any of the supposed customers in question. "My deepest apologies, miss," he said with a low bow. His flattering address did nothing to warm her, and her scowl only deepened. Then a thought struck him. "You must be quite familiar with this street and the goings-on here, I would imagine?"

She gave him a sidelong look from her rheumy eyes. "Ye might say that. They don't call me Sharp-Eyed Maggie for nothin'."

"Do you see that picture in the window over there?" He pointed to the shop, where the man had replaced the picture in its place of honor. "The one of the girl with the striking eyes and the flower brooch?" He doubted that "Sharp-Eyed" Maggie could see as far as her own nose, let alone across the street, but she surprised him by nodding vigorously.

"Oh, aye, I know that picture well. Knew the girl in it just as well, too."

Caleb's heart stopped in his chest. "You knew her? Who is she? Is she still living?"

"That's Miss Alice," the woman said, her expression growing soft and nostalgic. "I couldn't say if she's alive yet or no, as she moved away some years ago. She was a dear thing, though, always brought me sweets, she did."

"Where did she move?" Caleb couldn't believe it. He had thought that he would have to scour the city for information, and here this old lady was practically dropping the answers to his questions into his lap.

Maggie scratched at her matted hair. "Edinburgh," she said proudly. "I remember because I grew up there, an' I told her as much. Told her where she might get a strong whiskey should she be the imbibing type, and a warm-cooked meal. She thanked me right prettily, she did. Even gave me a token of her appreciation." Here she paused and fingered the very brooch that was in the picture. "Took herself off and I haven't seen her again."

Caleb didn't need to hear any more; he was already turning, the next steps of his plan falling into place. "You've been most helpful," he called over his shoulder.

He didn't know how he would do it, but he was going to Edinburgh.

Alice gasped and sat up in bed. Kicking off the tangled quilt, she shivered as the early-morning air hit her perspiring skin. She'd had that dream again, the one where she was wandering a vast, empty nothingness. No sound, no movement, no anything. Just a suffocating darkness pressing in around her from every direction. Then, just when she was certain that she was dead and would never awaken again, her name would ring out in the void. Each time she woke up sweating and heart pounding, an aching emptiness in her chest.

Glancing at the sleeping figure bathed in moonlight beside her, Alice quietly swung her legs out of bed and tiptoed to the window casement that overlooked the little square. Edinburgh glowed in the predawn light. It was beautiful, but no matter how long she had been here, it never felt like home. Perhaps it was because she'd seen a glimpse of her future life, and the little house she shared with a dark-haired woman had been in an unfamiliar city.

The flashes that she saw came unpredictably and without warning, sometimes entire scenes laid out like staged vignettes, and other times nothing more than a fleeting image, a buried memory that hadn't happened yet. But the image of the house and the woman had been as clear as a daguerreotype.

A rustle of blankets and then a groggy feminine voice. "Come back to bed, Allie. I'm cold."

"One moment," she said absently. Soon the sun would be rising and it would be time to go out with her tray of licorice and sweetmeats and hawk her wares. Another day just like all the others, a simple, happy-enough existence, but with something, someone, conspicuously absent. She wondered if her sister felt the same way, or if she hated Alice for what she had done.

She tried not think of Tabby too often, nor speculate on what might have become of her. It was better to look forward and not backward. Perhaps if Alice had tried harder, tried at all to use her gift, she would see her sister in her future. But she was afraid of what she might find, and so she did not attempt to open the door in her mind and see what lay behind it. Besides, like in her present life, any flashes of her future had been bereft of Tabby.

Climbing back into bed, she closed her eyes, hoping for a few more minutes of sleep. Her bedmate curled up against her, murmuring something drowsy and indistinct. Alice let herself drift in the place between wakefulness and sleep. She both looked forward to and dreaded the dream, on one hand hoping to hear the voice again, but also terrified of the endless darkness.

But one thing was certain: she knew the voice from her dream. And the day that she would hear that voice in person was coming.

22

IN WHICH A LONG OVERDUE INVESTIGATION IS PURSUED.

THE HARVARD MEDICAL School sat perilously close to the Charles River and was prone to flooding in the spring. But now the narrow strip of lawn that spanned between the building and the river sparkled with frost in the late-afternoon sun, and aside from a few students and a groundskeeper raking up leaves, it was quiet.

Tabby studied the unassuming brick building with its three-storied facade. It looked remarkably benign. Slipping into Mr. Whitby's house had been one thing, but here at the medical school, a young, unescorted woman would be incredibly conspicuous.

She fretted at the edge of her cloak. What was she even looking for? The rest of Harvard's campus lay across the river in Cambridge, but she had figured that the medical school would be more likely to yield answers. That was what the man at the Granary had said—The Spunkers Club, doctors and surgeons from Harvard who still practiced dissection. But surely such illicit activities would be hidden far from the public eye, wouldn't they? She could hardly expect to walk in and find a stolen corpse on a slab.

Well, if she wanted answers she would have to start somewhere. She was just about to gather her courage and head up the main steps when she recognized the groundskeeper as his raking brought him closer. She'd seen him before at Miss Suze's, a cousin or nephew of hers, perhaps, and though Tabby didn't know him well, she was grateful to see a familiar face.

"Mr. Dwight, is that you?"

The man straightened up as Tabby approached him and gave her a suspicious glance. "Miss Tabby, what're you doing all the way o'er here? Your pa's not in trouble, is he?"

Tabby shook her head. "How do you do, Mr. Dwight? No, Pa is doing well, thank you." She could only hope that she was speaking the truth.

He gave her a short nod. "All right then. Well, you take care now." He resumed his raking.

She was interrupting his work and he was making it clear that he wasn't interested in continuing their conversation. But she also knew that coming across him here gave her a rare chance for answers. Clearing her throat, she chose her words carefully. "Do you think anyone would stop me if I were to go inside and take a look around?"

He raised a brow. "Do I think anyone would stop you? Can't say for sure, but I wouldn't try it if I was you."

"Hmm." She considered the front steps again. "Have you ever heard the name 'Spunkers Club'?"

"No, I have not," he said without looking up.

She glanced around, her desperation for answers warring with her common sense that he just wanted to be left alone. In the end, the former won out. "What about resurrection men?"

This time he just shook his head, still raking.

"I'm sorry to be a bother, but it would be so helpful if you could—"

At this, he stopped his work and looked up. "Miss Cooke, I'm here to keep the grounds clean and keep my head down, not answer nonsense questions. We might break bread together at Miss Suze's table, but that's there and this is out here. You know what will happen if I get caught talking to a white girl on the job? I'll get docked pay, that's what."

Tabby bit her lip. "Of course. I'm sorry."

Muttering something under his breath, Mr. Dwight resumed his raking and she was just about to turn away when his voice stopped her.

"Around the back there's a door that leads to the library. Might be that someone left it unlocked. Can't promise there ain't nobody in there, though."

Tabby let out a long breath of relief. She would have to be careful once inside, no more mistakes like with Mr. Whitby. "Thank you," she said, wishing he knew just how grateful she was.

"Don't know what you're thanking me for. I didn't tell you nothing."

★ ★ ★

In the end, Caleb's wit and acumen had been all the capital he needed to rebuild his seed money. He'd found an easy mark at a card table in the dankest, dingiest pub in all of London, bet him that he couldn't hold his breath for twenty seconds, won threepence, and from there it had just been a question of continuing to make larger and larger bets.

As the coach rumbled through the Scottish countryside, Caleb massaged the lingering soreness in his jaw where he'd been hit. He hadn't realized how much London had been choking the life out of him with its heavy smoke and fogs until he was well out of the city and on his way to Edinburgh.

He knew that he had traded one improbable likelihood for another, but he couldn't help the cautious spark of optimism that took root in his chest. How many men got a second fresh start? How senseless would he have to be to waste this one, as well?

After a week in Edinburgh, he had easily tripled his modest amount of money. It was enough to fund his room and board at a clean, if not slightly small, boarding house run by an old widow. But he didn't want to spend his days playing cards; it was time to find work—honest work—and begin this new chapter of his life in earnest.

He'd never had to work for his keep before. Everything had always been handed to him, but with the assumption that he would fail if left to his own devices. But here, he had only his wits to rely on, and it was inebriating.

He could be whatever he wanted. He could make a new life for himself, a better life. A life where he was captain of his own destiny. He would have to leave behind Caleb Bishop of course—that was the name of a guilty man in Boston, and Daniel Cooke had likewise proven to be a disappointment. So it was Caleb Pope who found himself walking down the colorful Victoria Street in the old town on a cold, overcast day.

His first stop was a rickety little shop that sold all manner of dry goods, including drafting supplies. He ran his fingers over the thick, creamy papers, and inspected the charcoals the way a miner might gold or silver. The blank sheets of paper stock invited him to design the tallest buildings possible, to fill them with hope and progress and beauty. He had only to follow his imagination.

But before he could design new buildings, he would need to show that he understood the principles of design. When he'd procured what he needed, he tucked his supplies into his waxed canvas bag to protect them from the perpetual rain that fell from the low sky and headed out into the city. Finding buildings to sketch in Edinburgh was like shooting fish in a barrel. As carriage traffic flowed around him, Caleb sketched the new Walter Scott memorial, marveling at the intricate Gothic spires that pierced the clouds. His fingers working automatically as if they had only been waiting for free rein, entire sections of the city coming to life on his paper.

He settled into a routine; during the days he roamed the city, drawing and searching for the woman in the photograph, asking every street vendor and beggar if they had seen a woman with fiery red hair and eyes as clear and sharp as ice. At night he fell into bed at the lodging house after a simple meal of bread and stew prepared by the landlady. No more card games, no visits to the theaters that filled the city. Just work and hope.

A week later Caleb had a respectable portfolio not just of sketches of recognizable landmarks around the city, but also buildings of his own imagining. An unfamiliar sensation swelled in his chest as he flipped through the sketches, and with a start, he realized it was pride.

23

OF SISTERS AND SECRETS.

THE STREETS OF Edinburgh swarmed with red-haired women, sending Caleb's heart racing each time one crossed his path. But when they turned around, they were never Tabby, nor the young woman from the photograph.

What *would* he say to Tabby if he came face-to-face with her again? Would he apologize? Not just for absconding without saying good-bye, without thanking her for the warning, but for all the times he failed to see what was right in front of him. Failed to realize what the feeling in his chest was when she was near.

"Have ye finished with the Merritt papers?"

Caleb came out of his thoughts to find Hugh Sanderson, one of the firm's partners, looking at him expectantly from the doorway. An affable man of middle age, he had light brown hair, whiskers, and a pipe perpetually between his lips.

It had been nearly a month since Caleb had arrived at the firm with his portfolio tucked under his arm, delirious with hope. Hugh had gently explained to him that they didn't just hire men off the streets as architects, but that they were in need of a good clerk. It wasn't the vocation of drafting plans and designing buildings of which he had always dreamed, but it was certainly more than he could have ever hoped to do in Boston.

"Oh, right. Here," Caleb said, leafing through stacks of paper and handing him a packet of sketches and estimates.

Hugh glanced through the papers and gave a nod. "Good." Taking a long puff from his pipe, he glanced out the window. "I hate to ask, since it's downright miserable out, but we need more of that heavy stock, and—"

Caleb all but leapt out of his seat. "I can get it." He was desperate to get out, to resume his search, which he had all but abandoned since taking the job. Here in the office with the sound of rain on the windows it was too easy to slip into a melancholy, too dangerous to settle and never pick up his search again.

Hugh raised a brow. "Are ye sure? Ye'll have to get them to wrap it in canvas to protect it from the rain and—"

"Yes, yes. Didn't anyone ever tell you not to look a gift horse in the mouth?" He gave the bewildered Hugh a clap on the shoulder as he grabbed his hat and coat and headed out into the rain.

The brisk air was an elixir for his melancholy. He took the long way to the supply store, and found himself in one of the city's ancient cemeteries, a sprawling necropolis of mossy stones and picturesque ruins. How differ-

ent the elaborate crypts and monuments were from the
simple burying grounds of Boston, with their primitive
folk headstones. He had never thought death to be anything other than dreary and distasteful, but looking at the
expansive cemetery through Tabby's eyes, he began to
understand how a place like this could offer hope, peace,
and even beauty in its own right.

By the time he emerged through the back gates onto
the street again, the rain had transitioned to a soft miz-
zle, and the clouds were starting to part. He was making his way through the market square, when he caught
sight of a young woman with bright red hair hawking
sweets from a tray. If he hadn't been thousands of miles
across the ocean, he would have sworn that it was Tabby.

He stopped in his tracks. There was something in the
way she moved, the way she held her chin as she tried to
tempt passersby with her goods. She turned around, and
he caught a glimpse of icy, clear eyes. His neck went hot.
They weren't Tabby's, but he had seen those eyes before.

She stopped to banter with a cheesemonger, her bright
hair a splash of color against the drab and rainy surroundings. Removing her tray and handing it off to another
young woman, she started walking through the square.
Without thinking twice, he fell into step behind her,
trailing her like a hungry shadow.

When she headed toward a pub, he decided to make
his move. The supplies that Hugh was waiting for were
forgotten, as was everything else. The answers to the
questions that had been plaguing him for the past month
were so close that he could practically reach out and
touch them.

He waited a beat before pushing the door open and following her inside. He was just about to find an innocuous place at the bar to wait, when she spun around and faced him.

"Who are you? Why are you following me?"

Her voice was so like Tabby's that for a moment he was too dumbstruck to do anything but stand and gape at her.

"Well?" In a fluid motion, the woman had slipped a little blade out of her sleeve and was now pointing at him with unnerving confidence. "If it's money that you're after, you could hardly have picked a worse mark."

Before Caleb had a chance to assure her that he had no interest in her money—or her lack thereof—a burly man twice his size ambled out from behind the bar and put himself between the woman and Caleb. "This man botherin' ye, Allie?"

"I don't know," she said without taking her gaze from Caleb's face, or lowering the blade. "Is he?"

This was it. "I saw your picture in London, and I recognized you back there in the square. I only want to talk," he added. "I'm not after your money, or anything else, for that matter. I just want to talk."

The blade wavered. "That cursed picture," she said, more to herself than to him. Then she tightened her grip on the handle and jabbed it in the air in his direction. "Don't tell me that you followed me all the way from London. You aren't one of them, are you?"

"One of who?"

She only narrowed her eyes, so he continued.

"Your hair, and your...your eyes," he said in a rush. "I... It's just, you look like someone I know. Someone I knew. I've been looking for you, yes, but not following you. Well, only following you from the square, that is."

Hunching into his shoulders, he closed his eyes and braced for a blow to land, sure that he had insulted this stranger beyond all measure. But no blow came, and when he opened his eyes, she was looking at him with unmistakable interest.

"Was this someone..." the woman trailed off. "Your accent—it's American. This person that I look like, where did you see her?"

Caleb shot another glance at the mountain of a man who was still tensed and ready to beat him to a pulp before answering. "Boston," he said. "I'm from Boston."

She looked shaken, and he could see her struggling to maintain her composure as she turned toward the bartender. "I'm fine, Malcolm, thank you."

When the man had given him one last look of distaste and lumbered away, she turned back to Caleb. "What is her name?" she asked him in a whisper.

"Tabitha."

The woman's eyes snapped shut as she drew in a sharp breath. Then she was surveying him cautiously again. "And who are you to her? How do I know I can trust you?"

"I might ask you the same thing," he said, feeling suddenly protective of Tabby.

"You're the one who followed me. I hardly think you're in a position to demand information from me."

"And yet, I would know with whom I was speaking."

She studied him for what felt like an eternity before

saying, "My name is Alice." She swallowed. "Tabitha is my sister."

It was Caleb's turn to stare at her in silent shock. Tabby had never mentioned that she had a sister, had never even hinted at any living family beyond Eli. And yet, he realized that he had suspected, even if he had not fully admitted it to himself, that the picture could have been only one person.

He realized that she was saying something, and he shook himself out of his stupor. "What?"

"I said you had better tell me your name and how you know my sister, or I'll have Malcom have a go at you." She drew herself up. "I need to know I can trust you, that you aren't one of *them*."

"I don't know who *they* are," he replied. She was acting as if there was some conspiracy afoot, so he opted for honesty. "Caleb Bishop," he said with a neat bow, "of Bishop & Son Shipping. A friend of Tabby's." And, because he found that he was nervous and couldn't help himself, he added, "Mr. Pope if I owe you money from cards."

If she understood the joke, her expression didn't show it. His neck had grown hot under her scrutiny. All his hoping and work and prayers had come to a head, and now that he had found her, he couldn't leave without answers. Finally, she gave him a curt nod. "All right," she said, turning and briskly walking to a table in the corner. He let out a long, slow breath and followed.

He had barely sat down, when she was leaning across the table, gripping his hands with surprising strength. "Tabby is alive, then? She's all right?"

Good God, she really didn't know. "Er, yes. Last I saw

her she was fine." But was she still fine? Had Whitby caught up to her? A wave of guilt followed by regret crashed through him. How could he have just left her there? He had taken the lifeline thrown to him, and hadn't even paused to consider that he hadn't been the only one drowning.

Alice let out a breath and relaxed her grip. The picture had admirably captured her beauty and quiet dignity, but it hadn't prepared him for the intensity of her eyes. If Tabby's eyes were like green mountains shrouded in clouds, then Alice's were the sparkling reflection on a lake. Her expression was wary, guarded. "When was the last time you saw her?"

"One hundred and forty-seven days ago."

"That's an awfully specific number."

He cleared his throat and endeavored to look casual. "Yes, well, I have a head for numbers," he managed in a mumble.

Alice gave him a queer look. "Just what is your relationship with my sister?"

"She's a friend. A dear friend." Would that he had left Boston with something more, but dolt that he was, it had taken crossing the ocean to realize just what he had left behind.

"I see." Alice drummed her fingers on the rough table, suddenly looking younger, vulnerable. "Does…does Tabby ever talk about me?"

Caleb chose his words carefully. "She never mentioned that she had a sister, no."

Alice nodded, but did not offer any explanation. Hesitating, Caleb tried to decide the best way to coax the truth from her. But he was too curious to be tactful. "What brought you to London without Tabby? And now Edinburgh?"

At first it didn't seem as if Alice had heard him; she was staring at her hands, which were clutched around her cup. The sound of glasses clinking and the boisterous voices of the after-work crowd swelled up around them. When she spoke, it was sudden and in a low, urgent tone.

"What do you know of resurrection men?"

Taken by surprise by the sudden change of subject, Caleb frowned. "I know that grave robbing used to be a lucrative business in the medical field, and that there has been a spate of snatchings lately in Boston after a decade of nothing." He didn't mention that his own father had been a victim.

Alice nodded. "Edinburgh lives in the shadow of the murderers and body snatchers Burke and Hare, even twenty years later. But even before I came here, I'd heard stories of men digging up the graves of the freshly dead in Massachusetts for dissection and experimentation." She wrinkled her nose in a gesture that reminded him of Tabby. "I never thought that someday my fate would be so bound up in the actions of such men."

She took a long breath, and Caleb waited for her to continue. "I'm getting ahead of myself. Did Tabby ever tell you anything of her early life?"

Tabby knew so much about him, from his distaste for the shipping business, to his history with his father. But he knew very little of her aside from the fact that she was fiercely loyal to Eli and Mary-Ruth. He suddenly realized he was hungry to know everything about her, and ashamed that he had never asked when he'd had the chance. He shook his head.

"I suppose not, given that she never mentioned me." Alice sighed. "Our parents died in a carriage accident when I was ten years old and Tabby just seven. Our mother's sister and her husband took us in, being that they were our only family. It was no secret in town that our mother was a clairvoyant and they assumed that Tabby and I were, as well. We—"

Caleb nearly choked on his drink. "Wait. You're telling me that you and Tabby are… That you have…" he trailed off. Good God, had Tabby been telling the truth? Was it even possible?

Alice looked surprised. "Perhaps I shouldn't have said anything, but in order to understand the story I'm about to tell, you need to understand where we came from."

"Tabby said that she could speak to the dead, and that she had spoken to both my father and my fiancée on my behalf. But I rather thought she was, er, mad. Or at the very least, having a laugh at my expense."

Alice looked taken aback. "She told you all of that?"

He nodded.

"The Tabby that I knew would never, ever tell someone about her special abilities, not after what happened to her. If she did indeed tell you, then she must hold you in the highest of esteem."

Caleb sat in stunned silence. Regardless of whether Tabby did indeed hold some special power, she had confided in him about something that was deeply personal to her and he had been scornful and derisive, accusing her of lying.

Alice continued. "In any case, there was no love in that household, no nurturing or protection. Instead, my aunt and uncle saw us as a means to make money, and held séances and parties where we were forced to try to contact the dead for their friends and strangers alike. They envisioned a traveling act, with the two of us performing séances for audiences around the country. Tabby was more sensitive than me, and I knew that if we didn't get out of that house, that she would be permanently scarred. So I started stealing bits of money here and there from our aunt and uncle, and made plans to escape to Boston.

"The night that Tabby and I arrived in the city, I had gone to look for lodgings, for somewhere safe just to spend the night. Tabby was afraid that our aunt and uncle had followed us, and said that she felt like we were being watched. If I had been a better sister, I would have paid more attention to what she was saying. But as it was, I was tired and hungry and I thought I knew better. So I left her alone on some church steps while I went off to look for a place to sleep."

Alice paused in her story as the bartender came and refilled her cup. Caleb absorbed this incredible story; why had Tabby never mentioned her sister before? Or anything about her life before Boston, for that matter?

When the bartender had gone, she continued. "Tabby was right, of course. We were being followed, just not by our aunt and uncle. There was a ring of grave robbers, and they had heard of two sisters from Amherst that had clairvoyant powers. They thought that if they had these sisters that they could find more bodies, fresher bodies, faster. They must have been following us for some time, and when we ran away from our aunt and uncle, they saw their chance and took it. It wasn't until after I'd left Tabby on the steps that I realized I was being followed, and by then it was too late. I had to make sure that they didn't get Tabby. I had to lead them away from her and…"

She trailed off, and then drained her cup as Caleb sat, stunned. She'd sacrificed herself for her sister.

"I'll spare you the details," she continued, "but in the end, the men realized I wasn't the useful sister, that I didn't possess the kind of powers that Tabby did. It was only a matter of time before they killed me and put my body to use. I escaped with my skin and found passage on a ship to London. Eventually I found my way here."

"What do you mean, the 'useful sister'?"

Glancing around at the crush of men in plaid trousers and cinched frock coats drinking their ales and whiskeys, Alice lowered her voice and leaned forward. "What I am about to tell you is the gospel truth, and I don't care one whit if you believe me or not." She took a deep breath. "Where Tabby has a channel through which she can communicate with the other side, my channel connects me to the future, to things that have not yet happened." She paused and, when he didn't react, continued. "They didn't know this, of course. They only knew that I could not speak with the dead and, once they established that, decided that I was useless." She gave a shrug, as if it were the most inconsequential thing on earth.

Caleb opened his mouth, trying to find words. It was

almost too extraordinary to believe, but if he believed Tabby, then he must believe her sister, as well.

"So you never spoke to her again?"

Alice shook her head, studying the contents of her cup.

"But surely you could have written her, sent her some kind of message at the very least to let her know that you were all right?"

She gave him a withering look. "I haven't dared try to contact her or do anything that would draw attention to her. With all this renewed activity by resurrection men, I don't for a moment trust that they wouldn't have some sort of nefarious design on her. Her only protection is that no one knows about her gift. In Boston she can be anonymous."

But she wasn't anonymous, not anymore. He had told Officer Hodsdon about her, had let her fend for herself after she had run afoul of Mr. Whitby. Caleb thought about Tabby, about his mother, about Buttermilk, and how much he missed them. It must be torture for Alice and Tabby to be separated from each other.

They sat in silence, each nursing their own thoughts and regrets as laughter rose and fell around them and lamps were lit. It was Alice who spoke at last.

"How is she, really? Is she happy? Married? My only consolation is that she has gone on to live a full life. I cannot tell you how often I picture her with a baby and someone to love and protect her."

Caleb had never thought of Tabby as a mother, but the image he conjured of her dandling a baby on her knee made something inside of him hot with longing.

"No, she's not married. As for her happiness, I couldn't say. She has managed to make a life for herself in Boston, and she charms everyone she meets. My mother is exceedingly fond of her, and that is no small feat. For her part, Tabby likes everyone. Everyone except me," he couldn't help adding.

Alice raised a brow, but thankfully didn't probe any further. "Why haven't you gone back to find her?" he finally managed to ask. "Surely you could be careful, not draw attention to yourself or to her?"

Alice didn't answer, just stared into her cup. When she finally met his gaze, there was unspeakable fear in her clear eyes. "I don't know. I suppose that after all this time I assumed that even if Tabby were still alive that she would resent me for leaving her."

"I think she would want to see you." Caleb fiddled with his cuffs, saying the words that he hoped were true of him, as well. "She needs you."

"I don't know about that. Tabby is resourceful." Alice gave him a thoughtful look. "I don't know anything about your relationship, so you'll excuse me saying so, but it seems to me that you certainly need her."

Caleb swiftly shifted his gaze. "I doubt it. I was...that is, I acted the cad when last I saw her, and I wasn't exactly a gentleman in our dealings prior to that."

"But she obviously holds you in some regard if she confided in you about her ability."

Caleb wasn't so sure, and even if she did, he didn't deserve it. Like Tabby, talking to Alice was easy, and before he knew it, he was telling her about his father, about the other body snatchings around Boston. He told her about

Whitby and Rose's murder. He told her everything. Perhaps the more she knew, the more she would somehow be able to help. He already knew the answer, knew it because of the hot ball of guilt he felt deep in his gut, but he asked anyway. "You don't think that Tabby could be in danger, do you?"

"Tabby has been in danger since she was born, just by virtue of her gift. Our mother taught us never to share our gift with anyone, for fear that it would be exploited." She leveled a long look at Caleb and he felt his stomach drop even further. "But she shared it with you. I hope you guarded that secret like the treasure it is."

But he hadn't. He had traded it for his freedom, and now she was vulnerable, alone. He let out a groan and cradled his head.

Alice narrowed her eyes. "What."

"I—I may have told someone."

It was a moment before Alice responded. "And is this someone trustworthy?"

Billy was a policeman, and he had only wanted to contact his dead mother. Where was the harm in that? But what if he told others about her?

His silence must have been all the answer she needed, and Alice sighed. "I see."

In the din of the pub, a plan began to crystalize in Caleb's mind. He had managed to make the beginnings of a life here in Edinburgh for himself, but he could not enjoy it with the yoke of guilt on his shoulders. Clerking for Hugh in the firm wasn't the most fulfilling work, but it certainly was better than prison and a death sentence hanging over his head.

He had wasted his chance of love with Rose, and he wouldn't do the same with Tabby. And so long as he was considered a suspect in Rose's murder, there would be no justice. Rose deserved justice.

He studied the woman across the table, a vision of her sister, and knew what had to be done.

"What if we go back together?"

24

IN WHICH A LIBRARY YIELDS
AN OPPORTUNITY.

THE LIBRARY WELCOMED Tabby with the warm smell of books and leather. The door had been unlocked, just as Mr. Dwight had said, and then it was up two flights of stairs from the basement to the library. A small plaque informed her that the medical theater was next door. God willing, Tabby would not have to look there.

There was a hushed reverence about the great wood-paneled hall. A handful of students sat at desks with thick volumes spread before them, glancing up at her as she passed. If any of them were concerned with a young woman in their midst, they didn't say anything. She was used to being invisible, and nothing was more invisible than a lone woman in a shabby dress.

Tabby wandered the shelves of books. So much knowledge kept locked away for the privileged few, out of reach to those who were not born a man with white skin. She ached to pull the volumes down and learn all their secrets, but there was no time. She had learned her lesson the hard way at Mr. Whitby's house.

The floorboards creaked under her feet as she studied the shelves, the only other noise the soft rustle of pages as students read. She fidgeted with a loose button on her bodice, her skin starting to feel hot and prickly the longer she aimlessly wandered about. What was she looking for, exactly? There had to be books on anatomical study, some sort of chronicle of the history of dissection at Harvard. She had never been in a library before, and didn't know what kind of books might be available, let alone how to find them. Regardless, she could not simply take a book off the shelf and sit down with it like the men around her. Acting like a lost woman was one thing, but pretending to be a student was another altogether.

If only Caleb were there, he would have known what she was looking for. She was exhausted from nights of watching, weak from too little food and being cold all the time. What would she even do if she were to find out who the grave robbers were and what they were doing with the bodies? Who would listen to her? Tears of frustration started to build in her throat.

"Excuse me. Excuse me!"

Tabby looked up to see a barrel-chested man walking briskly toward her. She froze.

"Just what do you think you're doing here?"

"I—I'm sorry. I was just—" She moved to slip past him, but the man took her by the arm.

His tobacco-yellowed mustache curled downward as he frowned. "There are no women permitted in the library."

"I was just leaving. I'm sorry. I was only looking for—"

The man's grip on her arm relaxed. "I know what this is about," he said sternly.

"You do?"

"You've come looking for a position, haven't you," he said with a pitying, knowing smile.

She hesitated only a moment. "Yes, sir."

He nodded as if this confirmed his suspicions. "You'd have done well to come during business hours, but you're here now. My name is Mr. Quinn, and I manage the building. You look like a young woman in need of Christian kindness, and good, honest work. Can you carry a pail?"

She nodded. Though Tabby had never met Mr. Quinn before, she knew him all too well. He went to church every Sunday, puffing his chest as he belted out the hymns, thinking that it all but made him a saint on the days in between. When he looked at her, he saw not a person, but an act of charity.

"Good. Come back tomorrow at seven in the morning." He wagged his finger at her, a glimmer in his eye as if they were sharing some great joke. "This time no wandering about the library, eh?"

After a cold, sleepless night spent guarding her possessions at the boarding house, Tabby made her way back to the library. It didn't matter if she never slept a wink again; every time she closed her eyes she was assaulted with a barrage of pleas and grievances from spirits. Where were their bodies, they wanted to know? When would they be returned? When would they have their rest? Tabby could offer only harried promises, assurance that she was doing everything possible to help them.

Mr. Quinn was waiting for her at the back entrance of the library. He cast a disparaging glance at the dress she had been wearing the day before, and then gestured for her to follow him inside. Gleaming floorboards squeaked under her boots as they passed academic men carrying on hushed conversations. This time Mr. Quinn led her away from the library and up another set of stairs to a hall lined with studies and offices. He unlocked one of the doors and motioned for her to follow him inside, but she hesitated on the threshold.

Catching her uncertainty, he smiled. "Your modesty is a credit to you, Miss Cooke, but I can assure you, you are most safe."

She had no choice but to believe him if she wanted to learn what went on in this place, so she stepped the rest of the way inside. The office had an unpleasant vinegar odor, and the air was stale. Bottles with amorphous specimens floating in them lined one shelf, books stacked on another. She swallowed down her revulsion at the jars and forced herself to focus on what Mr. Quinn was saying.

As he explained what her duties would be, it dawned on her just how much a stroke of luck this had been. Not only would she be earning money, but she would have access to places about which she could have only dreamt. She would have to be on her guard, but if there were answers to be found, they would be here.

"It is of the utmost importance that you do not touch

anything, for what may look innocuous to you may in fact be crucial research, of which replication is not possible if destroyed. Your path should take you only to the grate, the lamps, and the bookshelves if they are dusty." He gave her a stern look. "Do I make myself understood?"

"Yes, sir."

"Good." He led her back out to the hall, closing the door behind them. To her amazement, he handed her key after key, explaining which rooms each one unlocked.

"Now," he said, beckoning to a woman bent over a mop at the other end of the hall, "I will leave you to the capable hands of Mrs. Cruikshank, who will show you where the supplies are kept." He paused, hands in his waistcoat pockets as if pondering some deep thought, before adding, "I hope that you will find the work honest and edifying."

"Of course," she said demurely.

When Mr. Quinn had left, Mrs. Cruikshank gave Tabby an assessing look. "Well?" she said, thrusting a heavily stained apron at Tabby. "Are you just going to stand there gawping, or are you going to work?"

She could feel Mrs. Cruikshank looking at her from the corner of her wizened eyes as she tied the apron on and began cleaning. She had endured worse before, and if working her fingers raw was the price of finding answers, then so be it.

The work was monotonous, but it was also soothing. She filled the scuttles with coal, swept the floors, and dusted the spiderwebs from the lamps. It was warm in the building, and there was a stall on the street outside that sold roasted nuts and potatoes for when she was hungry after a long day of cleaning. For the first time in weeks, Tabby didn't feel so desperately hopeless.

But on the fourth day she had still come no closer to learning what, if any, secrets lurked in this place, and she was beginning to wonder if she ever would. By all appearances, the men who worked in the offices were simply professors and doctors, the building simply a place of learning.

Tabby came out from one of the offices, her hands still black with coal, and found Mrs. Cruikshank on her hands and knees, scrubbing the floor. Taking up a rag, Tabby went to work beside her. She waited for two men in conversation to pass by before asking Mrs. Cruikshank, "Do you like it here?"

Mrs. Cruikshank let out a snort. "Do I *like* it? What a question. It's work, and the pay is fair. My feelings about the place don't come into it."

"What goes on here exactly? What sort of experiments do the medical professors conduct?"

"I'm sure I don't know and I don't want to know."

Mrs. Cruikshank's vigorous scrubbing didn't invite further comment, but Tabby was undeterred. "I've heard there are professors here who study the dead—anatomy and the like. I wonder if you have ever met any of them?"

"They don't pay me to consort with the faculty. Go in, keep your head down, and try not to get the shivers with some of the things they brine in the jars, that's my advice."

"What's in the jars? What do they do with them?" Tabby pressed. When she had hazarded a look at them, they had mostly been unrecognizable, but some she could identify as frogs and other small animals. There was something sinister about the bloated carcasses suspended in cloudy liquid, a life that should have lasted no more than a matter of months, preserved for eternity.

Straightening her creaking back, Mrs. Cruikshank wiped a dirty streak of water across her cheek. "What do they do with 'em? They do whatever it is men of science do. Now if you don't stop pestering me with these questions I'll tell Mr. Quinn that you aren't fit to work. Go on—" she nodded toward the end of the hall "—there's windows that need scrubbing."

Tabby sighed and took up the bucket to bring it to the water pump in the yard. She was taking it back inside when a man appeared in the doorway of an office she'd never been in before. Snapping his fingers to gain her attention, he called to her.

She set down the bucket, glad to give her aching hands a rest. "Yes?"

"The grate is empty and someone tracked mud onto the floor." He looked at her expectantly. "I have a meeting, but I'll be back within the hour."

Sighing, Tabby hauled the bucket into the office, water sloshing over the sides as she went. Her arms ached and her back was stiff as she lazily pushed the mop. Taking a quick glance into the hall to make certain that no one was coming, she rested the mop against the desk and took a moment to stretch and study her surroundings. There was a plush green leather chair that looked awfully comfortable, but she knew if she sat down, she would likely fall asleep and get caught.

The plaque on the desk told her that the man's name was Dr. Jameson. Unlike some of the other offices that were filled with specimens and medical tools, paintings dotted the walls of this one. Most were portraits of former deans and presidents, stuffy, important men who looked down their noses at the viewer, but one group portrait caught her eye in particular. She paused in front of the grandiose painting in a heavy gilt frame. Below it, a small brass plaque read:

MEMBERS OF THE BOARD OF
ANATOMY AND SCIENTIFIC ADVANCEMENT THROUGH DISSECTION
NON SIBI SED OMNIBUS

The name was certainly more official sounding than the Spunkers Club, but there was no mistaking their purpose. There was Mr. Graham in the front, his sickness charitably omitted by the artist. Next to him was a bearded man in a white apron that she recognized as Dr. Jameson, a scalpel in his hand. Her gaze stopped when she reached the last man in the group. A man with piercing blue eyes, one hand rested on a book, a skull in the other. A man who—

"What do you think you're doing?"

Tabby jumped at the voice and spun around to find Dr. Jameson standing in the doorway.

"I—I was just looking at the painting."

"You aren't paid to look at paintings." His eyes narrowed and he moved into the room. "You look familiar. Do I know you from somewhere?"

Tabby would not make the same mistake she had made at Mr. Whitby's. This time she ran.

Outside, she didn't stop running until she was well out

of sight of the building and had put the river behind her. She didn't know why she looked familiar to Dr. Jameson, but she didn't need to know. It had grown dark, and the cold air nipped at her cheeks and wormed its way in through the weave of her cloak. It was a long way back to the boarding house, but Tabby hardly felt the cold as she put one worn leather boot in front of the other.

She shouldn't have been surprised when her eyes had landed on the last man in the painting, but his face had still made her blood run cold. Mr. Whitby.

Mr. Whitby was tied up in the grave robbing; why else would he appear in a painting with Mr. Graham? She thought back to his personal library, the anatomy books which had seemed so out of place suddenly making sense. It seemed that wherever there were sinister deeds in Boston, there was Mr. Whitby. He was an evil man of giant proportions, throwing a long, menacing shadow over every aspect of her life.

She was so absorbed in her thoughts that she didn't hear the sound of footsteps matching her pace until they were practically upon her. Only now did she realize how far away from the bustle of the main roads she was. Her neck prickled in warning. Someone was following her.

She quickened her pace, passing deserted alleys and shuttered shop windows. It had to be Mr. Whitby—or, more likely, someone hired by him. Had he followed her to Harvard? Did he know she knew? Perhaps it was her uncle, sent by her aunt to find her and bring her back to them. Rabbit quick, Tabby made a sharp turn onto a busier street.

The footsteps quickened in response. Dodging a drunkard slumped on the ground and then a little boy selling walnuts, she hazarded a glance over her shoulder and caught a glimpse of her pursuer. The footsteps belonged not to Mr. Whitby, nor her aunt and uncle, but a big brute of a man she had never seen before.

Her breath came in sharp, painful gasps. Mr. Graham's words spun through her head: *Powerful men. Men you wouldn't want to cross.* But she had crossed them already, or one of them, and now he was after her.

Ducking into a narrow alley, Tabby closed her eyes and slumped against the wall, fighting to catch her breath. Her legs ached and her lungs were on fire, but she had lost him. She needed to get to Mary-Ruth. She would know what to do.

But she was too late. With a sickening sense of dread, Tabby realized that she was not alone in the alley. The sound of breath, not her own, rasped so close to her ear that she could feel it even in the dark. Her body felt strangely light and far away. Slowly, she opened her eyes, only to see something dark whooshing toward her. Her head exploded with stars, and then…black.

25

IN WHICH A PATH MUST BE CHOSEN.

THE NEXT FEW days moved quickly, with Caleb making inquiries about passage to Boston, and Alice disappearing during the day to sell her sweets.

Alice was an odd one, there was no doubt about it. Like Tabby, she exercised an abundance of caution, verging on paranoia, whenever she was out. Her knife was ever ready up her sleeve, her instincts as sharp and quick as a cat's. Unlike Tabby, she was strident and outspoken, spending much of her time in pubs enjoying spirits and debating the old men about everything from women's rights to the price of corn and its effects on transatlantic trade. If Caleb wasn't gainfully employed, he had a feeling that the two of them could have made a formidable pair at the card tables.

When Caleb at last found a packet that was calling at

Southampton, New York, and Boston, he was able to haggle for two tickets. With every step, the journey back became more and more real. He knew very well that when he walked off that plank on the Boston dock that he could be walking straight back into prison. He tried not to think of that, nor of the passage that would see him sick every day for the next six weeks.

Once he had counted out his hard-earned bank notes into the captain's hands, he began the long walk back to the city. There was one thing he still had to do before he left.

Caleb found Hugh hunched over his desk, compass in one hand, drawing charcoal in the other, a disorganized mass of papers spread around him.

Clearing his throat, Caleb knocked lightly on the door frame.

Hugh looked up, his pipe long extinguished, but still firmly planted between his lips. "There ye are. I was wondering where ye'd gotten to."

Caleb had hardly been a model employee the last few days as he'd hurried to make preparations for the journey back across the Atlantic. "Sorry, just had to step out for a moment." He glanced down at the drawing Hugh had been working on and raised a brow. "A mausoleum?"

Hugh gave a weary sigh, tossing his compass and charcoal aside as he leaned back in his chair. "Say what you will about Burke and Hare, but they did wonders for the funerary industry. Now everyone is clamoring for a crypt that will confound grave robbers. Buildings come and go, getting knocked down in the name of progress, but a crypt is sacred. It will last forever. Now," Hugh said, "what was it you needed?"

Caleb couldn't put it off any longer. "May I sit?"

Hugh gestured to the chair across from his desk, and Caleb seated himself, sinking down into the plush leather. He would miss the cluttered yet cozy office, and the man who occupied it. He would miss the dusty books and the shelves fit to bursting with papers. He would miss Hugh's deep brogue and easy companionship. Most of all he would miss feeling as if he belonged, of having a place and knowing that he had earned it with his own merit. Clearing his throat, he gathered his resolve. "Let me start by saying how deeply I appreciate everything you have done for me, and the chance you took when you brought me into the firm. I will never forget your kindness and—"

Hugh stopped him. "You're leaving."

"Regretfully, yes."

Hugh fumbled for a match and relit his pipe. "I had a feeling this was coming." Caleb's surprise must have shown, because Hugh gave an exasperated sigh. "I didn't hire ye because I'm kind, I hired ye because I know raw talent when I see it. I knew when I hired ye that you had aspirations higher than a clerk. Your sketches showed promise, and I was planning on promoting you to partner after ye'd proven yourself first. Well, you've proven yourself and then some. So I'd like to offer ye partner now."

Caleb sat, stunned. "Partner?" he managed to croak out.

Hugh nodded. "I was planning on waiting 'til the new year, but I don't want to lose ye, so there it is."

Everything Caleb had ever wanted was being laid at his feet, and all he had to do was pluck it up and claim it for his own. The cozy, cluttered office could be his. Buildings that had been born in his mind would become reality and bear his name.

Hugh gave him one of his rare grins. "You're speechless. Say yes, for God's sake. Jenny is with pup and I'm going to need a man I can rely on in the coming months before the bairn comes and I never sleep a wink again."

"I..." Caleb opened his mouth to decline it. He had to decline it. If he didn't, the temptation would be too great. But he couldn't find the words or the will to give up everything he had ever wanted.

"I've taken ye by surprise. Why don't ye take the afternoon to think about it?"

Before he could respond, Hugh was clapping him on the back and ushering him out of the office.

By the time Caleb emerged back out into the street, it was nearing dusk. Hugh's offer and what it would mean for him should have made him feel light as air, but instead it felt as if he had been burdened with a mantle of lead. He could have not just a new life, but a better life. By returning to Boston now he wouldn't just be giving up his freedom, but the future of which he had always dreamed.

As he walked through the now-familiar streets of Edinburgh, he cataloged each and every building and landmark as he passed. The Nelson Monument, designed by Alexander Nasmyth, 1807. Charlotte Square, designed by Robert Adam, 1792. The Scott Monument, George Kemp, 1844. Pausing at an empty lot, he envisioned a fountain of beautiful nymphs with long curling hair and marbled eyes, pouring bottomless basins of water. Bishop, 1860. What good could he really do in Boston anyway? Alice would still go back, and she would reunite with Tabby and make sure that she was safe. Who better to protect Tabby than her own sister? Tabby had made it abundantly clear that she didn't think very highly of him, so he would be going back to nothing but a warrant for his arrest. Perhaps it was better if he did stay.

He found himself walking well out of the city, and ended up back at the port. The ship that he had booked passage on for himself and Alice was bobbing gently in the water as the crew loaded it with trunks and barrels in preparation for its departure the next morning.

As he watched, his situation weighed only the heavier on him. By going back to Boston, he was giving up his freedom, not only to follow his own path, but to live his life at all. When he landed on the far shore, all that would be waiting for him was a noose. He shivered at the thought. Did they still hang people? Perhaps not a noose, then, but certainly a firing squad. If he was lucky they would kill him in one shot. And after his father's fate, he'd had the misfortune of learning what became of the bodies of convicts.

Someone touched his shoulder and he jumped.

Alice was standing behind him, dressed smartly in men's riding breeches and a nipped-waist frock coat.

"What are you doing here?" he asked. The port was a good distance from the city center, and he'd already as-sured her that he'd taken care of all their arrangements.

"I could ask the same of you."

He shrugged. A cold, brackish mist was rolling in off the water. "Just thinking."

Alice did him the courtesy of not probing any further into his thoughts. They stood together in comfortable silence, watching the crew move about the ship, a well-choreographed routine, as hopeful gulls circled looking for dropped food. He slid a glance at her out of the corner of his eye. What would she be leaving behind? What sacrifices of her own was she making to return to Boston? A sharp stab of guilt ran through him; if he stayed, he would be laying all the responsibility on her shoulders. But she at least would be free in Boston. She would have Tabby.

"Are you ready for tomorrow?" he asked, breaking the silence.

"I've packed and made all my arrangements, if that's what you mean."

"That's not what I meant," he said quietly.

She kept her gaze trained on the ship, nodding. "I know. No, I'm not ready. I'm not ready to go back and face the consequences of leaving my only sister to fend for herself, even if it was the right thing to do at the time. I'm not ready to leave behind the life I struggled to build for myself here. I'm not ready to go back to my old demons. But it's time. I can continue looking over my shoulder in Edinburgh, or I can do it in Boston where at least I have my sister. And if she's in some kind of trouble, I can do a lot more to help her there than I can here. It's time," she repeated.

Caleb swallowed, horrified to find that tears were welling up in his eyes. He hadn't cried when his father had beat him black and blue as a child, nor when he'd learned of Rose's death, or was imprisoned for it. He certainly hadn't cried when his father died. But as he stared out over the harbor lights winking in the dusk and the ship that would bear him back to Boston, he finally allowed the tears to fall. It was time.

26

IN WHICH NIGHTMARES BECOME REAL.

SHE COULDN'T FEEL her body. Cold darkness pressed in around her, and Rose's sweet, mournful voice echoed through the void.

She was dead. Oh God, she had to be dead. This had always been her fate—it was everyone's fate—but she simply wasn't ready. She would never feel fresh spring grass under her feet again, or Eli's warm hand squeezing hers. She would never smell the crisp scent of autumn mingling with the salty harbor breeze, or taste warm licorice melting on her tongue. She would never know what it was like to make love to a man, nor to be someone's one and only beloved. How lonely it was, and how much she suddenly realized why spirits were always so eager to be heard by her.

But just when she thought that ether would swallow her up completely, the fog dissipated, leaving her somewhere with the sharp scent of antiseptic, and a dull light behind her eyelids. Voices echoed as if coming through a tunnel, and she could feel the air shift as a person, or people, moved about her. She was alive, but the not knowing where she was or why was almost worse.

Gradually, the voices sharpened and became vaguely familiar. "You promised you wouldn't hurt her!"

The words were hardly comforting. She didn't dare open her eyes, for fear of what she might find. Perhaps these people thought her dead, or asleep. Best not to give herself away if she could help it.

The next voice was unfamiliar, but spoke with a crisp, upper-class accent. "Come now, it was just a light knock to the head. She'll be fine. After all, we wouldn't want to jeopardize that extraordinary mind of hers."

"If you don't let her go, I'll tell the captain of police."

This was met by grim laughter. "Hodsdon, I assure you that the captain already is aware. Who do you think looks the other way and allows us to operate with impunity?"

Officer Hodsdon. Her elation at recognizing a familiar voice quickly faded. How did he know about her? Had word gotten out after the séance? Why was he collaborating with these vile men?

She couldn't play dead any longer. Tabby struggled to open her eyes, but they didn't want to cooperate. Her legs were equally heavy, and with building panic, she realized that she was bound to the table. She might not be dead, but she was well and truly rooted.

Her efforts to free herself must have attracted the attention of the men because their conversation broke off, and there was the sound of footsteps on a bare wooden floor.

"Here she comes," said the unfamiliar voice, coming closer.

When she was able to make her sluggish tongue cooperate, her words were hoarse and small. "Where am I?"

"A safe place. A place of learning and enlightenment."

These cryptic words did nothing to reassure her. When her eyes finally opened and came into focus, she was looking up at a man with a neat brown beard, spectacles, and a white coat. Dr. Jameson. She could just make out the rows of steeply stacked seats rising up around her, the kerosene lamps dotting the walls. She was in some kind of theater or auditorium. "What do you want with me?"

Dr. Jameson gave her an almost pitying look. "You're a clever girl. You know exactly why you're here."

She did know. She knew with a cold and dreadful certainty she'd had since she was a scared and malnourished twelve-year-old stealing into the cemetery in the middle of the night. Her abilities made her valuable. Men could make good money off a girl who had a power like hers and no one to protect her.

"You're a difficult girl to find, Miss Cooke. When Officer Hodsdon said he knew of a young woman with clairvoyant powers, it was only a matter of looking in the right places. And your aunt was very helpful in that regard. Of course, she wanted compensation for the loss of income she would have made with you, which was easily arranged. Imagine my surprise when you walked right into my office!"

Tabby's heart dropped. She could not be surprised that her aunt had betrayed her, but she had thought Officer Hodsdon an upstanding young man. She should have heeded her instincts the first time he came to call on them: police could not be trusted.

Dr. Jameson followed her gaze around the empty medical theater and broke into an unnerving smile. "Incredible, isn't it? But no, Miss Bellefonte, the slab is not your fate. You are too valuable alive. For the longest time it was your aunt and uncle who provided us with the names of the recently dead. Clients would come to them seeking communication, and in turn your aunt would alert us of their loved ones' deaths and direct us to the body. But sometimes it would be days later, weeks even, before an eligible corpse could be located, and of course by then it would be too far gone for our purposes. With you, on the other hand, you can just take a peek in your mind, and alert us right away when someone dies, before they even have been carted off to the morgue."

The way his beady eyes bore into her sent chills running down her spine. He looked at her as if she was plated in pure carat gold.

"Yes, yes," a new voice cut in. Tabby strained to lift her head to see who it was but they remained just out of view. The voice that spoke was cool and even, and made Tabby's skin crawl. "That's all true, but you lack imagination, Dr. Jameson."

"I'm a medical man, Mr. Whitby. I do not bend to the whims of imagination."

Mr. Whitby answered this with a grunt and then moved into view, his steely blue eyes looking coolly down at Tabby. "Miss Cooke—or, excuse me, I believe it's really Miss Bellefonte—can do so much more for our cause. Imagine, if you will, having a line of communication to the dead. Imagine how invaluable it will be to be able to confer with the spirit during the reanimation process. The things they could tell us! Why, just think of all the crimes that Officer Hodsdon here could solve as sergeant if he could simply ask the dead who it was who killed them."

Reanimation. What a cold, terrible word, as if life were no more than a switch that could be thrown on and off.

"Like how you murdered Rose Hammond?" The words slipped out before she could stop them.

Mr. Whitby's lips twitched. "Sometimes we must do regrettable things for the greater good. Just think of the advancements we could make for all of mankind."

He had said something to that effect before, but Tabby did not believe that his motives were really so altruistic. How had Rose's death benefited anyone besides Mr. Whitby? Had he killed her simply for the purpose of framing Caleb and thus leaving the path to the business wide-open? Or was there some even darker reason? Besides, if the greater good required the death of young women, then how could that be considered progress?

But Tabby wasn't finished. She might die here, might never rise from this table again. Mr. Whitby's admission of guilt could be the closest thing to justice Rose would have. "She was an innocent woman! If you wanted the business so badly you might have just asked Caleb. He certainly didn't want it. But instead you murdered her."

Mr. Whitby was so still, so quiet, that she wondered if he hadn't heard her. Then slowly, he turned, his eyes blazing with fire.

"You understand little of the contents of men's hearts," he said in a hiss.

But he was wrong; she knew all too well what speaking to the dead could mean for their experiments in reanimation. The power that men like Whitby would wield if they could bring back the dead was almost too staggering to comprehend. The wealthy—who were already so afraid of dying prematurely and losing all their worldly riches—would pay exorbitant prices to live again, perhaps forever. It was all mankind had ever dreamed about, to be immortal. And Tabby was the key to the most precious treasure box that someone like Mr. Whitby could imagine. No, she understood more of the contents of men's black hearts than he ever would.

"And what if I refuse to cooperate?"

Mr. Whitby gave a bark of laughter and looked genuinely amused. "You think yourself very brave, do you not, Miss Cooke? Well, I think that you are naive, for I have some information that would prove very damaging if it were to be known."

What could he possibly know about her that she didn't know herself? "You're bluffing," she said.

He paused. "What do you know about the early life of your beloved adoptive father?"

Tabby's body went rigid. *No no* no. She had been so careful, but he had found Eli, and was prepared to do some terrible thing to him to force her hand.

"I can see by your face that you weren't aware that your father has secrets of his own. Just as I thought," he said. "Well, it might interest you to know that Eli Cooke is actually one Cato Walker, a fugitive slave from Virginia. Apparently, he was quite a favorite of his master. Unfortunately, the good Mr. Thorndike passed away six years ago. His son inherited his holdings and is quite determined that his father's property be returned to its rightful owner."

Tabby didn't need to hear any more, didn't *want* to hear any more. Eli had been a slave, and had somehow escaped hell and made his way to Boston, where he'd forged a new life for himself. She burned with fury at the unfairness of it all, that a gentle, kind man like Eli had to live in fear, while the Mr. Whitbys of the world were exempt from responsibility for their heinous actions.

She opened her mouth to tell him as much, but all that came out was a torrent of curses.

"Are you quite finished?" he asked. "Despite your assumptions about me, I'm a reasonable man. Your father has made a life here for himself, and has had the luck to thus far evade capture. I'm prepared to hold my peace, but you must cooperate."

At some point Officer Hodsdon had been removed from the room, and Mr. Whitby's silent presence radiated cold and menacing beside her. Dr. Jameson was hovering just beyond her field of vision, but she could hear the delicate clinking of silver medical tools.

So, it had come to this: her worst fear since she was a child. They had said they wouldn't hurt her, but they could poke and prod at her, try to find something in her that explained her powers, perhaps even harness them. Mr. Whitby had said he hadn't intended to kill Rose, and yet she had still ended up dead. Would the same thing happen to Tabby? And in the end, did it really matter? What had she to lose? Mostly she was sorry for Eli, that he would never know just how much he meant to her, and that he would think she had run away and left him. But she could not risk what Mr. Whitby said to be true, and so her fate was sealed.

27

IN WHICH THE FUGITIVES RETURN.

THE LAST TIME Caleb had been in Boston, he'd been stealing through the streets under the cover of darkness, his clothes filthy, his heart pounding, and a flight instinct propelling him toward the docks. Now he sat in a rather nice hack, the damp, ancient city of Edinburgh but a distant dream. They passed his club where Debbenham still owed him for cards, and then the theater where Caleb used to watch the pretty actresses from his box, waiting to catch their eye and secure an invitation to their dressing room after the play. How petty and small his old life seemed now. How much time he had wasted on a desperate and frivolous pursuit of what he had thought was happiness, and now knew to be only distraction.

Across from him sat Alice Bellefonte. She had been withdrawn and stayed below deck for most of the six-week journey, but now she sat on the edge of her seat, darting glances out the window and twining her fingers together over and over. The small hack vibrated with expectation, anxiety, and hope.

In the end, he had boarded the ship with Alice early in the morning, and watched the port disappear back into the Scottish fog. Fulfilling his dreams at the expense of abandoning Tabby in her hour of need would have been a hollow victory.

As they pulled up to his old home on Beacon Hill, his heart lurched. The flower boxes his mother took such delight in were empty in preparation for the winter, the windows dark and cold. The only sign of occupation was a thread of smoke coming from the chimney. Alice had wanted to go directly to the cemetery, had wanted to see Tabby for herself and make sure that she was all right. And though he ached to see Tabby like a marooned man aches to see land, he had reasoned that it had taken them nearly two months to reach home, and another hour or so wasn't going to change anything. His mother, on the other hand, would be wasting away from nerves.

He had been right. As soon as his mother saw him enter the parlor, she was on her feet, rushing to him with outstretched arms. She had lost weight, and the clothes in which she had always taken so much pride hung from her, like they were no more than rags tossed over the skeletal figure of a scarecrow. She folded him into her embrace, her arms thin and fragile, and enveloped him in her familiar scent.

But then she pulled back and delivered him a stinging wallop across his cheek.

"Ow! For Chrissake, what was that for?"

"That," she said, sniffing indignantly, "was for giving me the fright of my life. I thought you were dead!"

"Dead? Whatever would have given you that idea?" Word of his escape would have been in the papers, and he hadn't thought that his mother would think him so weak that he had immediately perished outside the prison walls.

Her lip quivered, but she drew her head up, defensive. "A medium told me."

"Oh, Mother," he said, rolling his eyes. "I *told* you not to waste a minute nor a nickel on those people."

"Yes, well, a widow with no children left has little recourse and I was desperate. If it wasn't for Miss Cooke setting me right, I would have lost all hope. But you will never believe this..." She leaned in conspiratorially. "The medium was none other than Miss Cooke's long-lost aunt!"

For the first time since they'd arrived, Alice made a noise. She took a hesitant step farther into the parlor, suddenly very pale. "Minerva Bellefonte? She was here?"

Mrs. Bishop's gaze finally landed on Alice. "And who might this be?"

"Mother, may I present Miss Alice Bellefonte. Tabby's sister," he added.

Alice gave an abbreviated bow of her head.

"I see," his mother murmured. "A pleasure. Yes, Minerva Bellefonte was here. She is supposed to be the best medium in Massachusetts. I didn't realize she was Tabby's aunt when I made the arrangements for the séance, but everything came to light in the most extraordinary manner."

Caleb's mouth went dry. "What happened?"

"Well, there was an awful row. Tabby exposed her in front of the entire assembly of ladies as a fraud. She said her piece, and before I had a chance to bring the room to order, she was gone."

Caleb exchanged an alarmed look with Alice. "You don't think...?"

His answer was written in the panic in her eyes.

"When was this?" he asked.

His mother frowned, thinking. "Oh, about a month ago now, I should think. It must have embarrassed Tabby terribly because she hasn't been back to call since then, the poor dear." Her eyes grew misty. "Miss Cooke has become a dear friend, a very dear friend. I don't know what I would have done without her. And Mr. Whitby, of course," she added. "He was here the day of the séance, come to see how I was doing since you'd gone away. I can't tell you what a trial it has been since you've been gone."

Caleb barely heard her. Tabby had been here, and Mr. Whitby, as well. And then she had disappeared, never to be seen again. It couldn't be coincidence.

"I knew we should have gone directly to the cemetery," Alice said as Caleb jumped into the hack behind her and rapped on the roof.

The hack lurched forward. He didn't say anything. Hot irritation crawled down his neck, the source more himself than Alice's accusing tone. They *should* have gone directly to look for Tabby, but he had wanted to see his mother. If he dug deep enough into his motives, he might have found that it was because he had also been scared to see

Tabby again. What if she didn't reciprocate his feelings? He didn't have experience with being rejected by women, and to be rejected by the woman he esteemed above all else—well, he was not eager to find out just how much it would sting. Now all those insecurities melted away as he thought of her in danger. "Can't this goddamn horse go any faster?"

"She could be anywhere."

"Don't you think I know that?" he snapped. "For God's sake, I've been gone for six months. I doubt that an extra hour will seal her fate." He said it for his own peace of mind as much as Alice's. He didn't add that it was his fault, that he was the one who had shared her secret gift with Officer Hodsdon, and then she had somehow found herself at his mother's house amongst a den of wolves. If Whitby had so much as touched a hair on her head...

Drawing a deep breath, he rubbed at his temples. "I'm sorry. It's just..."

The tension in Alice's shoulders softened and she gave him the ghost of a smile. Reaching across the seat, she squeezed his hand. "It's just that you love her," she said softly. "That's it, isn't it?"

He opened his mouth to deny it, the rogue inside of him rebelling against the idea of love and domesticity and all the nonsense that went with it. But then he closed his mouth, and gave a resigned nod. He did love Tabby, and God, it felt good to admit defeat, to bow down and lay his battle-scarred heart at her feet.

"Good," Alice said, looking back out the window. "It's about time you realized it."

28

IN WHICH OUR HEROINE IS A PRISONER.

OUTSIDE HER TINY room, Tabby could hear the faint tapping of rain on the window, the muffled clip of horses passing below. How much time had passed since she had been confined to the prison of this forgotten room? After her capture at Harvard, she had been examined and drugged, transported to this place without so much as an explanation of where they were taking her.

The cemetery had been a home, but it had also been something of a prison in its own right, a tiny, stagnant corner of the world where she was hidden away like a princess in a tower. But now she missed the peace, the safety of it, and would have done anything to be back there. She closed her eyes and thought of the day she and Mary-Ruth had run amongst the graves, racing for flowers in the pollen-sweet air.

When she opened her eyes again, the scene that met

her could not have been farther from the gentle colors and subdued ambiance of the cemetery. The air was stale and damp, the chinoiserie wallpaper faded. There was a cobwebbed cradle in the corner, a relic of when this room must have been a happier place, filled with the laughter of children. The only window faced another gable so that there was no hope of being seen below. When she had tried to open it, she'd found it was nailed shut and would not budge.

In an effort to preserve her sanity during her imprisonment, she had undertaken a census of the room, counting every nick in the wooden bedposts, every blue tuft of wool in the flowers on the Oriental carpet. There were exactly seventeen hairline cracks running the length of the plaster molding. It was still by far the most luxurious place she'd ever slept, but even so, she would have preferred a dank crypt to the mind-numbing boredom and melancholy of her prison.

On the wall, a row of tiny scratches marked the number of days she had been confined here. Although it had been thirty-seven days, she still had no idea where exactly she was. Twice a day, a dour serving woman came in with a tray of food. Every single time Tabby had pleaded with the woman to help her, but if she understood Tabby's pleas for mercy and escape, she gave no indication as she went briskly about the business of changing the linens and emptying the pot. It didn't matter anymore; there was nothing worth escaping for. To escape would be to sign Eli's fate over to the cruel slave hunters. She thought about Caleb, wondered where he was. No doubt some sunny, faraway coast with a blushing girl on his knee. Why had she been so resistant to him when he was here? Even if he was only interested in a romp, why had she denied herself the only chance she might ever have? She had been so concerned with what made her different that she had forfeited all the little normalcies she had taken for granted.

Tabby waited for the brisk knock followed by the key in the lock that meant the serving woman was coming in. Although she didn't have a clock, she could hear the chimes of one in the hall outside the room, and the woman always came at seven in the morning with a tray of food, and then again at seven at night to collect it.

It was a boring, numbing routine, but it was infinitely better than the days when Mr. Whitby came up to the chamber with Dr. Jameson to ask her their questions and scribble notes in their books.

They wanted to know if she could simply reach into the void and encounter a spirit? Or did she need to know the name of the deceased to find them? Did she ever see the dead walking among the living? Could the dead tell her how they died? Why did she not use her gift for profit when all of Boston was ripe for such spectacles? Hadn't she heard of the beautiful and gifted Cora Hatch, who'd made a small fortune touring the country and relaying messages from the other side? Day in and day out, a hundred variations of the same questions.

Today was different, though. Today was to be the day.

Tabby knew because instead of her usual brown calico dress, the woman brought in a dress of blue silk and matching slippers with dainty heels. Instead of the simple fare of brown bread, beans, and cold chicken, Tabby was served beef medallions in a rich, creamy sauce with capers and a warm pudding for dessert. And when the clock outside the hall struck three, a man she had never seen before appeared, with the maidservant hovering behind him.

He gave a short bow, as if she were not a prisoner being kept against her will and he was not a complete stranger. "Miss Bellefonte, I come on behalf of Mr. Whitby. I would be most obliged if you were to put on the dress that Mr. Whitby so kindly provided for you. You have a very special engagement today."

Tabby glared at the dress. It was the most beautiful frock she had ever seen, but it was from Mr. Whitby, and so it might as well have been made of burlap. The only dress that could rival it was Rose Hammond's dress. As her gaze ran over the lace accents on the skirt, she realized with a start that it *was* Rose's dress. She had seen her wear it at the cemetery, had remembered it because it had looked like it had waltzed right off the page of a fashion plate. Her stomach collapsed in on itself. Was this some sort of sign that she was to meet the same fate as Rose?

"Where are my manners? My name is Dr. Ferris, and I will be assisting Mr. Whitby and Dr. Jameson today. They are both busy making preparations, or Mr. Whitby would have been here himself."

When she didn't say anything, the man gave a *tsk*. "We want to look nice for our grand debut at the surgeon's hall today, don't we? It wouldn't do to insult Mr. Whitby after all he's done for you."

"Perhaps *you* should put on the dress if you have such

warm feelings for the venerable Mr. Whitby," she said, shoving the balled-up silk at his chest.

The man's cheeks went red. "Miss Cooke, it would behoove you to cooperate. I don't need to tell you that Mr. Whitby has something of a temper, and I would hate to see it turned against you."

He was right; it wouldn't do to go against Mr. Whitby. She had learned that the hard way over the past months.

"Well?" he prompted.

She snatched the gown back. "Well, I can't very well change with you in the room."

When he had gone and locked the door behind him, Tabby slumped onto the bed, the dress growing damp in her grasped hands. The silk was smooth and cool, blue as a sapphire. It was a dress meant to be worn to a ball, where its full skirts could billow out as the wearer twirled in carefree circles. It was a dress meant to be enjoyed. But instead, she would wear it to a dreary theater, surrounded only by the morbidly curious.

She sat there for what might have been minutes or hours, the light from the window gradually growing dimmer and dimmer. "Miss Cooke, are you decent?" came a voice from the other side of the door.

"A moment," she managed to make herself say.

She knew what would happen tonight; Mr. Whitby had been promising it for weeks now. For her part, it wouldn't be anything she hadn't done before. All he would ask her to do was open her mind and make contact. But there was one very important difference; tonight, there would be a corpse beside her. Tonight, she would see the body of the person with whom she must speak.

Stepping into the skirt and attaching the bodice, Tabby felt like Anne Boleyn dressing before her execution. There was a cloudy mirror hanging from a nail on the wall, and she studied her reflection, feeling as far away from her body as the spirits to which she spoke. Then, she took down the mirror, and smashed it against the corner of the washbasin, sending a cascade of slivers onto the floor.

"Are you all right? Miss Cooke?"

No, she was not all right. She was alive, but she was not living. She missed her sister. There was no one for her on this side of the veil save for Eli and Mary-Ruth, and she couldn't see either of them without endangering them. Why had it taken her so long to realize what must be done? Bending down, she selected a long, jagged shard and slipped it into her stocking garter. The rest she kicked under the bed. She might be leaving this spectral plane, but she would not go alone. She would not go without a fight.

"Miss Cooke, I'm coming in there."

The key turned in the lock, and when the man opened the door, he found her perched demurely on the edge of the bed, hands clasped on her lap.

He narrowed his eyes. "I thought I heard something break."

"Did you?" She cast a serene gaze about her. "I didn't hear anything."

"Well, never mind that now. We're going to be late. Are you ready?"

Taking one last cursory glance around the room, she stood and smoothed down her silk skirt, taking comfort in the cool weight of the mirror shard against her leg.

Escape was not an option, not corporeally speaking, in any case. But what could they do to her if she was dead? What could they do to Eli? Would they betray him and send him back to the south? It was a risk, but so long as she was alive, she posed infinitely more of a risk to him.

"I am ready as I will ever be."

29

IN WHICH A SEARCH PARTY IS FORMED.

ELI MUST HAVE been coming back from church
when the hack came to a stop on the steep hill in front of
the boarding house. He looked older than Caleb remembered, much older, his gray hair thinner, his gait stiffer.
More than that, though, he looked tired. Dressed in a
dark wool suit, he was escorting an older black woman,
smiling down at her as they spoke, but as soon as he
looked up and saw Caleb, his expression turned sour.

"Miss Suze, you'll have to excuse me," he said, tipping
his hat to the woman.

The woman gave Caleb a wary look. "You sure?"

"I'm sure," Eli said without taking his stony gaze from
Caleb. "I know this boy. He's trouble, but he wouldn't
be so stupid as to try anything with me."

When she had gone, he turned back to Caleb. "Oh, but
you have some nerve coming here, boy," he said. "Your

face is on every broadsheet between the harbor and the river for your jail break...where you were being held for *murder*," he added in a hiss.

Caleb hadn't expected a warm welcome, but he had at least hoped that the old caretaker would give him a chance to explain. He raised his palms in a gesture of peace and nodded toward Alice. "I'm not here to make trouble. I can explain everything later but there's no time right now. This is Alice, Tabby's sister."

At the introduction, Alice stepped forward, and Eli seemed to notice her for the first time. His face went gray. "You...you look just like her. Tabby never said anything about a sister."

"Is she here?" Alice demanded, without reciprocating the introduction.

Mr. Cooke dragged his gaze away from Alice, before turning to Caleb and giving him a long, hard look. Caleb took an involuntary step back. "I haven't seen Tabby for over a month. She just up and disappeared one day. The police are no help, and no one has seen neither hide nor hair of her."

Caleb felt as if someone had kicked his legs out from under him and he was free-falling. "A month," he repeated. Tabby had been gone for a month. How could he have ever even considered not returning? How could he have thought he could live carefree in Edinburgh while Tabby was in danger?

"Do you know where she's gone?" he asked stupidly.

"If I knew where she was I sure as hell wouldn't tell you," Mr. Cooke said, fumbling in his pocket for his key and climbing the crumbling front steps to the boarding house.

"Please." Alice stopped him with a hand to his sleeve. "Caleb has told me all about you and Tabby, about how you took her in when she was just a girl. I know you only want what is best for her. Please let us help. We think she might be in danger. Do you know of a man named Mr. Whitby?"

Slowly, Mr. Cooke placed the key back in his pocket and stepped off the stoop.

"I don't know of any Mr. Whitby," he said. "Just what kind of danger do you think she's in?"

Caleb opened his mouth, but no words came out. Where to start? Luckily, Alice took over. "We think that there are men behind recent grave robberies in Boston who have her and want to use her for her abilities. We think that she is being held somewhere against her will."

Eli frowned. "Abilities? What are you talking about? Why would grave robbers want Tabby?"

Good lord, Eli didn't know. Tabby had entrusted her secret to Caleb, and not even her own father. He was both humbled and ashamed, but he was spared having to explain any further by footsteps behind him. Caleb turned to find Mary-Ruth standing behind him with arms crossed, her face pale and tight with worry. Wonderful. The only other person who trusted him even less than Mr. Cooke.

Mary-Ruth put her basket down and gave Mr. Cooke a kiss on his cheek. "These folks say Tabby is in some kind of trouble," he said.

"Miss O'Reilly," Caleb said with a tight smile. "How good to see you."

She gave him a scowl and then her lips parted as her gaze landed on Alice. "You look just like her," she said in a whisper.

"Tabby's sister," Caleb hurried to explain. "We think she may be in trouble. There's a man, a Mr. Whitby, who—"

But he didn't have a chance to finish. "Mr. Whitby?"

"You know him?" Caleb asked.

Mary-Ruth nodded, looking uneasy. "Well, I don't know him, but Tabby mentioned him. She was convinced that he murdered Miss Hammond, and was after her, as well. Oh God," she groaned. "She told me she was going to hide, to stay out of sight. I figured that was why I hadn't seen her in so long."

Caleb shared an alarmed look with Alice. This was worse than he'd thought, so much worse. Why had he taken the coward's route and gone to England? Why hadn't he stayed and tried to protect her?

"She had been doing watching for me," Mary-Ruth continued. "The last time I heard from her she had been at Robert Graham's house. She was supposed to send for me when he had passed, but I never heard from her again. I searched everywhere." Mary-Ruth paused. "I had thought…that is, I had hoped that she had left town and was lying low."

Mr. Cooke had lowered himself down onto the step, his face in his hands. "We all of us failed her," he said.

The sky was heavy, looking like it might finally let loose its snow any moment. The day when Caleb had kissed Tabby in the gentle spring air seemed decades ago. He closed his eyes and took a deep breath. It was no use wallowing or giving in to despair. They were going to find her, it was only a question of when and how. They had to start with what they knew. "Who's Robert Graham?" Caleb asked.

Mary-Ruth pushed a dark strand of hair out of her tired eyes. "He is—was—a dean at Harvard, and from a very prominent family. He had a wasting condition and died about a month ago."

A prominent family with ties to Harvard. Caleb gave a dry swallow. "Might…might he have been acquainted with Richard Whitby?"

Mary-Ruth's gaze sharpened. "I would be surprised if they hadn't been acquainted. You don't think…" she trailed off.

"Well, we aren't going to find her standing around here and speculating," Alice said with an impatient huff.

Mary-Ruth nodded. "She's right. We need to go to Robert Graham's house, find out where she might have gone after that."

As Caleb stepped out onto the street to find a hack, he looked around at the small group. They were an army that was prepared to defend Tabby and do everything they could to keep her safe. Wherever she was, he could only hope that she knew how much so many people cared about her.

A small weight lifted in Caleb's chest now that they had the beginning of a plan. The hill was not heavily trafficked, but eventually a hack strained its way up the street and he hailed it.

Mr. Cooke was adjusting his hat, moving toward the hack, and Caleb realized he meant to come. "Someone should stay here in case she comes back," he said.

Scowling, he jabbed a finger at Caleb's chest. "That's my girl, and if you think I'm not going to do everything I can to get her back, then you're thick as they come."

Caleb opened his mouth, but it was Mary-Ruth who put a gentle hand on Mr. Cooke's arm. "Mr. Bishop is right," she said. "This is Tabby's home and when she comes back, she'll want her father there. You won't be helping her by running around the city and putting yourself in harm's way."

With obvious reluctance, Mr. Cooke nodded. "All right. I'll go put some coffee on just in case she's wanting something warm when she comes back. I've been doing the same every day for a month, but maybe today will be the day."

"You two go to the Graham house," Mary-Ruth ordered after Mr. Cooke had gone back inside. "There are some places around the city I can look, and some people to talk to who might know something," she added cryptically.

Caleb didn't like the idea of letting her go off by herself, even if she did seem to be a woman of unusual boldness. What if she ran afoul of the same men who were after Tabby?

Mary-Ruth must have seen the conflicting emotions on his face, because she scowled and said, "I know this city backward and forward, and if anyone can find Tabby, it's me."

There was no use arguing with her; besides, she said this with such conviction that he couldn't help but trust her.

He nodded and watched her hurry down the hill as he and Alice boarded the hack.

What, exactly, would they do when they found Tabby? The best case was that she was simply out of town, staying safe and far away from Mr. Whitby. But he had a feeling that it would not be the best case. Deep inside, he knew that something was very, very wrong.

30

INTO THE LION'S DEN.

"THEY'LL ARREST YOU, you know," Alice told him as they took the brick steps up to the front of the Graham house.

"I know."

"You won't do Tabby much good with a noose around your neck."

Caleb swiped an impatient hand through his unwashed hair before replacing his hat. "And what, exactly, do you propose I do?"

Alice didn't say anything, just pressed her lips together in disapproval as Caleb slammed the brass knocker harder than was strictly necessary.

"What do you know about Mary-Ruth?" Alice asked as they waited.

"Miss O'Reilly?" Caleb frowned. He knew that she guarded Tabby like a precious jewel and that she did not care for him, but that was about all. "She's a friend of Tabby's. Does something with corpses, if I'm not mistaken."

He was about to ask her why she was interested, when the door opened and revealed a clean-shaven man of about forty in a black mourning suit. He raised a brow, no doubt taking in Caleb's unkempt appearance and Alice's travel-worn dress. "Yes?"

Time was of the essence, and it seemed silly to cling to manners and convention, but if there was one language that men of his class understood, it was that of etiquette and manners. Caleb pasted on an apologetic expression and gave him his most winning smile. "Excuse me, I'm so sorry to trouble you, but I believe that you employed a young woman about a month ago to watch a Mr. Graham. I am trying to find her as my uncle is not long for this world, and my aunt specifically requested the services of Miss Cooke."

The man gave him an assessing look, flicked another glance at Alice, and then nodded. "Yes, she was here with my father when he passed." The man paused. "But as you said yourself, that was a month ago. I have not the slightest clue where you would find her now."

Caleb's heart sank. What had he expected? That the man would know exactly where Tabby had gone after and where she was right now? "I'm sorry for your loss," he said. "And for imposing on you during this sad time."

The man shrugged, and was just about to close the door when he paused, his expression turning thoughtful. "Do you know, you're the second person to come looking for her. I wonder if there's not something going around Boston and her services are in high demand. God help us if it's the yellow fever again."

Caleb froze. "Who...who was looking for her?" he asked, trying to sound casual.

But the man didn't seem to hear Caleb's question. He was looking at him with unnerving scrutiny. "You look extraordinarily familiar. Have we met?"

Damn those broadsheets advertising Caleb's escape that Mr. Cooke had mentioned. Caleb flicked his tongue over his dry lips. "I believe we're neighbors. We have probably passed each other in the street a dozen times and then some."

The man was still staring at him. "Yes," he murmured. "I suppose that is it."

Before Caleb could say anything else, the door closed and the man disappeared. Alice shook her head. "I'd say we only have a matter of days, if not hours, before word gets out that you're back in the city and the police come looking for you."

Caleb stopped halfway down the steps, a thought striking him. "The police—that's it!"

"What are you talking about?"

"Come on," said Caleb, taking her by the elbow and practically dragging her the rest of the way down. "We're going to have to go into the lion's den."

They stood outside the police station, their breaths coming out in white puffs in the chill air.

"Are you sure you want to go inside? You could wait out here while I make inquiries."

Caleb nodded. Alice had made a sacrifice for Tabby all those years ago, and now it was his turn. "I have to do it."

Walking with more confidence than he felt, Caleb headed into the station, Alice hesitantly following him.

He had envisioned a swarm of officers descending on him, yelling and clamping him in irons. But on the contrary, he and Alice passed inside with only the briefest of nods from a couple of men loitering in the hall.

Approaching the desk, Caleb had to clear his throat to get the officer's attention. The man looked up from his newspaper, irritated. "Yes?"

"I'm looking for Officer Hodsdon. Is he here?" He assumed that by now Billy's arm had fully healed and he was no longer on guard duty in the prison. If he wasn't, then Caleb risked being arrested before finding him.

The officer gave him a long, hard look before answering. "Sergeant Hodsdon is in his office," he said, jutting his chin vaguely to the hallway behind him.

Sergeant Hodsdon. So, he had gotten his promotion after all, though only God knew how after he had let Caleb escape. Sending up a brief prayer to some higher power, Caleb led Alice down the hallway where they found Billy's office with his name and title neatly stenciled on the door. Caleb lightly rapped.

He almost didn't recognize the man who looked up from his papers at their entrance. Officer Hodsdon had been young and eager, bright eyed and clean-shaven six months ago. But Sergeant Hodsdon had dark smudges under his eyes and a patchy dusting of stubble that spanned from his overgrown side-whiskers down his neck.

If Caleb didn't recognize Sergeant Billy Hodsdon, Billy

certainly recognized Caleb. The pen he had been holding dropped from his hand and he stood bolt upright,
upsetting his chair. "W-what are you doing here?" He
gazed frantically around the small office as if looking
for a weapon or some way to defend himself against this
murderer who had escaped from his custody. Caleb had
only a few seconds before Billy probably started holler-
ing for reinforcements.

"I'm here because of Tabby," Caleb said quickly, putting himself on the other side of the desk.

At this, Billy stopped in his tracks, his face paling to a
worrying shade of green. "What about her?"

"We believe she may be in danger," Alice cut in.

Billy was stock-still for a prolonged moment before he
crumpled back down into his seat and cradled his head
in his hands. "She is, and it's my fault, goddamn me."

Caleb shared an alarmed glance with Alice. "What do
you mean? Where is she?"

Drawing his hands down his face, Billy gave a hopeless shake of his head. He looked like he wanted to bolt
from the office. Alice must have seen this too, because
she stationed herself more squarely in the doorway.

"You need to tell us, now," Caleb said in the sternest
voice he'd ever heard come out of his mouth.

Billy closed his eyes. "Whitby," he finally whispered.
"And Dr. Jameson." He brought his gaze up to meet
squarely with Caleb's. "Do you know who they are? Do
you know *what* they are?"

"I know that Whitby is a conniving son of a bitch,
and that he killed Rose Hammond." He knew it, but
he wanted to hear it from Billy's lips. He wanted vindi-

cation, he wanted justice. But nothing could have prepared him for what came next.

The sound of men talking in the hall drifted in, and the air in the office strained with heavy expectation as Billy finished telling his tale of grave robbers, mediums, the resurrection men, and their morbid exploits trying to bring the dead back to life. Eyes cast down and fingers drumming nervously against the desk, he ended with his role in exposing Tabby to the worst possible people. Caleb and Alice shared a look; it all corroborated what she had told him in Edinburgh.

"You protected them," Caleb said, breaking the silence. "You looked the other way, and then when I told you about Tabby and her gift, you delivered her up to them." His fists flexed at his sides, his blood rushing hot and fast to his head. He could never take on a man like Billy in a fight, but still he imagined his fists connecting with his jaw, pummeling him into a bloody pulp.

"They paid me handsomely for turning a blind eye, and made sure that I climbed the ranks. And I wanted to contact my mother, was desperate to speak to her one more time. I knew the information about Tabby would be valuable to them, and that I could use it to my benefit, as well." His voice dropped and to his credit, he looked genuinely miserable. "I was always fond of Miss Cooke, exceedingly fond." He paused. "I'm not proud of what I did."

Alice spat on the floor. "You're pathetic," she ground out.

"I'm prepared to make amends, but I have to know for certain before I do that you are truly innocent. I cannot have something else on my conscience." He hesitated. "Did you kill Rose Hammond?"

"On my honor, I did not," Caleb said, before adding: "I think we both know that it was Whitby."

Billy gave a slow, heavy nod. "With this kind of work, you develop a sense for these things. You want to believe that the charming and the wealthy are above such barbarity, but often they are the ones hiding the darkest sins. I saw Whitby watch as that doctor strapped her to the table. I should have known that they wouldn't be true to their word, but I so badly wanted to believe that their goal was admirable." He looked up at Caleb. "We played cards together, and I came to think of us as something like friends. You betrayed that trust, but whether it makes me a fool or not, I believe you."

Caleb's heart raced, went light, and felt as if it might fly away from him. He wouldn't have to go back to prison. He wouldn't hang for a murder he didn't commit, and Rose would finally have justice.

Billy must have seen the hope on his face, because he shook his head. "I can't let you go. Even if you are innocent of the murder, you still escaped custody. That's a serious crime in and of itself. I can't expect that they will be so lax as to overlook my letting you go a second time."

"But Tabby—" Caleb started, only for Billy to stop him.

"I am giving you her whereabouts in exchange for your freedom." Billy took out a leaf of paper and scrawled something on it before handing it to Alice. "Take this and find her before something terrible happens to her." He turned back to Caleb. "But I cannot let you go, and I think you know that."

Well, what had Caleb expected? That he would waltz in, apologize for escaping, and then go on his merry way? Given what he knew about Billy's involvement in the scheme, Caleb would be well within his rights to threaten him right back. But was it worth risking any harm coming to Tabby? Reluctantly, he turned to Alice, took her by the shoulders, and looked straight into her clear eyes.

"Go find Mary-Ruth and take her to that address." He was entrusting Tabby's well-being—and possibly life—to two young women who would have no one to protect them, no one to fall back on should anything go wrong. The police certainly couldn't be trusted.

As if reading his thoughts, Alice drew herself up and gave him the same obstinate tilt of her chin that Tabby so often employed. "She's my sister, and I assure you that no one will fight for her harder than I will."

The past months should have taught Caleb that there were so many more things beyond his control than he would have ever thought possible as a young man of wealth. It was a hard lesson to learn, and one that he had to learn over and over. More than anything he wanted to be able to go to her, to make things right. He nodded reluctantly and then, on impulse, gave Alice a kiss on the cheek. "I know."

31

IN WHICH THE DEAD DANCE.

WITH A MAN on each elbow, Tabby was escorted into the auditorium, the reassuring weight of the mirror reminding her with every step that her nightmare would be over soon. They led her up the same back steps Tabby had taken that fateful day when she had gone to the library, only one floor below. They must not have wanted to risk taking her up the main stairs where she might try to escape, or plead with a passerby for help. Tabby stifled a bitter laugh; they might have known by now that she was completely and utterly broken. She would not try to escape even if they left her alone in the middle of a busy road.

After the first few interviews Mr. Whitby and Dr. Jameson conducted with her, Tabby was allowed to sit in a chair with no restraints. But today it was back to the table like the first time. They had given her a drink, told her that it would relax her and make her more receptive to messages from the other side. Tabby drifted in and out of consciousness, whatever had been in her drink making her drowsy and sluggish.

Her palms were clammy, her mouth dry as cotton. A fly was trapped somewhere in the room, its nervous buzzing an incessant assault on her ears. The silk dress with its cotton underpinnings felt like burlap against her skin, every breath painful and labored. Everything felt at once magnified, yet impossibly far away and distant.

The sound of feet shuffling in and excited murmurs filled the small theater with echoes. It appeared there would be an audience. Did these men have no shame? They might have unearthed corpses under the cover of night, but they were brazen in their experiments, treating them like nothing more than the removal of an appendix or extraction of a bad tooth.

Mr. Whitby was addressing his fellow members of the society, making expansive hand gestures and pontificating about the noble pursuit of eternal life. He was more animated than she had ever seen him before. It was only a matter of time before she would be expected to perform her party trick, and memories of sitting in her aunt's parlor with sweaty palms and a pit of dread in her stomach came storming back.

Eventually the sound of wheels rolling on wood cut through the taut silence of the theater. Lifting her head as much as her restraints would allow, Tabby caught a glimpse of a gurney being pushed by Dr. Ferris. A sheet covered the gurney, but Tabby could make out the outline of a body beneath it, and despite the stale, antiseptic air, a shiver ran down her spine.

"Now, Miss Bellefonte," said Dr. Jameson, coming into view. "We only have a few preparations to complete, and then we'll be needing your services. Is there anything I can fetch for you to make the process smoother? Anything that will help facilitate contact?"

He sounded as if he were hosting a dinner party and she was simply his esteemed guest. Tabby stared up at the thin face and brown beard to see if he was joking, but she was met with only a probing gaze. When she didn't say anything, he gave a sigh and shook his head. "It's unfortunate that such an ability should be bestowed on someone of the weaker sex, though I suppose the female's sensitive nature is what makes them more conducive to receiving communication from the other side."

It had been years since Tabby indulged in missing her mother, but she missed her now with a longing that shot through her body like hungry fire. Even Eli seemed distant, like he belonged to a life lived long ago. What she wouldn't give to be far away from this cold, sterile place, and back in the cemetery with the familiar headstones and the sounds of the city, Eli singing a hymn under his breath as he weeded.

Someone had wheeled the gurney so close to her that she could smell the faint scent of lime and decay. The sheet had been removed, revealing the prostrate body of a woman, and a wave of nausea came over Tabby.

The way Tabby saw it, she had two options.

One: Lie. Tell them it didn't work. How would they know if she had opened her mind or not? She could simply say she had and that no communication had come through. Perhaps she could lie about what the spirit said, tell them just what they wanted to hear. But what exactly *did* they want to hear?

Two: be a good girl and open her mind, faithfully relaying everything the spirit said, thus helping Mr. Whitby reach his abhorrent goal.

As far as options went, they weren't ideal. She felt a surge of protectiveness for the spirit of the dead woman. How would she reassure this poor spirit that she would be all right? *Would* she be all right? Or were Whitby and Jameson damning her to some kind of unspeakable hell? In the previous experiments, Tabby had simply had to open her mind and make contact. There had never been a corpse in the room. She thought of Mr. Graham's dying words, and fought another wave of nausea at the memory of bodies dancing with electricity.

A hush fell over the small assembly, and Tabby had to squint against the blinding light that suddenly shone in her face. Dr. Jameson cleared his throat and thanked Mr. Whitby for his opening words before launching into his own speech.

"Today we are gathered here to witness a new stage in the cycle of life. We are familiar with birth, with death, and now we seek to understand *re*birth. I know that there is frustration at the perceived lack of progress, but I would be remiss in not pointing out that there is no such thing as a wasted experiment. Every experiment that we ran in the past that did not give us our desired outcome led us one step closer to this day." He gestured to Tabby. "But we now have a valuable new tool that will bring us even further in our search. Will we see the spark of life re-kindled today? It is possible, but not likely. Again, I urge patience and to remember that the scientific process is a slow, methodical one, as it should be."

He sounded so reasonable, so logical. Tabby wished she could see the faces of the men in the audience, see how they reacted. How long had these experiments been going on? How many people in Boston were privy to the grotesque pageantries played out in this theater?

His speech concluded, Dr. Jameson bowed to light applause. Tabby twisted her neck to the side so that the corpse on the gurney filled her vision. Though the deep lines etched around the woman's eyes and mouth spoke of a hard life, she was not old, perhaps thirty at most. She was covered by a sheet up to her neck, but in a dramatic flourish, Dr. Jameson flicked it down, revealing her bare chest. Tabby closed her eyes, unwilling to partake in the titillating spectacle that drew murmurs from the audience of men.

He spoke as he moved about the corpse, applying all manner of clamps and wires to the cold, hard flesh. When he was finished, he called for absolute quiet from the audience. "Now, Miss Bellefonte. I am going to ask you some questions about the woman beside you, just to establish that you're truly in possession of the abilities attributed to you. If you answer these to satisfaction, I will remove the bindings and you may sit in a chair, or however is most conducive to you."

She would cooperate, for now. She did not believe that anything she did would actually help them achieve their goal of reanimation. How could it? Taking a deep breath, she focused her intention, and tried not to think about the men leaning forward in their seats to watch her. She would pretend she was on the church steps as she had so many other times, the reassuring nocturnal sounds of Boston around her. Grudgingly, she gave a small nod.

"Good. Now, tell me the name of the woman beside you."

It was not easy to clear her mind, to make it an open vessel, not when her heart was pounding with fear and there were dozens of men watching her. But if she was going to do this, she was going to do it right, for the sake of the poor woman beside her.

Closing her eyes, Tabby let go. Let go of the tension in her body, let go of the fear and worry swirling in her mind, let go of the hatred and anger she had for these men. Gradually, the glare of the kerosene lamps dimmed to nothing, and the stifling blackness encroached on the corners of her mind. When she could no longer hear the coughing and shifting of the audience, Tabby reached out through the darkness.

Hello? My name is Tabby, and I know you must be very frightened right now, but I must speak to you. I promise to do everything in my power to help you, whether that is relaying any messages you may have, or helping you find peace.

There was no response. *Please*, Tabby tried again, *tell me your name.*

She waited. Still nothing. Perhaps the spirit had moved on, far beyond the reach of even Tabby's abilities. What would Dr. Jameson do if she was unable to provide answers to his questions?

Just when she thought the darkness would suffocate her,

the smallest of stirrings blew through the ether, and before her stood a woman, not naked and stiff and covered in wires, but unmistakably the same fair-haired woman as on the gurney.

The woman looked at her with dark, bottomless eyes. *Why do you call me? Where am I?*

Tabby might have told her that she was in an operating theater, that she was the unwitting subject of a dreadful experiment, but she could not risk frightening her off.

You have passed on, Tabby said gently. *I have called you back to the in-between place so that I might speak with you.*

A taut, nervous smile spread over the woman's colorless lips, even as her eyes dilated with panic. *You must be mistaken. I am simply sleeping. Surely you can see my two little babies that I tucked into bed so sweetly last night? Surely you can see how they wake and stir and look for their mama? I was only feeling so tired that I had to lie down and rest. It is only for a little while, and then I will wake up and rock my babies in my lap and sing them their favorite songs.*

Tabby winced. The dead who knew not that they were dead were the hardest to speak to. They were ever hopeful, though hope could quickly turn to desperation. *Of course. You are right, I must be mistaken*, Tabby said in soothing, placating tones. *But please, what is your name?*

I am Nancy Doyle, wife of Peter Doyle. I live above a dry goods shop in the West End, and I am twenty-eight years old. Her voice was hollow. *I don't see why you need to know this, though.* The spirit looked about her at the dark void. *This is truly the strangest dream*, she mused. *I can almost feel the cold upon my skin as if I walked through a frigid winter's night.*

Tabby bowed her head in thanks and prepared to return to the land of the living. *Thank you. I may have yet more questions to ask you when I return.*

The spirit's eyes went wild as she stretched out a skeletal arm toward Tabby. *Wait! Where are you going? Please, don't leave me in this dark place!*

Tabby pushed aside her guilt. If she had not been doing this for Mr. Whitby, she would have taken her time, soothed and assured the woman. *I will come back. I promise.*

The darkness receded, and with it, the terrified face of the woman, her echoing pleas. Opening her eyes, Tabby found Dr. Jameson staring down at her with a mixture of wonder and impatience. She hated giving him what he wanted.

"Well?" he asked. "What is her name?"

"Her name is Nancy Doyle. She has—had—two children, and lived above a dry goods shop in the West End."

A gasp rippled through the audience and even Dr. Jameson looked fleetingly surprised before his expression changed to one of smug satisfaction. "Very good, Miss Bellefonte. Now," he said, extending a hand, "would you care to have a seat?"

Tabby hesitated. She fingered the mirror shard through her skirt, the promise of release only a quick cut away. She could go now, join Nancy on the other side and never look back. She could join Rose, and finally be reunited with her mother and father. Dr. Jameson had his back to her as he pulled out a chair, and Mr. Whitby was speaking with Dr. Ferris. She flexed her fingers. All it would take was one quick motion and she would have it in her hand. But she thought of the frightened woman wandering the darkness, and with a sinking feeling, she knew that she could not run until she had seen this through. Mute, she nodded.

Mr. Whitby faced the audience. "You have seen that she is indeed able to establish contact with the spirit of the deceased. Now we will introduce a current of electricity to the corpse, bringing about a marriage of the flesh and the spirit, reunited again."

As Dr. Jameson helped her to a seated a position, a wave of dizziness went through her at being upright. From her new vantage point, she could see the faces of the men in the audience, a homogenous sea of pale skin and dark suits.

"Miss Cooke, this time when you make contact, it is imperative that you call the spirit back. She must return to her body. When the moment is right, we will start her heart. Convince her to manifest herself once again in her mortal shell."

Tabby did not think that it would be so simple, prayed that it would not be so simple, but once more she steeled herself and entered the ether. She had never been quite sure how time worked in this in-between space, and didn't know if Nancy had thought her gone for a few moments, hours, days, or some other measure of time entirely. But no sooner had she slipped all the way under than a commotion in the theater yanked her back to the here and now.

There was something happening at the door, causing a great amount of excitement in the audience. "Excuse me," Dr. Jameson said, rushing forward, "this is a closed theater. You must be a student of mine, or a member of the club." His face grew red as he saw just who was at the door. "And there are *certainly* no ladies allowed."

At this, Tabby sat forward and followed Dr. Jameson's line of sight to where a flustered man in a white apron was trying to hold back two women from entering. All she could see of the second woman was a glimpse of a brown plaid skirt, but she immediately recognized Mary-Ruth, and she caught her breath. Was she dreaming? Was this some cruel effect of the draught they had given her?

"I'll take care of this," Dr. Ferris said, striding to the door. "Begin the current. I don't want any more delays."

"Tabby!" Mary-Ruth cried as she struggled to twist free of Mr. Whitby's grip.

Tabby's heart at once leapt in joy at seeing her friend, and recoiled at the same time. "Mary-Ruth?" she croaked before finding her voice. "You shouldn't be here! Go!"

The audience was on their feet, the corpse beside her jerking and dancing like a limp marionette. This had to be some sort of hallucination, a terrible dream.

"Let go of me!" Mary-Ruth said, swatting away Dr. Ferris. "Tabby, come with us!"

The mirror forgotten, Tabby struggled to force her sluggish legs to move. But no sooner than she was out of her seat than Dr. Jameson was lunging toward her, a balled-up rag in his hand. He caught her by the waist and, despite her struggles, pressed the cloth against her mouth. Her head went light and just before the world went completely black, she could have sworn that she saw her sister's face.

32

IN WHICH THE FUTURE COMES TO PASS.

THERE HAD BEEN a brief, preternaturally calm moment before all hell had broken loose in which Alice had locked eyes with her sister for the first time in over twelve years.

Alice had expected the theater to be bright and clean, but when they had entered, they were met instead with dimmed lamps throwing dramatic shadows on the dark walls. It felt more like a performance than a medical experiment.

It had all happened so fast; first she and Mary-Ruth were on one side of the door, holding their breath, and then they were pushing through, an eruption of male voices greeting them. She'd known that their presence in a medical theater would have raised a few brows at least, but she had not been prepared for utter chaos that two women could cause simply with their entrance.

"Out!" The man in the white apron was propping up an unconscious Tabby with one arm, and gesturing wildly at them with the other. The feeling of pure hot anger came flooding back to her, the way she used to feel when she shielded Tabby from one of their aunt's stinging blows.

Mary-Ruth had broken free of the doctor and was tugging her arm. "We don't leave under any circumstances," she hissed. "This may be our only chance."

She didn't need to convince Alice; there was no way that she would let Tabby out of her sight now that she'd found her again.

The other man, the one who had been watching from the side, turned toward her. He had cold blue eyes and an angular face that radiated arrogance and contempt. It could only be Mr. Whitby.

As soon as those eyes locked on her, he went pale, as if he had seen a ghost. Then he was striding toward them, up through the wooden balcony seats. "No! They do not leave." He motioned to a man, and before she knew what was happening, the door was being closed behind them.

Alice threw a look at Mary-Ruth, panicked. But in the short time of their acquaintance, she should have learned that Mary-Ruth was tougher than her tall, slender figure and delicate features belied.

"I am sure these esteemed gentlemen do not want to be party to kidnapping," Mary-Ruth said.

Mr. Whitby smiled, a surprisingly charming and genuine smile. "These esteemed gentlemen understand that scientific advancement sometimes demands extreme measures."

The men in question seemed intrigued and a little non-plussed, but hardly shocked or outraged. Did they not understand just what they were witnessing? "Mr. Whitby and this—" she gestured at the man in the white apron "—this *doctor* are holding my sister against her will, using her for grotesque experiments!"

She waited for the men in the audience to object, to spring into action, but if they were concerned with the ethical ramifications of what was happening, no one said anything. Mr. Whitby threw a look at the doctor, some silent signal passing between them.

A moment later the man in the white apron was taking Alice by the arm, and tugging her toward the auditorium floor. She dug in her heels, but it was no use. From behind her she could hear Mary-Ruth's vain protests.

All those years ago Alice had left her little sister cold and alone, sitting on the steps of a church in an unfamiliar city. She'd done it because she'd thought it was the only way to keep her safe, to protect her. But now, as she gazed helpless at Tabby's limp form, she knew with a heart-wrenching certainty that she had been wrong. They should have stayed together, no matter what.

"Remove her," Mr. Whitby ordered with a nod toward Mary-Ruth. "Somewhere she can't cause any trouble. And send for the police—Sergeant Hodsdon will take care of this. He's one of ours."

Alice watched helplessly as Mary-Ruth was roughly escorted from the auditorium. She wanted to go after her, but Mary-Ruth would be all right. It was Tabby who needed her now the most.

The men took their seats again. Normalcy returned,

as if they were simply attending the most mundane of lectures, and two women hadn't just barged in, another drugged before their eyes.

"I apologize for the interruption," Mr. Whitby was saying. "Unfortunately, as our subject had to be subdued with the use of drugs, we will not be able to continue with her."

An older man with full white side-whiskers and a long, austere face stood up with the help of a cane. "How long will you continue to delay? It's been nearly fifteen years, and I expect to see some return on my investment before I find myself on the slab."

A few other men murmured and nodded their agreement.

So the audience was more concerned with money than the well-being of a young woman. Alice's heart sank even further; no one here would help them.

Mr. Whitby held up a hand to silence them. He may have been an evil man, but he had a commanding presence and knew just the right words to say to calm his wary investors. "Gentlemen, I understand your frustration, and I share in it. But as is the nature of this kind of work, we are beholden to the whims of nature and womankind. Fortunately, we may yet see a demonstration today."

It took Alice a moment to realize just what he meant as all gazes shifted to her.

"Miss Bellefonte, perhaps you do not remember me," he said as he forcibly guided her to a seat on the auditorium floor. "But I remember you."

Alice stilled, taken off guard. She did remember him.

He had worn a beard then, and in her child's eye he had appeared almost larger than life. But she would have recognized that slippery-smooth voice anywhere. It had been the voice that had ordered her out of the carriage after she had been snatched from the Boston street. It was the voice that had demanded that she speak to the dead, and then had berated her in disgust when she could not. That voice had haunted her for years, and now here he was, in the flesh.

If Tabby had not been sitting mere feet away, prostrate and vulnerable, and the door not sealed, Alice would have given him a sharp kick where it hurt the most, and bolted. But she would not leave without her sister, so she allowed herself to be roughly handled and seated.

"I also remember that you do not possess the same gift as your sister," he continued. "Pity." He leaned against the marble slab where the corpse still lay, and crossed his arms. "I did always wonder if perhaps you simply needed some motivation in finding your powers."

Alice had never been able to harness her second sight, not the way Tabby had been able to harness her clairvoyance, but then again, she had never really tried. She'd allowed the future to come to her in flashes, dreams, and that had been enough. But Mr. Whitby didn't know about her second sight, and probably didn't care. He wanted her to speak with the dead, as Tabby did.

When Mr. Whitby turned around, he was brandishing a menacing silver instrument. "We all of us contain a great reserve of power, yet most of us will go through life without ever trying to mine that reserve. Perhaps we all have something of your sister's gift, but have just not yet learned how to access it. Perhaps we are all of us conduits to the great beyond." He paused, clearly moved by his own words. "Miss Bellefonte, this is my gift to you—the motivation to find within yourself the extraordinary gift that you have heretofore taken for granted."

Alice spat, hitting Mr. Whitby neatly on his polished brown shoes. It was satisfying in the extreme, but the only acknowledgment he gave was a slightly raised brow. "You're only making this more difficult for yourself. You only have to open your mind, accept the message that this spirit wishes to impart."

The corpse beside her was still, but she had caught a glimpse of it jerking around when she had first come in, as if it would sit up and get off the table. Dr. Jameson caught her gaze. "The simplest thing in the world, Miss Bellefonte," he said, not unkindly. "Relax your mind and your body, let yourself become an open receptacle."

"Relax my body, should I?" she said, jutting her chin at the silver tool Mr. Whitby still clutched in his hand.

The doctor frowned. "Richard, perhaps we could forgo the forceps?"

When Mr. Whitby had placed the instrument back on the table, Alice made her decision. She would mine her reserve, as Mr. Whitby had instructed. She would relax her mind and invite her intuition to take over. She would do everything they said, just not for the results they were hoping for.

With a curt nod, Alice closed her eyes. Her heart was pounding, her worry for Tabby nearly debilitating. She just needed time. They might think that Sergeant Hodsdon was one of their own, but she prayed that his revelation of conscience was strong enough. She just needed time until he got there.

"Good, *good*, Miss Bellefonte. I am so glad to see that you are willing to cooperate in this most noble venture. I thank you, and the scientific community thanks you. Now, please tell me the name of the woman beside you."

Alice had no idea what the woman's name was, and she certainly had no idea how to find out. But she would give the men here a show that they would not soon forget. Rocking back and forth in her seat, she began a low hum that grew into a wail, the eldritch sound of it making even her hair stand on end.

"What are you doing?" Mr. Whitby asked urgently. He turned to the doctor. "What is she doing?"

Her eyes were still closed, but she could hear the doctor. "Perhaps this is her method. We must let it take its course."

The humming had been strictly for the benefit of the men, but the wail that continued to spill from her throat was real, the result of her mind being yanked and wrenched in unnatural directions. Then the voices grew fuzzy and faraway. Alice was standing in a white expanse so like the void of her dreams, and yet different. Light where the void was dark, open where that was suffocating.

An image flashed before her, a tall, raven-haired woman that she now recognized as Mary-Ruth. She was standing on the bank of a river, wind in her hair as she smiled up at Alice. Her heart swelled with love. Then the image shifted, and Alice was looking out over a vast battlefield, the aftermath of a terrible skirmish. Though carrion birds pecked and squabbled amongst the carnage, there was no sound accompanying the images. There was a war coming to this country, and soon. She wanted to retch, the sheer magnitude of it all becoming unbearable, but then the image was shifting again. Scene after scene, some containing recognizable faces and places, others so foreign that she could hardly believe they were real. *Whitby. I need Whitby.*

It was not the future that would give her the answers that she needed about Mr. Whitby, but the past. Her conversation with Caleb in Edinburgh came back to her and she remembered the jest about his alias, how stupid she had thought it at the time. She remembered the conversation they'd shared about the grave robbers, and all the details therein.

Her head pounded, the white of the expanse blinding her. And then there it was. Everything she needed.

33

THROUGH THE VEIL AND BACK AGAIN.

TABBY'S EYES WERE heavy and dry, but she forced herself to open them. For a disorienting moment, she expected to see the cracks in the ceiling of her prison room, but instead it was the dimly lit rafters of the auditorium that greeted her.

Voices. No, just one voice. A feminine voice that tickled at the edges of her memory. Then she recalled the glimpse of face that had flashed before her. Alice. Could it be? Was her sister really here?

Still too weak to move much, Tabby gingerly turned her head so that she could see the red-haired woman in the brown plaid dress, careful not to draw any attention to herself.

Alice was sitting straight as a board in the chair, eyes closed, mouth moving. She was more beautiful than Tabby remembered, mature and dignified, and all at once the magnitude of the time they'd lost together hit her. But there was no time for sentimentality. Tabby forced herself to focus, to parse out her sister's words from the ringing in her ears.

"I have made contact with a spirit, though it is not the spirit that you wished me to reach." A heavy, drawn-out pause. "A man."

Mr. Whitby's voice, eager. "What man? What is his name?"

"A Mr. Pope," she said. "He comes bearing a message for you, Mr. Whitby."

"Are you certain?" Tabby could hear the frown in his voice. "I know of no Mr. Pope."

"That may be, but he knows you, and what you have done."

As soon as Caleb set foot back in the holding cell, it was as if the last six months had never happened. The leak in the corner was still dripping, a fresh crop of drunkards was lazing about, and the air was still damp and heavy.

He sat down on the bench, but was too nervous to be idle for long, and jumped up again, pacing back and forth. He hadn't liked watching Alice disappear out the door and he liked the idea of her confronting Mr. Whitby even less. The worst part of being imprisoned again wasn't the foul air or the pungent belches of his cell mates, but that he had no clue what was happening in the world beyond the damp stone walls.

He was wearing grooves in the floor with his pacing when Billy approached the bars. "They're going to move you to Charles Street, they're just waiting for the cart."

Caleb nodded. It was off to the big new prison across the city for him. He'd known that he couldn't expect any liberties or concessions. He was an escaped convict, wanted for murder. The drunk cell was too good for him.

"Sergeant? Sergeant!" A man, out of breath and hatless, tumbled into the hall. He looked around and, on seeing Billy, panted a big sigh of relief. "Sergeant Hodsdon," he said. "You're needed at the Harvard Medical School. There's been an incident."

Caleb stopped his pacing, and a silent, alarmed look passed between him and Billy. Tabby was there, and they had sent Alice and Mary-Ruth. He rushed up to the bars.

"What's happened? Is there a young woman—women—involved? Is everyone there all right?"

The man ignored him, instead whispering something into Billy's ear. Caleb could have bent the bars and taken the man by the shoulders, shaking the information out of him.

"Billy, please." Caleb reached for his sleeve through the bars, aware that he was very close to being thrown in some dank, forgotten cell in the basement. "Regardless of whatever anger you still have toward me, you have to help her."

Billy looked down at his hand on his sleeve and slowly removed it. The look he leveled on Caleb contained no hint of kindness or understanding.

"Mr. Bishop," he said, and Caleb's heart sank at the formality of his tone. "You overreach yourself." Without a backward glance, Billy strode purposefully after the man, sliding his club into his belt.

"You have to stop them!" Caleb shouted after his retreating back. "Whatever happens, you have to save Tabby!"

Alice was magnificent. Tabby didn't know where the words were coming from, but each one found their mark with biting accuracy.

"Mr. Pope knows your darkest secret, knows that which you would keep hidden."

Mr. Whitby shot a worried glance at the spectators before composing himself. "You may tell your Mr. Pope that I am an open book. I have no secrets, and what's more, I am not interested in unfounded, malicious accusations. We are here to create new life. If Mr. Pope will not help us, then he must step aside so some more obliging spirit can make contact."

Dr. Jameson stayed Mr. Whitby with a hand. "It's remarkable that she was able to make contact at all, given her history with such things. We should allow her to progress as she sees fit."

Tabby's eyes had finally adjusted, and she could not look away from the spectacle, never mind that they might discover she was awake at any moment. Mr. Whitby muttered something and tugged at his collar, the roots of his hair dark with perspiration.

Alice continued, raising her voice to be heard over the bickering of the two men. "Who is Rose?" she asked. "Mr. Pope keeps speaking of a Rose."

Mr. Whitby's face went pale green, a spasm at the corner of his mouth the only indication that he had heard her.

"Rose Hammond," she continued. Then she tilted her

head, as if listening to something no one else could hear. Her hand flew to her mouth. "He says you killed her. You killed her in cold blood."

A murmur ran through the audience. It took Mr. Whitby an overlong moment, but then he was exploding from his vantage point beside the table. "Lies! I don't know what you're on about. I—"

But he didn't have a chance to finish. Alice was rising from her seat, shouting over the din of the audience and Mr. Whitby's outburst. "He says you killed her, and that you will rot in prison for it! You murdered her as sure as you kidnapped and drugged my sister!"

Dr. Jameson turned to Mr. Whitby. "Is this true, Richard? We agreed from the start that there would be no blood on our hands."

"Of course it's not true!" Mr. Whitby roared. "She's a fraud. She can no more speak to the dead than I can!"

Be careful, Tabby willed her sister. In baiting Mr. Whitby, Alice was teetering on a dangerous precipice.

"It was Caleb Bishop," Mr. Whitby ground out. "The boy murdered her. If he wasn't guilty then he wouldn't have been arrested—twice—and escaped from prison."

Alice gave a thoughtful shake of her head, her eyes still closed. "Mr. Pope is quite insistent that it was you. He says there was an earring, a sapphire. You kept it after you killed her, as a sort of trophy."

How on earth did Alice know about the earring? Tabby had assumed that her sister was putting on a show, but she knew details, things she couldn't have known otherwise. Did she, in fact, have the same abilities as Tabby?

But when Tabby searched in the ether for a Mr. Pope, there was no spirit of that name.

Mr. Whitby scoffed. "An earring? That doesn't mean anything."

Dr. Jameson was listening, rapt. "Richard," he said, finally pulling his gaze from Alice. "It's true, isn't it."

"You killed her for your late partner's business," Alice said evenly. "You killed her in the parlor, choking the life out of her, and then you stabbed her dead body again and again."

"Miss Bellefonte, I am warning you. If you—"

But Alice continued, speaking over him. "You didn't mean to kill her, did you? It just happened, and before you knew it, it was too late. I know that you loved her. It must have hurt to see her with the very man who had taken your business from you, as well. You stayed silent, but all the while the woman you loved cared for you no more than the most casual of acquaintances. You could never hope she would return your love, of course. How could any woman, let alone a gentle, sweet woman like Rose Hammond, love a monster such as yourself?"

In an instant he was rushing toward Alice, just as he had done to Tabby in his study. He was going to hurt her, kill her, right there in front of all those respectable men. Tabby willed her sluggish body to come to life, but she had no more feeling in her legs than she did in her heavy tongue. She was going to watch Mr. Whitby kill her sister and she was helpless to stop him.

Dr. Jameson was just stepping in front of Mr. Whitby, hands out, when there was a heavy thud from the gallery.

"Open the door!" came a muffled cry. "In the name of the police, open the door!"

Mr. Whitby stopped in his tracks, his fist still raised as if he had only just stopped himself from swinging it.

"That will be Sergeant Hodsdon," Dr. Jameson said. "Come, Richard. Be reasonable and leave the girl alone."

She watched as a spectrum of emotions wrestled across Mr. Whitby's face. At his outburst, all sounds had stopped in the theater. Kidnapping, coercion, and drugging were all acceptable in the name of science, but it seemed that the murder of a young woman was a bridge too far, even for the learned men gathered there.

Mr. Whitby's expression turned introspective, as if he'd forgotten where he was. His hand trembled as he absently adjusted his crisp neckcloth. "I didn't go there with the intent to kill her, only to talk. I had to make her understand how I felt about her, and why it was so hurtful, so *disrespectful* that she would continue her engagement to Caleb, the man who had inherited the business that should have been mine. But she wouldn't listen, and things grew heated between us. I put my hands around her neck, just enough to make her listen, but she wouldn't stop struggling. I never meant to kill her," he repeated dully. "It was pure luck that she and Caleb were heard arguing earlier in the evening. That helped me immensely."

Tabby somehow found the strength to hoarsely ask: "But what about the stabbing? Why stab her once you had already strangled her?"

Mr. Whitby frowned at her, then gave a little shrug. "I of all people know what can become of a pristine corpse.

It was my last act of love, to save her from such men as myself."

The old man with the cane stood up again. "When I invested in this venture, it was with the understanding that all the bodies used would be those of criminals or the insane. I will not be party to such depravity. I want my money back." More men stood up, shouting their displeasure and waving hats in the air.

It was then that the gallery door finally gave, and Sergeant Hodsdon came storming in, a half-dozen uniformed officers behind him. Like rats scattering from a sinking ship, the men in the audience fled, no doubt afraid that their own participation would be grounds for arrest.

"I think we've seen enough," Sergeant Hodsdon said, a pair of irons open and ready in his hand. "Richard Whitby, you are hereby placed under arrest for the murder of Rose Hammond."

Mr. Whitby came back to himself. "You can't arrest me!" he roared. "We paid you! You are just as complicit as any man here!"

Sergeant Hodsdon was silent as he placed the irons around Mr. Whitby's wrists. More officers were pouring in now, and Dr. Jameson sadly held his hands in front him, waiting for his own set of irons to be placed around them.

Tabby finally met Alice's eye from across the floor. A current as strong as electricity passed between them. But what little strength she had found to confront Mr. Whitby had long since dissolved, and when next she closed her eyes, she did not open them again for a long time.

34

"WHEN WE TWO PARTED."

"SHH, SHE'S WAKING up!"

She had been floating, her body light and inconsequential. This was not the pressing darkness of the in-between place, and she couldn't be dead because her head was pounding like the devil, her bladder was full, and there was a sour gnawing in her stomach. But she let herself drift a little longer, clinging to this comfortable nothingness like a dream, afraid to wake up and find herself in that horrid place again.

This time when the world slowly came into focus, it was not the kerosene lamps nor the sterile wood gallery of the operating theater, but the familiar eaves of her small room in the boarding house attic. The dim light coming through the little window was too much, though, and she closed her eyes again. Around her, she could feel the heat and presence of people gathered in the tiny space.

"Tabby, can you hear me?"

The Irish voice was low and sweet, like liquid velvet, and Tabby had never heard anything more welcome in her life. "Mary-Ruth," she croaked.

"That's right, dearest. And Alice is here, too."

"Hello, Tabby."

It took Tabby a minute to place what she was seeing, *who* she was seeing. Had she slipped back into the ether? Had she finally made contact with the one person who had eluded her after all these years? But no, there was no darkness, no terrible wind, no creeping sense of dread. She was tucked safe in her room and the woman who stood before her was as real as the cold rain that fell in needles against the window.

Tabby gave a little cry and, mindless of her sluggish legs and aching head, was out of bed and across the room in a flash. All resentment, all loneliness was forgotten as she felt her sister's arms close around her.

"I'll wait outside," Mary-Ruth said, closing the door behind her.

"Oh God, Alice," she said between sobs into her shoulder. She was twelve years old, scared that if she let go she would never see her sister again.

Alice was stroking her hair, then holding her at arm's length and surveying her with her clear, sharp eyes. "I'm so sorry, Tabby. I never meant to leave you. I only wanted to make sure that you were safe. If…if you can't forgive me, I would understand."

All these years she had lived with a hole in her heart, a wound that would not heal. Her sister had not been quite a ghost, but not quite living either, so Tabby had neither body to mourn, nor hope to cling to. As she looked at Alice now, she felt the raw edges of her heart begin to fuse and heal. So this was what those mad resurrection men sought to do. This was the second chance that they strove to bring about. But their reasons were tainted by money and power; Mr. Whitby, Dr. Jameson, and the rest would never understand the tender beating of a heart and what it meant. They would never understand that only love could cross such a divide.

"There's nothing to be sorry for." She allowed herself to hold Alice for as long as she could, before her legs began to tremble and she had to get back into bed. When she was warmly tucked back in, she gazed at her sister, committing to memory the clearness of her sharp, intelligent eyes, the way her lips curved up ever so slightly in the smile that she'd given to Tabby when trying to reassure her as children.

"Where have you been? And why are you back now?"

"I think that may be a conversation for another time," Alice said. "A time when the dust has settled from the last few days."

Though Tabby was burning with curiosity, she knew her sister was right; there would be time now, all the time in the world. "What happened in the last few days, exactly?" Memories of a faceless audience of men, of a chalk-white corpse beneath a sheet flitted through her pounding head.

There was a brittle silence before Alice spoke. "You were part of some experiment, taken by Mr. Whitby to help him communicate with the spirit world in his quest for resurrecting the dead."

Tabby didn't need to be reminded of all that. She would have the tang of chemicals, Dr. Jameson's greedy eyes, and Mr. Whitby's cold, dispassionate voice bored into her memory until the day she died, and perhaps beyond.

"He was arrested, and when the public gets wind of everything that has been happening at Harvard, Mr. Whitby and his associates' names will be in every paper, their good characters dragged through the mud," Alice added smugly.

So, the world was not completely bereft of integrity. Even the richest, most powerful men still had to bow before the scales of justice. With the resurrection men no longer a threat, perhaps she could work to prove Caleb's innocence. Hope surged through her. Then Caleb could come back a free man—if he hadn't already started a new life for himself somewhere with a wife and family. She pushed the stomach-turning thought away.

"Alice," she said slowly, "how did you know all those things about Mr. Whitby and Rose? And who is Mr. Pope?"

The smile faded from her sister's lips. "For all his mad ideas, Mr. Whitby was right about one thing: I only had to go deep inside of myself to find what has always been there, what I have never before tried to harness."

"You used your gift," Tabby said. "You looked into the future." Alice nodded, and Tabby considered this. "What did you see?" she asked.

Alice looked swiftly away. "I saw what became of Mr. Whitby."

"And Mr. Pope? Who was he?"

"A man to whom I owe money for cards," Alice said.

Then she brightened. "Eli is waiting in the other room. He said he didn't want to interrupt our reunion."

Tabby couldn't help smiling; that sounded like him. "Would you send him in now, please?"

Alice gave Tabby's hand one more squeeze before she went to fetch Eli.

The door creaked back open, and Eli's familiar scent of pipe tobacco washed over her. "Hello, Tabby cat. You gave us a fright."

Reaching out her hand, Tabby felt Eli's close around hers, reassuring and firm. "I know, I'm sorry," she said. "It was the last thing I wanted to do."

Eli gave a little snort. "There you go again, worrying about me when it's supposed to be the other way round." He smoothed back her hair, looking at her with something between pride and awe. "I always knew my Tabby cat was special."

"You know…" she said before trailing off.

"Alice and Mary-Ruth told me everything."

So, he had finally learned about her sight. He didn't seem hurt, yet Tabby couldn't help the guilt that sat heavy on her heart. "I should have told you, I don't know why I didn't. It's not that I didn't trust you, it's just that—"

He stopped her. "Hush now, I understand. It's a hard world and you got to do what you got to do to protect yourself. No reason to feel guilty about that." He looked down at his hands, massaging the knotty fingers. "I do wish you would have told me. Hell, I wish you would have felt safe knowing you could trust me, but I understand. I know how a secret can sit with you, weigh you down, and eat at your soul."

Nodding, she fiddled with the edge of her worn quilt. When she was younger, she had traced the faded geometric pattern of pink and blue triangles with her fingers, marveling at the dainty appliqués and relishing the feeling of something soft and homey after the coldness of the crypt. Her secret had been a cold and heavy mantle, but Eli's secret had meant life and death. How could she begrudge him keeping it from her?

"There's something that I've kept from you, Tabby," he said, as if reading her mind.

She would do anything to spare him the heartache of saying it. "They told me," she said softly.

He nodded, as if this didn't surprise him in the least. "Huh. So you know. They know, too. Here I thought I was invisible."

"I don't think they would dare send you back, not now."

Eli let out a long breath, tenting his fingers and looking off into the corner. "When I reached free soil, I thought that it would all be over, that I would start new and leave the past behind. But it haunts me, how could it not? That pain is in my bones, my blood. When I found you, I saw something of myself in you. I wanted to help someone, and you were there, an orphan just as I had been."

Tabby blinked back tears. Eli was being kind, as he always was. Tabby had been made an orphan by tragic circumstances, yes, but they had been by chance, a terrible accident. Eli had been made an orphan by systematic cruelty, by an institution that took pleasure in ripping children from their parents. That he saw the two of them as kindred spirits spoke more to his bottomless well of compassion than anything else.

Silence lapped up around them, until Eli stretched out his legs, the chair creaking. "Well, if I'm to stay, there's things I put off too long as it is. There's something I need to tell you."

"What is it?"

He rubbed at his graying tufts of hair as he often did when he didn't want to come right out and say something. "The thing is, I've asked Miss Suze to marry me."

Tabby blinked, stunned, as Eli rushed on, uncharacteristically tripping over his words. "She's plenty of room for the two of us to be comfortable. She says she doesn't want me working anymore, not with my back the state that it is. Of course, I'll make sure that you're looked after and you'll always be welcome and—"

Tabby stopped him, throwing her arms around him and burying her face in his neck. "I'm so happy for you. And just try to keep me away."

Alice and Mary-Ruth had returned, the small room crowded with laughter and well-wishes. When they quieted down again, Mary-Ruth reached out and placed a hesitant hand on her leg. "Tabs, there's something else you should know. Well, two somethings."

"Just how long was I asleep for?" Tabby said, trying for a light tone. "It seems that the world has been quite busy."

She expected that Mary-Ruth would smile at this, but her friend's usually sparkling demeanor was dead serious.

"Caleb is back in the country. In Boston, in fact."

Mary-Ruth looked like she had more to say, but Tabby

was already scrambling upright, questions falling off her tongue as fast as her mind could form them.

"How? When?"

Caleb was back in the same city as her, under the same sky and walking the same streets. The last time she had seen him he had laughed at her, accused her of that which she had always been afraid. Some stubborn corner of her mind told her that he didn't deserve a second chance. But something else, something deeper and centered in her heart, told her that she needed to see him one more time, to give him one more chance.

"He's in prison, Tabby. He walked right up to the police station in an effort to find out where y—"

Mary-Ruth stopped herself, but Tabby knew what she was going to say. He had walked into the police station to try to find her. She sank back into the pillows, her elation evaporating. Stupid man, to come back here when he knew he would be thrown right back in jail. Yet she couldn't be angry at him, not when he'd done it for her.

Dressed in her Sunday best, Tabby called on the prison the next day. Her best was still rather shabby, but when she thought of the beautiful blue gown that she had worn at Mr. Whitby's demonstration, she was grateful for its familiar comfort. The worn heels of her boots softly clicked down the dreary prison corridor, the warden at her side.

They turned onto the corridor where Caleb was being held, and the damp walls, the stench, the shouts of men, all fell away as soon as her gaze landed on him.

His curly hair had grown shaggy and his face narrower, but he was still the beautiful, golden boy who had brought light with him into the cemetery all those years ago. He didn't look older, but more poised, sober.

But what if he didn't feel the same? Alice had told her that they'd met in Edinburgh, and that he had been working as a clerk in an architectural firm. He'd come back, yes, but now he was in prison; would he resent her?

His face slowly transformed when he met her gaze. "Tabby," he said on the back of his breath. "You look…" he trailed off, but his eyes said everything that his words could not, and heat rushed to her cheeks as his gaze swept over her. He cleared his throat, looking as dazed as Tabby felt. "Mary-Ruth visited me, told me everything. I hope that you're not hurt from your ordeal?"

Tabby shook her head. "Just a little tired. I'll be fine."

"I'm glad," he said.

Why were her feet suddenly made out of lead? He was standing right up against the bars, his hands clasped tight around them. The warden was chatting with an officer a little way away, and the moment was as private as they were like to have, so why couldn't she go to him? And why wasn't he saying anything more than the barest pleasantries?

"You shouldn't be here," she said bluntly. "You did nothing wrong." What little faith she'd had in the police and the rule of law was further shaken every time she saw Caleb sitting in his cell. "They've arrested Mr. Whitby and his accomplices. They must know you're innocent."

"Innocent of murder, perhaps, but I am still an escaped convict. I made the police look incompetent." He gave her his old roguish smile. "I doubt that they're eager to see me on the streets again."

The straw rustled as a rat scurried across the cell, and Tabby took a deep breath, willing herself to be patient. "Surely your mother can speak on your behalf to the court?"

He shrugged.

"But Caleb," she said, her voice rising, "you must at least *try*!"

He looked away, watching as the rat gnawed on something in the corner. "Has it occurred to you that perhaps I am right where I belong? That I deserve to be here?"

"What are you talking about?"

He gave a heavy sigh and kicked at some straw. "Do you know what gave me the will to survive my exile?"

She shook her head.

Exasperation edged his voice. "*You*, Tabby. The thought of you happy and in my arms."

"Then let me petition the court," she begged. "Let your mother rally her wealthy friends. There's no need to sit here a moment longer. You have no shortage of resources to—"

"Tabby," he said quietly.

"You could bribe the police!" she continued, heedless of his protest.

"*Tabby.*"

She finally stopped.

"Listen to me. There's something else I need to tell you. Something I did, that, ah, I am not proud of. If you knew, then you would understand why I deserve my sentence."

She frowned. "I know that you have a certain...colorful history," she said diplomatically.

"It's not that," he said. "I know I was a bit of a cad. I

kissed you when I was engaged, I left you alone when you were most vulnerable. And…"

She did not like where this was going. "Go on."

"The thing is…" He rubbed at the back of his neck. "I may have told Billy—that is, Sergeant Hodsdon—about your…your ability. I may have leveraged it to help me escape."

She could see sweat gathering at his temples despite the damp prison air. She waited for him to finish.

"I think… I think it was my fault that they found out about you and that you landed in Whitby's hands."

So Officer Hodsdon had found out about her from Caleb, not the séance. Tabby didn't say anything, didn't move a muscle. Not only had he not believed her when she'd told him, he betrayed her trust. How high her heart had soared, and now how quickly it plummeted.

"Please, say something," he pleaded.

"What would you have me say?" She struggled to retain her composure, but her voice rose, her face growing hot. "You broke my trust, you sealed my fate by offering me up right to Mr. Whitby. I lost all hope. Do you know how close I was to taking my—" She cut herself short, biting down on her tongue and swiftly looking away.

Caleb took a step closer, but was stopped by the bars. His face was deadly serious. "How close you were to what, Tabby?"

"Nothing," she mumbled, crossing her arms. "It doesn't matter."

He reached out a hand as if he would touch her, but then dropped it again with a heavy sigh. "It does matter, Tabby. *You* matter. What I did was terrible, unforgivable. I know that. If you can't forgive me, I understand. But please know that what I did was out of my own miserable nature, and was not a reflection of you. You are a hundred times the person I could ever be, strong and loyal and loving. I—"

"Stop," she said, cutting his pitiful speech short. "I don't want to hear it anymore."

She called for the warden. Her eyes stung with tears as she hurried away, heedless of Caleb calling after her.

Stupid man. Stupid, stupid man.

As soon as the prison expelled her onto the gray, slushy street, she began walking across the city to Beacon Hill. The sky was low and moody, a cold sting in the air that had men bundled up to their noses in thick mufflers, mothers holding their bundled children by mittened hands. Tabby had still not grown accustomed to walking without fear through the streets. Did the people she pass sense that she was different? Were her aunt and uncle still out there, looking for her?

One thing had not changed, though: Caleb still possessed the unique ability to drive her mad while simultaneously making her want to crawl into his arms and never let go. If he wanted to keep company with rats and drunkards as some sort of misplaced penance for the rest of his days in prison, that was his prerogative. But if he thought that Tabby was going to sit idly by, then he was mistaken. Him sitting in prison did Tabby no good. It didn't bring Rose back. It didn't erase the memories of the medical theater and the men leering at her. It didn't erase the loneliness and crushing desperation of the past months. If he wanted to be a martyr, then he could do it out in the real world like everybody else.

Larson let Tabby in and showed her to the parlor. Mrs. Bishop sat in her chair, plucking listlessly at a loose thread on the arm of her chair. Her hair was thin and greasy, her coiffure unkempt.

"Hello, Mrs. Bishop," Tabby said softly. "How are you?"

The older woman looked up at Tabby with glassy eyes, a vacant smile touching her lips. "You've come to see Caleb, haven't you? I'm afraid he's gone away and not likely to come back this time. He found his way back home, only to be arrested for his flight."

"It's you I've come to see, actually. About Caleb."

Mrs. Bishop gestured vaguely to the sofa. Tabby had to push aside a pile of Caleb's drawings to make room to sit. Measuring her words before she spoke, Tabby leaned forward. "You must know that I think rather highly of your son."

At this, Mrs. Bishop looked up, some of the glassiness leaving her eyes. "I've always liked you, Tabby Cooke. My Caleb would be a fool if he didn't, too."

Tabby managed a small smile before continuing. "I tell you this because I think it's possible for Caleb to be freed. He is innocent, after all, but he refuses to press his case, or even try for that matter."

Mrs. Bishop had returned to picking at the thread, gazing sightlessly out the window. "I don't know," she said. "I just don't know what to do. Thomas was the one who would know what to do in this situation, and that wretched Mr. Whitby was always the one to look after our legal affairs."

"With all due respect, I believe you are more resourceful than you give yourself credit for. I was at the séance and saw for myself the influence you exert over the ladies in your circle."

"Perhaps," said Mrs. Bishop. She gave a heavy sigh. "But the business has all but collapsed in on itself. There simply isn't the money."

Tabby eyed the expensive furniture, the Oriental carpets, and lamps dripping with crystals. Mrs. Bishop followed her gaze. "It's all bought on credit," she said. "Every stick of furniture and piece of bread in the larder." She buried her face in her handkerchief. "Why, I couldn't even pay the grocer's bill this month. Soon the creditors will come banging on the door, demanding their money, and then what shall I do?"

Tabby stood and crossed the room. She had come this far, and she wasn't going to let Caleb brood about in prison while his mother withered away.

"What are you doing?" Mrs. Bishop watched as Tabby sat down at the writing desk in the corner, pulled out a sheaf of paper, and dipped the pen into ink.

"I'm writing a letter to the good ladies of the Benevolent Society," she said, as she began to pen her missive. She thought of something. "And the ladies at the temperance coffeehouse."

Buttermilk jumped up beside Tabby to supervise. "What can they do? We are just women," Mrs. Bishop said with a sniff.

"*We* can accomplish quite a lot." Tabby scribbled as

fast as she could despite her poor penmanship and the wet, splotchy ink.

Mrs. Bishop's interest had finally been piqued, and Tabby could feel her come up behind her and read over her shoulder. Buttermilk's purring filled the silence until Mrs. Bishop finished reading. "Another séance? I'm sorry, my dear, but what will that achieve?"

Tabby sprinkled the wet ink with sand before reading over her work.

Mrs. Dorothea Bishop Humbly requests Your Presence
For an evening of Spiritualism & Mystery
With the medium Miss Tabitha Cooke
Private readings available for a small fee.

The replies to the invitations came flying back. After Tabby's first performance exposing Minerva Bellefonte, every lady in Boston was eager to have a private reading, and paid generously for it. With Alice and Mary-Ruth's help, Tabby transformed Mrs. Bishop's parlor, draping silks over the lamps until the room glowed with other-worldly elegance. Larson circulated the parlor with trays of cakes, and Tabby offered discreet readings to one lady at a time behind a screen. At the end of the night they had raised a stunning one hundred and forty dollars—more than enough to retain the best lawyer in Boston. Caleb would be a free man yet, whether he wanted to or not.

35

IN WHICH THE LIVING LIVE
HAPPILY EVER AFTER,
AND THE DEAD REST IN PEACE.

SKELETAL TREES FEATHERED against a gray sky, and a cold, fine mist hung suspended in the air. In its own stark way, December in the cemetery was no less beautiful than spring, and equally full of life. Squirrels darted between the stones, birds huddled on icy branches, quietly chirping, and three young women stood bundled against the gloom, as solemn as a funeral.

"This is the one," Tabby said, pointing at the overgrown crypt with rusty hinges. She had given Alice the broadest strokes of how she had survived those first days, trying to paint it more as an adventure than as the harrowing experience it had been.

Mary-Ruth trailed a respectful distance behind them. Every once in a while, Alice would look back over her shoulder at her, and when Tabby asked her what she was smiling about, she only smiled the more.

Alice shook her head. "I never thought that you would make a home for yourself amongst the dead, not after what we went through in Amherst." She stepped around a crumbling stone covered in lichen as they moved away from the crypt. "Are you sure that you want to stay here?"

"It's the only home I know. Besides, with Eli retiring, someone will need to look after this place. There aren't many burials here anymore, but there are plenty of souls who still need to be remembered." She glanced over to the far end of the cemetery, where a sea of unmarked men and women were buried, abused and enslaved in life, and quietly forgotten by all but Eli and a few others in death. Perhaps she could learn their names, their stories, make sure that they were always remembered.

"And how will you get by? Mary-Ruth told me that you were embroidering and doing watching."

Tabby had been worrying over just this predicament. "I was thinking," she said slowly, "of using my sight." At Alice's horrified expression, she hurried on. Her sister had been skeptical of the séance at Mrs. Bishop's house, saying she worried that it would take too great a toll on Tabby. "I wouldn't charge a lot of money, and only to people who can afford it. If there are messages I can pass on to the poor bereaved, then I shall always do so free of charge. But there are plenty of well-to-do people who would pay good money for the benefit of my gift," she said. And it was a gift, even if it had always felt like a burden, a secret shame. Even if men tried to exploit it and use it for their own selfish means. She could use it to help people, and the thought gave her comfort. She and her sister could rent some rooms together, maybe with Mary-Ruth, and provide the bereaved and curious with messages from the other side for a small price. For as much as Tabby had always feared and abhorred speaking with the dead, she had done so out of necessity many times in the past months, and so long as she was in control, it had lost some of the terror of those early days.

She threw Alice a sidelong look. "And what about you? Do you think you would use your sight?"

Alice had always been quiet about her gift, holding it close to her chest, just as Tabby had hers. Her aunt and uncle had never suspected that Alice was any different than Tabby, that she was simply following Tabby's lead at those terrible séances. They never suspected that Alice's gift was a different sort of rare jewel. God only knew what they would have done if they had.

Sighing, Alice pulled her cloak tighter around her and stared down the misty hill. "I don't know." She paused, worrying at the ribbon of her hood. "There are dark times ahead for this country in the near future."

A shiver ran down Tabby's spine, but she dared not ask what Alice meant. She'd rather the future remain a mystery. If what Alice saw was truly terrible and came to pass, then she was at least glad that she would have her sister by her side.

She was just about to tell Alice as much, when the sound of voices and footsteps made her look up. Mary-Ruth was speaking to someone. Someone she recognized instantly.

Her heart sped up, the sounds of the city fell away, and

suddenly it wasn't a cold, foggy day in December, but that soft spring night all those years ago when the most dashing man had stumbled into her world of death and darkness, bringing with him light and hope.

The last she had heard, the lawyer was working to have Caleb's sentence commuted for time served. She had assumed it would take months, perhaps even years. But here he was after only a few days.

Alice followed her line of sight and gave a small smile. "He's a good man," she said. "I wasn't sure about him at first, but he proved himself when it mattered the most."

It was all Tabby could do to nod. He *was* a good man, if impulsive and reckless. After all, he had risked everything to come back. But his betrayal was still a fresh wound. She had wanted him out of prison for his mother's sake, but now as she watched him approaching, she realized how many things she wanted to say to him.

Alice squeezed Tabby's hand. "I'll leave you alone."

Tabby watched as her sister linked arms with Mary-Ruth and walked along the fenced perimeter of the cemetery, their heads bent together. A moment later Caleb was approaching her, hesitation in his step.

It took everything in her not to run to meet him and throw her arms around him and hungrily inhale his scent that had lingered on the edges of her memory these past months.

He came to an abrupt stop a few feet in front of her, his hat in his hands, his hair tousled and damp from the harbor breeze.

"My mother told me what you did."

Tabby managed a shrug. "It was nothing."

"You know very well that it was not nothing. You've saved me, three times now. First, when I was a scared young lad. Again when you warned me of Mr. Whitby and persuaded me to escape. And now by rallying her wealthy friends."

When she didn't say anything, Caleb continued. "The shipping business is dead. After the scandal with my arrest and escape, and now its association with Whitby, no one will touch it."

"Oh," she said, trying not to let her surprise at the abrupt change of subject show on her face.

Caleb shrugged. "I certainly can't say I'm sorry. I thought perhaps I might try my hand at architectural design." He gave her a shy look. "It's always been an interest of mine."

So he would return to Scotland, to the freedom of pursuing his dreams. "I saw your sketches at your house. They were very good," she said grudgingly.

Pink touched the tips of his ears and he cleared his throat uncomfortably. "Ah, yes. My mother is inordinately proud of anything I sign my name to."

Above them, a crow rasped a call into the damp air, taking flight, and they lapsed into silence. Frigid mud was seeping into her boots, her toes growing numb.

"Tabby…" he started, before trailing off and scrubbing his hand through his fair stubble. He tried again. "Look, here's how it stands. I don't want to wait another ten years to see you again, or ten days for that matter. I don't want to think of you wandering this cemetery like some sort of spirit, worrying about you and if you're all right."

She opened her mouth to assure him that she might

have once been a lost spirit, but that she'd found a family, made a life for herself. As if reading her thoughts, he hurried on.

"I know that your sister is here now and you have Mary-Ruth and Eli. I know you have no need of a man, let alone a useless man like me, but I just need you to know that I would do anything to make you happy and lift your burdens from you. I would do anything just to catch a glimpse of you every day and would cross a thousand more oceans if it meant being with you. What I did was unforgivable, but I hope you can endeavor to forgive me all the same."

His words washed over her, but it was like waiting for the thunder clap that followed lightning, and she dared not let out her breath until she was sure of what he was saying.

"Please say something," he said, his eyes imploring. "I've never stood before the woman of my heart and given an impassioned speech before and I'm not sure I've done even a passable job at it."

"Of course you've done a passable job at it," she said bitterly. "Pretty words are your strength. But I need more than words. I think… I think you should go."

He opened his mouth, but then must have thought better of whatever he was about to say, and just nodded. "I understand." Turning, he replaced his hat, and began walking away.

He had hurt her. He had done what she always feared, and yet as his figure grew smaller, all she could think of was how much she wanted to be walking hand in hand beside him. Perhaps he would hurt her again, but what love, what happiness, might she miss if she did not give him another chance? She didn't *want* to love him. It was inconvenient at best, and downright destructive at worst. But she couldn't deny the truth any longer.

"Wait! Caleb," she called after him. "Wait."

Stopping, he slowly turned around. She ran as fast as her numb toes would allow her to until she was right in front of him, her breath coming in short puffs that evaporated on the warmth of his coat. "Wait," she said again. "I don't care." At his hopeful expression, she hurried on. "Well, I do care. I care very much. You betrayed my trust, but what's more important, you didn't believe me. I need to know that you would have believed me anyway, if not for what happened at Harvard. I need to know that you will take me seriously, and that I can trust you."

He nodded so vigorously that his hat nearly fell off again. "I will. I can."

"Good," she said. "You have a lifetime to prove your words with actions."

He looked at her, his eyes alighting with hope. "You'll have me, then?"

"Caleb," she said softly, "I made a home for you in my heart since the first moment I saw you all those years ago. I've just been waiting for you to come and take your place in it."

This seemed to take him by surprise. He took a step back, his lips twitching into a frown. Perhaps he hadn't actually expected her to return the sentiment and was at a loss for words. But there was no denying the look of smoldering longing in his eyes.

"Well?" she said expectantly. "Is there something you'd like to ask me?"

"I suppose I… That is, I'm asking if you would marry me," he said, the words seeming to surprise him even as they came out of his own mouth.

Her heart stopped in her chest, and for a brief, terrible moment, she was sure that he was playing some sort of cruel trick on her. But one look at the desperate vulnerability on his face told her that he was in earnest.

"Of course I'll marry you," she said, unable to stop the laughter from bubbling up in her throat. If the trials of the past months had taught her anything, it was that happiness was fleeting, and it could be found only within oneself and the love one shared with others.

"Oh, thank goodness." His shoulders sagged in relief and he closed his eyes. "My mother would never forgive me if I came home without an answer in the affirmative from you."

At this, Caleb finally broke free of where he had been standing, and before she knew what was happening, he was leaning in to kiss her. Instead of a hungry embrace, he simply brushed his lips reverently against her temples. She closed her eyes, relishing the sweetness, the warmth of him. But no sooner had she opened her eyes than her world threatened to break apart again.

"What is it?" Caleb followed her line of sight to where two figures were picking their way over the ice at the cemetery gate. He frowned. "Do you know them?"

Tabby knew them all too well. "My aunt and uncle." She could feel Caleb stiffen at her words.

"The nerve of them," he muttered, moving to put her behind him. But she held her ground.

Her aunt looked thin, drained of color with her dark hair pulled severely back under a moth-eaten fur hat.

"Tabby," she said with a tight smile. "Dear, dear Tabby. I know we left on less than ideal terms, but I come bearing no ill will."

Tabby didn't say anything.

"I understand why you ran away all those years ago, but it can be different now. You're a grown woman and I've seen for myself how you have come into your powers. Come back and join us, and you'll share equally in the profits. Just look at Cora Hatch and the fame she has achieved."

"Your aunt is right," her uncle put in. "Just think of the profits."

Tabby ignored him. "You must have heard that your good friends from Harvard have been apprehended and charged with all manner of crimes. I wonder what would happen if your role in their despicable scheme was known."

Her aunt's face went even whiter. "What...what do you mean?"

"I know that you helped them. I know that you provided information to them, gleaned from your clients about when and where they could find bodies. I know that you helped them apprehend Alice. I have no interest in seeing you jailed, but neither have I interest in ever, ever crossing paths with you again, or hearing that you are cheating money out of the bereaved."

She hadn't needed him there, but it felt good to have

Caleb's steady presence behind her as she confronted the monsters of her childhood.

"I see," her aunt said, her dark eyes shining with hatred. "Well. You always were a wicked, ungrateful child." She sniffed. "Come along, Harold."

"Tabby," her uncle said with a tip of his hat, before her aunt could yank him along by his arm.

When they had gone, Caleb slipped his arm about her waist. "Well done," he murmured into her ear. She leaned into him, her legs shaking.

Mary-Ruth and Alice were returning. "Was that..." Alice looked back at where the figures of their aunt and uncle were retreating through the gravestones.

"They won't bother us again," Tabby told her.

"They should be put on trial, just the same as Mr. Whitby," Mary-Ruth said.

Now it would be her aunt and uncle forever looking over their shoulders, too afraid to set down roots.

"We're going to go find some hot chowder and strong ale. Are you two lovebirds coming?" Mary-Ruth asked with a raised brow at Caleb's arm around Tabby's waist.

"You go on ahead," Tabby told them. "There's something I need to do."

She watched as Caleb turned to join Mary-Ruth and Alice. "Wait," she said, reaching out and taking him by the arm. "Come with me. Please."

Using her gift with other people present had always been fraught with terror and unwillingness, but she trusted him, and realized that she wanted him there. Besides, Rose had been an important person in his life, and he deserved closure as much as she.

Surprise flickered across his face, but then he was following her to the other side of the cemetery. It didn't matter where she tried to contact Rose, and this was a secluded, pretty spot with the foggy harbor just beyond. Tabby moved to take off her cloak to spread on the ground, but Caleb stopped her, removing his coat and laying it over the knobby roots of an elm. Helping her down, they sat side by side, shoulders touching.

She had scarcely closed her eyes when the darkness came. This time it was not a rushing, pressing flood, but a gentle lapping that slowly crept over the corners of her mind.

Tabby didn't need to call her name or reach out very far to find who she was looking for; almost instantly the delicate smell of spring flowers filled the space around her.

I promised that I would help you, she said into the darkness, *and I think I can, now that Mr. Whitby has been exposed for the villain he is. You'll have justice, and you will not be forgotten.*

Rose stood with an aura of light shining from behind her. Tabby had never known the dead to smile, but Rose came the closest she had ever seen, her face placid. The light grew stronger and brighter, gradually enveloping Rose's form until Tabby had to look away.

Her relief that Rose had found peace was tinged with melancholy for the life on earth that had been so violently interrupted. Would Rose and Caleb have married had she not been murdered? Would she have borne children? Written poetry? Become one of the most sparkling socialites in Boston? Tabby pushed the thoughts away; it did no good to dwell on what might have been.

When nothing remained of Rose except the lingering scent of flowers, Tabby slowly opened her eyes and came back to the land of the living. Ahead of her, Mary-Ruth and Alice were laughing with heads bowed closed together at some private joke. Caleb took her arm and tucked it into his elbow, and they passed out of the misty cemetery and down the hill, leaving the dead to their eternal slumber.

★ ★ ★ ★ ★

AUTHOR NOTE

While exploring an old cemetery on the North Shore of Massachusetts, I discovered an informational plaque that mentioned a local man who had been found guilty of robbing corpses for medical research in the 1810s. Intrigued, I began researching the history of grave robbing in Massachusetts, and learned that it persisted much later into the nineteenth century than I had originally realized. While Mr. Whitby and his exploits are fictional, Harvard really did have a macabre history of employing grave robbers to provide their medical students with bodies for dissection. The resurrection men and the Spunker Club were real, and took their job of procuring the bodies of the recently deceased seriously. In 1999, construction workers at Harvard found the bones of at least eleven individuals, believed to have been deposited in a basement after dissection in the early 1840s.

I based Tabby's "Cemetery Hill" on Copp's Hill Burying Ground in Boston's North End, a quiet cemetery that sits on a hill on the historic Freedom Trail. Copp's Hill Burying Ground is the final resting place of many notable early Bostonians, as well as over one thousand free and enslaved Black peoples (most in unmarked graves). After the end of slavery in Massachusetts in the late eighteenth century, the Copp's Hill area became an enclave of free Black people, known as New Guinea. While these people were largely displaced by the influx of Italian and Irish immigrants, the Copp's Hill area was still home to a small African American community through the late-nineteenth century. Today you can visit the African Meeting House on the Freedom Trail to learn more about the history of the African American community in Boston.

In 1848, the Fox sisters of Rochester, New York, became a national sensation after word of their uncanny ability to channel the messages of the dead spread across the country. Soon other mediums, such as Cora Hatch (nee Scott), would mesmerize audiences with their abilities to speak on esoteric subjects while in a trance. Boston, already a hotbed for new philosophies and movements, was soon swept up in the craze that was known as spiritualism.

Spiritualism only increased in popularity as the Civil War raged. No one in the United States was left untouched by the conflict, and many were desperate to reach loved ones who had died in battle. Even Mary Todd Lincoln visited the spirit photographer William H. Mumler, and received a photograph that appeared to show her late husband hovering reassuringly over her shoulder.

In 1854 in Lynn, Massachusetts, a spiritualist named John Murray Spear claimed to be receiving messages from the spirits of prominent men such as Benjamin Franklin and Thomas Jefferson. These spirits advised Spear to build a "mechanical messiah" that would usher in a new utopian age of enlightenment. An angry mob ultimately destroyed the metal being. It's a wild story, and if you're ever in Lynn, you can still visit the tower where these events transpired.

Many spiritualists and mediums of this time period were publicly disproven or revealed to be frauds, with Maggie Fox confessing that the supernatural sounds and messages from the other side had been manufactured by her and her sisters (though she would recant this confession a year later). Mumler likewise was put on trial for fraud, and though he was acquitted, his career never recovered.

I first learned of Mary-Ruth's profession of "watching" from a *Splinter* article by Isha Aran titled "The Death Midwife: Women Were the Original Undertakers" (it was published online October 23, 2015, and I highly recommend giving it a read). I also found the article "When Death Was Women's Business" by Livia Gershon incredibly informative. Being a watcher (or, "watch woman") was a real vocation in the nineteenth century, and was almost exclusively filled by women, sometimes as a paid position and sometimes as an unpaid extension of their other domestic duties. Being buried alive was a common fear of the time, and there was a need for someone to not only care for the dying, but to make sure that they were indeed dead when the time came. But more than that, there was no real funerary industry like there is today, and the business of death was carried out in the domestic sphere. This changed after the Civil War with the popularization of embalming, and so, like many other professions before it, embalming became the work of men once there was money to be made from it.

Another resource I found helpful when writing *The Orphan of Cemetery Hill* was *Widow's Weeds and Weeping Veils: Mourning Rituals in 19th Century America* by Bernadette Loeffel-Atkins. If you are interested in mourning embroidery, hair art, and basically anything to do with the fascinating social system of mourning in the nineteenth century, then this is the book for you. Atlas Obscura likewise provided lots of interesting and arcane material, such as the story of High Rock Tower. And of course, much of my inspiration simply came from the old cemeteries of New England, their crumbling stones, and the forgotten stories they commemorate.

ACKNOWLEDGMENTS

There are so many people who not only helped make this book a reality, but have supported me in my writing journey in one way or another. Chief among them are my editor, Brittany Lavery, and agent, Jane Dystel. I am truly humbled to have two such amazing women on my team, helping me grow my craft and advocating for me.

My thanks to everyone at Graydon House, as well as the Harlequin art department, who time and again so brilliantly bring to life the atmosphere of my stories. In the UK, I have an equally wonderful team at HQ led by Sarah Goodey.

My heartfelt gratitude goes to the booksellers and librarians who read and promote by books. Special thanks to Belmont Books in Belmont, Massachusetts; The Open Book in Warrenton, Virginia; and the Malden Public Library. I am also thankful for all the book bloggers and bookstagrammers who feature and share my work.

Love and thanks to Trish, my wonderful critique partner and first reader. Also Jeannie, the best cheerleader and friend a writer could ask for. Jenny, Debby, Bev, and the rest of the 1linewed crew. As always, I am incredibly grateful to my friends and family who come out to support me at my events.

All my love to my little team, MF & FF.